LOGAN

#SEX MACHINE

KADE

Edited by Jessica Royer Ocken

Proofread by: Paige Smith and Chris O'Neil Parece
at Parece Consulting

Cover image from Scott Hoover

Cover designed by Tijan Meyer

Interior Formatting by Elaine York,
Allusion Graphics, LLC/Publishing & Book Formatting
www.allusiongraphics.com

ISBN: 9781682304976

BOOK ORDER

Logan Kade is written as a standalone, but he is from the Fallen Crest Series. This series does not have to be read before reading, but if a reader wanted to be fully prepared for Logan's awesomeness, the order is:

Mason (prequel novella)
Fallen Crest High
Fallen Crest Family
Fallen Crest Public
Fallen Fourth Down
Fallen Crest University
*Logan's book fits here in this timeline

For up-to-date information on this series and remaining books/
novellas, visit
www.tijansbooks.com

DEDICATION

Logan is so loved and this book is dedicated to all of the Logan Lovers out there! This book is also dedicated to a certain eighteen year old who has been patiently waiting for years to find out Logan's middle name. I revealed it to her a while ago, but I wanted to dedicate this book to her as well.

Nichole Green,

Happy birthday!

From, Logan Lucas Kade

CHAPTER 1

THE FIRST
LOGAN

"Logan Motherfucking Kade."

I heard the slow and sensual drawl behind me and smirked. I'd always know that voice, no matter what frame of mind she was in. Tate Sullivan had screamed underneath me, at me, and behind my back. Anyway there was, I'd had her. Lover. Enemy. Friend. Fuck buddy. We were all of those, and she dropped a bomb on her way out the last time she was in my life. Turning around, she was walking towards me with a sexy stroll, midriff showing under a white halter top and swinging those hips encased in tight-as-skin jeans. I narrowed my eyes and leaned back against my Escalade, sliding my hands inside my front pockets. "Tate Mother Slutting Sullivan." There was no warmth in my voice. "What do you want?"

She stopped and lifted an eyebrow. "You're mad."

I grunted. That wasn't a question, and she knew better than to give me an opening. I'd fillet her alive, but instead, all I said was, "You fucked with my relationships the last time I saw you."

"Uh. Yeah." Her frosted pink lips pressed together, and her eyes glanced away for a second. "About that, you know that wasn't to get at you, right? That was to fuck things up with your brother. He's the asshole I wanted to hurt."

"Not making it better, Tate."

"Well." She gestured behind me to the lit up mansion. Hip-hop music blared, even sounding loud where we were, a few yards away in the parking area. "I saw Mason and Samantha inside. They seem happy and still sickeningly in love, so all's still good in the Kade/Strattan trio."

"You told Sam that I was in love with her."

"To my credit, I thought you were."

"Bullshit." I pushed off from the Escalade and started toward her. Her eyes widened, and she backed up. I kept advancing. I wasn't going to hurt her. With all the history between us, physical violence had never been present. Manipulation. Backstabbing deceit. Her just being a slut as she propositioned my brother when we were dating—yeah, that had all been there, but when Tate came back in our lives, she and I became friends. Well, we were fuck buddies, but those were the best types of friends in my opinion.

"You're scared of me now, Tate? Not when you told my brother's girlfriend that I was in love with her. You didn't just hurt Mason. You screwed with all of us. I love Sam. Always have, but only as a friend and a future sister. How'd you feel if I did something like that? If I fucked with your family, the people who you hold most dear?"

She stopped, her back against a truck, and I stepped closer. Looking down, holding her gaze, I let her see the anger there. She didn't look away. There was shame in her blue eyes, but resolve, too. Her chin trembled and then hardened, and she lifted her chin higher, standing higher as we stood toe to toe. "You did fuck with my life."

"You mean when we dated for two years, I was in love with you, and you went to my brother's room to have sex with him? You mean after that, when he called me while you were propositioning him and my dad was nice enough to get you a driver to take you home?"

She bit down on her lip, her eyebrows pinching forward together. "I was naked, and you were both going to cast me out like that."

I shrugged. "Who was the one who took your clothes off?"

Her. The truth was silent from Tate, until she said, softly, "I thought we were okay, Logan. That's why I came out here." She leaned forward, grazing her breasts against my chest. "We were friends when I left."

We were more than friends, and I reached up, cupping the back of her neck. She shivered, closing her eyes as I said, "When are you going to learn, Tate?"

Her eyes opened. She waited.

"When you fuck with one of mine, you fuck with me." I leaned forward, my forehead resting against hers. "And you fucked with my family."

She knew this wasn't going anywhere. She pulled her head back, out of my hold, and leaned against the truck again. Her shoulders lowered a centimeter. "I didn't think you'd get hurt by what I said. I really didn't mean that. I just wanted to hurt Mason. He's the asshole."

"No, Tate. We're both assholes. You just like how I feel inside of you."

"God." She shoved me back. Her eyes flared. "You can piss me off."

My lips curved up. I was being the asshole she liked to screw, and we both knew it. I saw the old lust coming back over her. Her skin was warming. Her lips parted. Her nipples hardened under her shirt. But I meant what I said. "What are you doing here, Tate?"

Her bottom lip stuck out. "You're going back to Cain U tomorrow." She rolled her eyes, shaking her head. "I thought one last night, but I can see that's not going to happen." She gestured around the parking area. "I thought you were waiting for me. That's what we used to do. The party's inside, and you're out here."

"Who said I was waiting for you?"

She opened her mouth, then stopped. No sound came out. "God, you're a prick."

I rolled my shoulders back. "You're lucky this is all you're getting. Did Mason see you inside?"

"No. I saw 'em in the back with Nate, then saw you heading out here. I thought maybe you saw me, too, and here I came."

My mouth twitched. I could do so much with that last statement, but I held back. She'd take it as flirting. "I came out here for a chick, but it wasn't you. Sorry."

"Same old Logan." Her eyes slid down me and back up, a soft sigh leaving her. "Screwing girls, partying, and," her eyes fell back to my hand and lingered there. She touched my red knuckles. "still fighting."

I pulled my hand away. "You say that like it's a bad thing."

She sighed, touching the corner of my mouth before letting her hand fall back to her side. "I'm sorry for hurting you. I know I did."

She was sincere and I frowned at that. "That was a long time ago. I got you back. We made your life hell in school afterwards."

She groaned, grinning up at me. "You did. Holy shit, you and Mason both did, but I still want to apologize for what I did. I did you wrong, and I'm sorry for that."

"Apology accepted." I waited. Tate didn't do anything without reason. She probably did come out here to proposition me for one more night, and if this had been two years ago, I would've taken her up on that, but she hurt my family. There was no going back from that. "What's going on with you, Tate? Why'd you really come out here?"

"I really did come out to get in your pants, but I know that's not going to happen." She lifted up her slim shoulders. "I came to this party to find you and to apologize again. I heard through the grapevine that what I said to Sam had hurt you too. I'm off to my college tomorrow, too, so who knows the next time I'll get the opportunity to do this in person again."

I nodded, my suspicions still clouded in my mind. "Okay. Thank you for apologizing again."

"Logan!"

Tate glanced over her shoulder, seeing the real reason I'd come out to this parking lot, and she rolled her eyes before meeting mine. The girl didn't matter. She had a good rack, and I loved how she gave blow jobs, but who she was wasn't important. Both Tate and I knew that even if the girl thought she was, I never lied to them. I never made promises where they'd be my girlfriends. On the rare occasion, I'd have to hurt their feelings, but more often than not, they accepted what I offered. A good time. That was all, and with this girl, I'd forget her name in the morning, or even in an hour depending how good she was. For once, a shadow of doubt crossed my mind. I had loved Tate, or I thought I had. She was my first serious girlfriend and I only had one other since her. I loved sex. I loved to party. And yes, I loved to fight, too, but I never considered changing...until I saw the disappointment in my first ex.

Then I shrugged that off. That was crazy.

"Okay. Well, see you, Logan."

I nodded. "See you, Tate."

She turned, one hand hooked in her jean pocket as the other girl slowed, passing her by. Tate ignored the girl and said, "Give me a call if you ever change your ways."

My side-grin turned cocky. "Tate, if that ever happens, you'd be the last girl I'd fall for."

She laughed. "And there's the asshole again. Thanks. I almost forgot for a second there."

"No problem. I'm here if you need an asshole."

She shook her head and sauntered away, holding two fingers up over her shoulder. "Deuces, Kade. I never thought I'd be saying this, but I really do hope your next year is a great one." She paused, glancing back, and her voice came out softly, "I hope you fall in love. You can feel what the rest of us feel."

She left after that, and I shook my head, before pulling the girl against me. That was never going to happen, and then I lowered my head, my lips finding hers, and I stopped thinking altogether.

CHAPTER 2

BEEEEP YOURSELF
TAYLOR

"Broozer! You're hilarious. Why didn't I know this?"

Listening from around the corner, my nails sank farther into my palms. That woman had been saying that same phrase over and over for the last thirty minutes. Even though I was in college, I felt some middle-school tendencies rearing up. I wanted to get up from my perch on the stairs, march in there, and do something I'd regret later.

"Broozer!" She laughed, and her hand pounded the table. "You are too funny."

Okay. That was it. I stood up, but the gods shined their favor on me. My friend's headlights lit up the house.

"Bruce," a male voice from the dining room said, "I think someone just pulled up in your driveway."

"Oh." A chair scraped over the floor. "That must be Taylor or her friends. I didn't know she was here."

That wasn't surprising. There was a lot he seemed not to know anymore.

"Taylor?"

I was at the door and reaching for the door handle when he came around the corner. I paused and glanced back. I loved my dad. I had moved back almost nine months ago to be here with him, but we were roommates. The father/daughter dynamic wasn't there anymore. It hadn't been since my mother died and we dealt with her loss in two different ways. He became engrossed in his job as one of the coaches for Cain University among some *other* activities. If he wasn't thinking about football, he was watching tapes, he was planning plays, he was on the phone with a player, he was on the phone with a coach, he was—the list went on and on. He'd been promoted to defensive coordinator last spring, and I knew it was a product of all his extra work.

I didn't recognize this man who let some woman call him Broozer, like that was his name. He was known as Coach Broozer, but his name was Hank. Hank Bruce. Coach Broozer had always been his alter ego. Wild. Yelling. Passionate. That was Broozer. Hank was quiet, kind, loving to my mother. Hank was my father. But Coach Broozer stood in front of me now, looking like he regretted coming out to check because now he actually had to talk to me.

"Is that a date in there?"

His eyebrows pinched together, and the corners of his mouth strained. I looked away from his eyes. He kept his body trim, his dark brown hair didn't have any graying strands, and he had a strong jawline below clear blue eyes. He was dressed nice: a pastel blue polo over trendy jeans. He and Mom had me when they were eighteen, and he was only thirty-eight. I knew that made him prime dating material, but that didn't mean I liked it.

He glanced over his shoulder, giving the dining room a wary look before he lifted a shoulder. He still held his cloth napkin, and his hand closed a fist around it. "I don't know, to be truthful. Mike and Evelyn brought a friend over, but it's just a night with friends for me."

Beep! Beep!

"Is that Jason and Claire?" My dad gestured to the car outside.

I nodded. "Yeah. Hold on."

Opening the door, I stuck my head out. Claire waved from the driver's seat, smiling widely at me while Jason leaned his head out his window. He made an impatient motion.

"Two seconds," I yelled.

His eyes rolled. Claire gave me a thumbs-up.

"I should go," I told my dad. "We're going to a party."

"Taylor Laurelin Bruce!" Jason yelled from outside. "Get your cute patootie out here. We've got parties to attend and beverages to regurgitate. Let's get a move on, *son*."

My dad chuckled, waving me off. "Go ahead. Have fun. We can catch up later." He chuckled, then said, "Oh—"

I stepped back and waited.

"Did you need a ride to campus tomorrow? I'll be leaving around six. Early practice."

I cringed. "I think I'll take my own car and deal with the parking lots. Thanks for the offer, though."

"Anytime. I'm there every day. I'm sure we can figure out times when we can ride together."

I nodded before slipping out the door, but I doubted it. As of today I attended Cain University technically as a transfer freshman, but I knew I'd be going it alone most of the time—unless Claire got a bug up her rear and wanted to ride together. That seemed unlikely, though. She lived a block off campus in an apartment with three other girls. Driving all the way to my house, through traffic, and back to campus would be an hour's venture. She'd only driven tonight because the party was outside of town.

"About time." Jason twisted around as I slipped into the backseat. "Were you contemplating world peace in there? I could've joined the local monastery and became a nun by now."

I grinned as I clipped my seatbelt in place. "Monasteries are for monks."

"Hmm-mmm. Not for me they ain't." He wiggled his eyebrows, flashing me a smile and his dimples. He waved a finger at me. "You know I'd be the only non-practicing nun in there, too."

"Was that your dad?" Claire looked in the rearview mirror at me after she had pulled out into the street. Ten and two. Her hands were positioned perfectly on the steering wheel. Even her posture was perfect. Her back was straight. Her head stood tall and confident, like the rest of her.

Claire had almost-white blonde hair, and it was wavy and spiraled like she had a perm that would never go away. With the right shampoo and a little bit of gel, hairspray, and fluffing, her hair fell past her shoulders and down her back like she'd stepped out of a hair commercial. She had the golden tan, a light smattering of freckles, and blue eyes. If anyone was going to joke about being a nun, Claire had the best chance of persuading someone to believe her. She actually looked angelic.

Not that she was a nun, though. I'd been the one with the steady boyfriend all through high school—from eighth grade until the day my mother died. Claire had had her fair share of boyfriends. She averaged two a year, and one time, after a night of too many daiquiris in high school, she confessed that she enjoyed starting the school year with a new guy and ending with a new guy. She said things never got too dull, but they lasted long enough to get into a comfortable routine. She only started blushing our senior year, so I figured that was when she lost her V card.

Jason was the opposite, not just with his sex life, but also how he dressed. Claire was elegant, and Jason was anything but with his pink collared shirt and red plaid shorts. I was a little more conservative in a black tank top and frayed jean shorts. Claire liked to point out that it didn't matter what I wore, I usually wore it best—her words, not mine. I thought she was ludicrous whenever she said that. We all stood at the same height—around five feet, eight inches—though Jason's hair was currently gelled up into something like a Mohawk. Claire's hair was loose, and I had my light brown hair back in a messy fish braid.

"Tay?"

I remembered her question about my dad. "He came to check on me. He has friends over tonight."

"Well, that was…" Jason shared a look with Claire. His mouth flattened into a disapproving line. "…sure nice of him."

They shared another look, and I pretended not to notice. They'd helped me pick out the casket and finalize all the funeral details while my dad watched football tapes. Yes. They didn't need to say anything at all.

And it was time to change the topic. I cleared my throat. "Where's this party again, Claire?"

"It's not far from your place, a couple of miles. I heard about it from some friends at school."

"Will I know people there?" Jason asked.

She took the car in a careful turn, pulling onto a gravel road. "I'd be surprised if you didn't."

"Wait. Friend or foe?"

Claire didn't reply.

"Claire," he urged, leaning closer to her. "Friend or foe? You know my enemies."

She flicked a strand of hair over her shoulder, glancing at him from the side of her eye. "Um…"

He sat back in his seat, his back resting against the door. "You're kidding me."

"It might not be that bad—" she started.

He finished. "Park's enemies? Right? That's who it is? That's who's throwing the party?"

She cleared her throat and readjusted her hold on the steering wheel, as her little chin grew firm. "Sebastian Park is not on campus anymore, so that means you're not indebted to him. You can do whatever you want, and that includes—"

He rolled his eyes, cutting her off. "I know how ruthless he can be. I think not. Park's gone, but he's not out of commission. Not fully. He still has some connections, and I'm not going against him.

No way. If those guys who went against him last year are there, you know I'm done for. I won't even be allowed into the party."

"That's not true." Claire's voice grew louder. "You'll be fine, and you're going in as my friend. You're not working for him anymore, and besides, believe it or not, I doubt they even remember you. You do go to a different college than us."

"Kade will."

I sat up, recognizing the name. "Kade?"

Claire let out a soft, irritated sound. "It's not even like that, and Kade won't remember you. I'm sure of it. He's…" She held her hand up, lifting it close to the car's roof. "…up here, and you…you're…" The meaning was clear. Jason was not a blip on this guy's radar.

I kept my mouth shut. No way was I stepping into that.

"Thanks, Claire."

"Well, it's true." She shrugged. "I'm sorry. You had one run-in with Logan Kade last year, and Park's beef wasn't even really with him. It was with his brother. So yes, I think Logan Kade will be at this party, but I don't think you have to worry about him."

I didn't know who this Park was. Kade sounded familiar, though.

He folded his arms over his chest and fixed Claire with a brooding stare.

"Stop it." She gave him the same stare right back. "I mean it. That's all over and done with. You have nothing to worry about, and if you do, I'll step in. Or Taylor will."

"What?" My head swiveled between them. "Step into what?"

"It's fine. If these guys come after Jason, just tell them who you are, who your dad is, and they'll stand down. People know your mom died last year, and they respect your dad. So they won't do anything you don't like tonight."

"Great." Jason's sarcasm was thick. "Just wonderful. I have to be saved by some girls."

"Hey!" Claire and I cried.

"Nothing against vaginas, even your vaginas, but despite how I dress, I'm still a guy. I can handle myself."

I leaned forward. "Do they know *how* my mom died?"

A sudden hush came over the car, followed by a slight wave of tension, and I knew why. It plagued me for the last nine months, but I hadn't talked about *it*. No one asked, and I never offered. A counselor had asked my feelings once, but I spent the entire hour in silence. My friends never questioned me. They knew better. I'd talk when I wanted to. The last and only time I spoke on the subject was my statement to the police—until now.

Claire shifted in her seat. "Uh...no," she murmured. "It was kept out of the papers, and I've never heard any word about it on campus."

"No one talks about it on my campus either," Jason added.

I was relieved to hear it, and as quick as I brought it up, I shoved it to the back of my mind. Seeing lights from a house growing brighter and brighter as we approached, I said the only other thing I wanted to do that night.

"Good," I told my friends. "Now let's get drunk."

CHAPTER 3

MOTHER F&CKER LOGAN KADE
TAYLOR

The house party had spilled out into the backyard. A river, down from the backyard's slope, was lit up by floating candles anchored in place. It was beautiful. It gave the entire scene an almost magical feeling. My last college had parties—for the short time that I'd been there—but they were distinctly different from this. They were about beer, wine, rum, and deep conversation. I'd gotten into a few philosophical debates about religion and society's selfishness, with Eric, the boyfriend, at my side.

He'd been at my side in high school, too. Those years had been about pretending to be mature while people hooked up, got drunk on whatever they could score, and kept one eye out for the cops. No one was running around naked tonight. A few were making out, but all in all, this Cain U party seemed tame. People were drinking and talking. Those who were swimming were doing just that: swimming. A few guys were pretending to dunk some girls, but that was the closest to shrieking anyone came.

Claire headed off to find her friends, and when she came back, I took the drink she offered. Gesturing with it around us, I asked, "Why couldn't we have parties like this in high school?"

"We were too busy pretending to be cool?"

"Oh, yeah."

Jason came over then, a scowl on his face. "I couldn't get one. You were wrong, Claire. They *do* remember me."

She almost choked. "You're kidding."

He rolled his eyes, and took the one she was holding. "Nope, sweet chickadee. They remember me. This is Blaze's party. I didn't know this house was his. He moved. He was closer to Cain campus last year."

Claire held her hands up. "Chill, okay. I'll get you a drink, and stop worrying. If they were going to throw you out, you wouldn't have been allowed back here."

"Mmm-hmmm." He glowered at her retreating back over the drink he still held. "She's off to get her *own* self a drink." He raised the glass to me. "And I'm no idiot. They're waiting for Logan Kade to get here. Then they'll see what *he* wants to do with me."

"Okay." I shifted closer to him. "What happened, and who is Logan Kade? His name sounds familiar."

"His name's familiar because his brother is a football god around these parts: Mason Kade. I'm sure your dad's mentioned him."

I scratched at the corner of my mouth. Was that where I'd heard that name before?

"So his brother is a big football guy. What does that have to do with Logan and whoever this Park guy is? How were you involved?"

"Mason Kade hated Sebastian Park last year, so that meant his brother hated him, too. I don't know the reason why. There are rumors, of course," Jason said, fluttering his hands through the air. "But who really knows? What I do know is that I took bets on some fights for Park last year. Logan Kade wanted me to open it up to his buddies at a party, and I wouldn't do it. It was a conflict of interest. I owed Sebastian. Everyone knew about the beef between the two. I was protecting myself."

He ran a hand over his face. "Since then, I've not been invited to any Cain University party. Park basically got run out of town, and the Kades took over, kind of. I mean, a lot of people have no clue about the rivalry, but everyone who matters knows, and they paid attention. Once Kade gets here, they're going to throw me out…" His voice trailed off as his gaze fixed on something over my shoulder.

He suddenly resembled an owl. His eyes got big, and his chest rose as he sucked in a quick breath of air.

Someone new had arrived at the party, and turning around, I assumed it was Logan Kade. I could only see the back of him. He was talking to a group of guys right outside the back door, and someone motioned in our direction.

Jason groaned.

Logan lifted his head, looking right at us.

From the back, he was the finest specimen I'd seen in a long time. Tall. Lean. Broad shoulders. Trim waist. His shirt clung to his form, outlining his lithe build. He was obviously an athlete. Guys couldn't get that look unless they played sports on an almost-daily basis and for hours at a time. Others might try to mold and sculpt their bodies to look as good as this one, but their efforts never played out.

Even the back of his neck was delicious. His shirt hugged the muscles of his shoulder and the ridges where his neck and shoulders became one. His hair had a crew cut. When he finally glanced over his shoulder again, looking in the direction the other guy had pointed, his eyes found mine. They held firm.

I swallowed, feeling like I'd just gotten the wind knocked out of me. He was breathtaking.

Dark chocolate eyes. Long eyelashes I would've killed for when I was younger—hell, I still would. He had an angular face with high cheekbones, and the front of him matched his back. His biceps bulged, and his shirtsleeves tightened around them for a second before they relaxed. The outline of washboard abs was visible through his shirt. His jeans sealed the image, making my mouth water, and I finally pulled my eyes away.

I had to. I hadn't reacted to a guy like this in a long time. It didn't feel right. A breeze picked up, sliding across the back of my neck, and goose bumps formed. I felt a shiver go through my body, and I turned, as if to shield myself from the wind. Maybe I was shielding myself from this guy. I didn't know. He was just…too much. His charismatic pull still tugged at me, even when I wasn't looking at him.

I swallowed over a knot. Claire hurried over toward us, holding two big glasses in front of her. She almost tripped in her haste. "He doesn't even remember you, Jason," Claire said once she arrived. "You don't have to leave."

"No." Jason shook his head. "I'm going. I'm not sticking around and waiting for whatever Kade is going to do."

"Come on—"

"He starts fights, and he finishes them," Jason said firmly. "Don't try to tell me you're not hoping he'll come over. I know you've got the hots for him. Honestly, Claire. He's a manwhore. He's had a different girl with him every time I've seen him. And look at him." Jason pointed as Logan Kade approached. "Tonight's no different. There are two girls with his group. I'm not—"

Claire huffed. "Believe it or not, not every girl is enamored with him. I've got my own set of friends and—"

Jason's voice rose higher as Logan approached. "Like you said before, he's up here…" His hand rose to his head, then lowered to his waist. "And we're down here. Isn't that the way it is?"

Ten feet away.

Jason's breaths came in quick gasps.

Eight feet.

Claire threw him a look. "Maybe we can remember why we even came tonight?"

Six feet.

Jason wasn't listening anymore. He was frozen, his gaze fixed off to the side. He watched Kade coming from the corner of his eye and let out a shrill breath through his nose.

Four feet.

I didn't know the guy, but now I was on edge too. I turned so I couldn't see him, but I could still feel his approach. His presence was even more overwhelming up close. Two feet away—one—and he walked right past us. His group followed, taking over a bunch of loungers that surrounded an empty bonfire pit. A keg sat in the center and as Kade got a drink, his friends filled theirs after him.

Jason wheezed. "I was pissing myself there for a moment."

Claire cursed under her breath. "I told you it'd be fine, and look what happened. He asked where the keg was. They pointed it out for him. If you would've let me talk, I could've explained that, and also that no, they didn't bring up your name." Her eyes blazed. "Whatever. I'm going inside to hang out with friends who are actually nice to me."

She took off, and Jason rolled his eyes. He shifted closer to me, his arm brushing against mine. "She's the one who told me I was beneath Kade. Whatever, my ass. Maybe he is above me. Maybe I'm small potatoes compared to him, but so is she. She hangs out with the philosophy club." He laughed. "Does that sound like someone Kade would date? Someone who's into philosophy? He's all about sex, fighting, and having his brother's back. There's only one girl I've heard he's ever been loyal to, and it ain't her. That's for sure."

My insides had begun to churn. My mother. My dad. Even my ex. I didn't need this. "Can you stop? I thought we came to get drunk tonight."

Jason caught himself before he could speak further and swung his gaze my way. "I'm sorry, Taylor. I...Claire..." He finished his drink, and after tossing the cup on the ground, he wrung his hands together. "We've grown apart since school."

The knot was back. It took root at the bottom of my throat. "I'm beginning to see that."

I should've asked what happened, why they'd grown apart, or how they had put up a good front for me over the last nine months, but the truth was that I didn't care. I would someday, but I didn't that night. I looked over at Kade and his group, my eyes lingering on a beautiful girl who sat next to him. She had jet-black hair and a stunning face that could've graced any magazine cover. She wasn't touching him, he wasn't touching her, but they were close. That was obvious.

I jerked my head toward them. "Looks like you don't have to worry about him now."

"Yeah. Guess not." He linked elbows with me. "Come on, friend. You said you wanted to party, so let's go do that. Let's drink ourselves all the way back to high school."

"That sounds fanfuckingtastic."

Jason chuckled, and a couple of pitchers later, we were in two lounge chairs on the front lawn. I lost track of time, but I was happy. Or I had the buzz to make me feel happy. The world was a little blurry, just how I liked it. Jason just came back with the third pitcher and he plopped down when a girl came around from the back of the house. She was headed for the street, but before she could slip through two cars, some guys surrounded her. They seemed to have materialized from the road, stopping the girl.

She backed up at the same time Jason leaned forward in his chair. "Oh no."

I looked. "What?"

"Move, assholes. I'm leaving," the girl said. She wasn't scared. She was annoyed.

Jason said to me, standing up, "That's Samantha and those are Sebastian's guys. This is so not good. Not at all. Hold on."

"Who's Samantha?" I asked, but he didn't answer. I looked over and saw he wasn't there.

As he disappeared around the house, a few people had followed Samantha to the front. Those people stopped, saw what was going on, and turned back to their friends. Pretty soon, more and more people started to come around the house. Soon a crowd started to fill in around her. I stood up, going over too. Maybe it was the beer in me, or maybe it was because of my own tragic douchebag ex-boyfriend, but I wasn't going to let her stand there to be gawked at alone. My confidence that anyone would help was at an all-time low, so fuck it. I was going to help.

Damn the consequences.

I stepped closer, recognizing the girl now as Jason's words clicked. This was the girl who came with Logan Kade. She stood now with her hands at her sides, her feet set apart. Her shoulders were back and ready as she watched the guys. She was ready to fight, and a nervous flutter moved through me, but there was an excited flutter right next to it. No. That was an angry flutter, but it was bordering on excitement. I was ready to fight, too, and remembering a time when someone who hadn't stuck next to me, who should've, spurred me on.

"Get Logan," someone yelled.

Another girl asked, "Where *is* Logan?"

I heard other people saying the same thing, but I focused on the girl.

She raised her chin, and a warning flashed in her eyes. "Touch me. I dare you."

There were three of them, all tall and, not to be stereotypical, but they looked like preppy douchebags. Each was good looking, with bodies built like they rowed every morning for hours. They looked like money. It practically dripped from their clothes. Their jawlines were rigid enough to form glaciers.

Their eyes were icy, too, as they stared back at the girl. They weren't backing down.

I broke from the crowd, planning to go stand next to her. But before I could move, the crowd broke in half. An actual opening formed, and Logan Kade strode forward.

My foot jerked back into its spot, stepping back as he brushed past me.

Kade stopped beside her, and the three guys turned their attention to him. They didn't move or say anything, but the air shifted. It'd been dark and ominous before, and I still felt a battle brewing.

"Kade starts fights, and he finishes them."

A low tingle went through me, warming me. I remembered what Jason said and the nerves/anger/excitement took on a whole other feeling. My mouth was almost watering. I wanted to see what would happen. I wanted to see this Logan Kade in action, and for some reason, I was thirsting to see this fight.

"Kade," one of them grated out his name.

Kade glanced at the girl, and then settled back on the spokesman. "What are you doing here?"

"It's a party. We were invited."

"And that's why you're facing off with Sam?" He moved forward a step.

"We weren't facing off..."

Samantha folded her arms over her chest. "Yeah, right. You were just walking past me? That's why you wouldn't let me get past you to the car. We just 'happened' to block each other and you didn't hear me when I told you to move."

A little laugh slipped from me.

Kade threw me a sideways look.

I should've clamped a hand over my mouth. I should've let them know I wasn't involved, because really, I wasn't. I didn't know this girl. It wasn't my place to say anything or join in, but I didn't. A dark part of me had opened up, seeing that this girl might need help. I wanted something to happen. I was almost egging it on in my head and as Kade watched me, his eyes lingering, the dark part grew into something else. My body grew warm and my pulse started to pick up. It was like he knew what was going on in me, and I swallowed over a lump, because that wasn't right. He couldn't know. He didn't even know me...

But I felt like he did. I felt like he knew exactly what was going on in me, and a flash of anger flared up in me. I turned away. He could see inside of me, and that was too much. I didn't want that so I slipped back into the crowd. As I pulled further away, enough so I wasn't on the front line, my insides were still charged up.

"Come on. Who invited them?" someone near me asked.

"Who are these guys?"

"Park's lackeys," another voice answered. "And they weren't invited."

More and more partygoers were talking. They were annoyed, and an excited buzz filled the atmosphere. People wanted a fight. They wanted to see some action.

The three douchebags scanned the crowd. Two stepped back. They seemed wary, but the third focused his attention on Kade. He moved closer, stepping so he was right in Kade's face. His lip curled in derision, and his mouth moved, saying something I couldn't hear.

Oh boy. I swallowed.

I recognized the look in Kade's eyes. His anger wasn't fading; it was increasing. And then it didn't matter.

Kade's hand flew and punched the guy right in the face. Douchebag One's head flung backward, and he stumbled a few steps before recovering. His two friends shared a look, seeming unsure what to do, but Douchebag One made the decision for them. He wiped the back of his hand over his mouth, locked eyes on Kade, and charged.

The fight was on.

"No, no, no!" Jason shoved his way through the crowd. "Cops have been called," he yelled. "Everyone scatter—"

Before he finished talking, sirens began to wail. They were faint, still in the distance, but he was right. They were coming.

Douchebag One reared back. He was going to hit Kade.

"Stop!" I yelled.

Kade heard me and turned to look. I pointed behind him. Before he turned around, he ducked, and Douchebag One's arm went over his head. Kade caught it, twisted around, and rammed his elbow into the guy's gut. He hit him with an uppercut, then bent over and tossed him over his back. The two other guys ran to their friend and pulled him away as they took off with the scattering crowd.

I watched, frowning. We weren't in high school. We didn't really need to worry, did we? But Jason grabbed my hand and yanked me after him.

"Come on," he said. "There's illegal shit here. We don't want to get caught. Trust me."

I was still revved up. I didn't know what from: from Kade or from the fight, but Jason took off and I followed right behind. As we zipped past a car, Kade was right there. He was heading to a different vehicle and for a moment, our paths crossed.

Kade looked at me. His eyebrows furrowed together, like he wanted to say something, but Jason yanked on my hand and we were past him.

"Logan!" Samantha called from farther down the road.

She waved from an Escalade. Jason veered toward them, pulling me along. I wasn't sure what he was doing, but he continued right past the vehicle. I glanced back and watched as Kade sprinted for it. He leaped, took hold of the top of the Escalade, and somehow threw himself into the front seat as Samantha clambered into the back.

Once inside, Kade reached out and pounded on the top of the vehicle. "Let's go," he barked.

The driver took off, and they were past us in two seconds, just as Claire pulled up.

Jason hurried into the passenger seat, and I threw myself into the back. Claire gunned the engine, and we turned off the block and onto another street as the cop cars began pulling up in front of the house.

"That was close."

I wasn't sure who said that, but it didn't matter. We were all thinking it.

Then I grinned. I wanted to do it again.

CHAPTER 4

SOC 101: MINDF'CKING A GROUP
TAYLOR

The house was dark when Claire dropped me off.

Empty wine bottles sat on the kitchen table, along with half-empty glasses and a platter with cheese and crackers on it. A few grapes remained in a bowl, along with some crumpled-up napkins and three beer bottles where I assumed my dad's co-worker had been sitting. A couple of the glasses had lipstick stains near the rim.

I plopped down in a chair and surveyed the scene. Judging from the dirty dishes in the sink, the food was plentiful. And based on a few more empty wine bottles in the garbage, the booze had been flowing all night long.

Speaking of booze, some of the beer started to trek its way back up my throat. I grimaced and swallowed as I cleaned up the kitchen quickly. My dad wouldn't have time in the morning, and I had no doubt he was already knocked out now, sleeping the booze off. When I finished and headed upstairs, I was surprised to hear the sounds of his television coming from his office.

But he was zonked out. I was right.

An old football game played, while my dad snored in his chair. His head was back, his mouth open, and another eruption sailed out. I shook my head; I'd found him this way so many nights—either this way or he was gone. When being a workaholic didn't help with forgetting, he'd find other ways: alcohol. Strip clubs. I was pretty sure he'd had a brief affair with a married woman.

The house reeked of cheap perfume and cigarette smoke, and I'd found notes written on napkins in the trash. Most had hotel names and room numbers on them, but I didn't have the heart to follow him to those places. I'd thought about it once. I'd had my phone ready to go. I was going to call Jason and make him go with me—Claire wouldn't have understood. Her parents were still together, and alive. But Jason was different. He got it, but after I brought his number up, I couldn't hit the call button.

So coming home and finding my dad here? I was okay with that. At least he was here.

I got to work. The television was turned off and I wheeled his chair down the hall to his bedroom. Thank God for wooden floors. Lining the recliner up next to his bed, I put his feet on the mattress, folded up the rug underneath the wheels so the chair wouldn't go anywhere, and hit the controller so the chair folded down. He was next to the bed if he wanted to roll in there, or he could sleep the rest of the night the way he was. Either way he'd be hurting in the morning.

I grabbed a water bottle and a couple of painkillers and set them on the nightstand before heading to bed.

When I woke up the next morning, the chair was back in the office, and he'd taken the water with him. The painkillers were gone, too. After getting dressed and ready, I sat at the kitchen table drinking my coffee. It was peaceful. It was quiet. It was relaxing, but that didn't last once I left and got to school. I was late. Really late.

The door to my first class was about to close as I sprinted around the corner. A guy was reaching for it, and when he saw me a frown appeared, but he waited. I sailed past with a breathless, "Thank you."

I slipped into the first empty chair, which was in the front row. The door closed and the guy walked past me...right to the front of the class. Lovely. He could glare at me all through class. I snuck a look over my shoulder, but I didn't see any other open chairs. I was stuck.

Note to self: Leave twenty minutes earlier tomorrow.

The guy cleared his throat. His hands rested on the podium, and his eyes lingered on me for a moment before sweeping the class. "Welcome to Abnormal Psychology. My name is Jeremy Fuller," he said. "I'm Professor Gayle's assistant, so I'll be helping out with most of the teaching and testing for this class."

He had striking features. Blue eyes, light blond hair that held a little curl, and an almost too-thin face, but he was handsome. He looked a little like Jude Law, which would normally have made me frown, but as far as I was concerned, this guy was my teacher. I'd be friend, not foe.

We got the syllabus, an explanation of everything contained in the syllabus, and when no one could think of a question to stall the arrival of our first lecture, we got that, too. The lesson filled the rest of the hour. He dismissed the class, but I was putting my laptop away when he came up to me, clearing his throat.

"You're Taylor Bruce?"

"Yeah?"

"Hi. I'm Jeremy Fuller—" His lip twitched, and he pulled back his hand. "Sorry. Habit. We already did introductions, and I swear, I'm not a creepy teacher dude." He paused, closing his eyes for a beat. Then he shook his head. "I'm coming across like an idiot. Okay. Let me try again. I knew your mother."

My heart stilled.

"No. Sorry. Wow. I'm bumbling this, aren't I?" He tried another smile. "I'm really sorry. I didn't realize who you were when you first came in, but once you introduced yourself... I'd been meaning to find you before class started. That's what I'm trying to say. You don't have to be here."

A boulder lodged inside my chest. Someone had opened me up,

stuffed it in there, and now they were trying to stitch me up around it. "What?" I couldn't move.

"No, no, no," he said again, hastily. "This is all coming out the wrong way. I recognized your name on the list, and Professor Gayle asked me to double-check, because she recognized your name, too. She's a friend of your dad's, and she remembered hearing that you were in a nursing program already. I double-checked your transcripts and called your last professor."

My chest grew tighter as he spoke.

He called my last professor…

He knew…

He had to know…

I licked my lips. They were chapped. When did that happen? A slight buzzing sound started in my ears, and I shook my head, trying to clear it. When I spoke, my voice was hoarse. "I took an incomplete with that class, the one like this one."

"Yeah." He nodded. "The professor explained where you went when—"

I tensed, waiting for the blow. He was going to say it.

"—you had to take your incomplete. He told me it was late in the semester, and you had a ninety-eight percent in the class overall. He would've passed you, but you didn't take the final you assured him you'd be back to finish."

This was like a nightmare.

My hands sank into my bag, holding on to it tight. "I left school altogether."

He paused, his mouth open, then his eyes darted to my face. "Uh, yeah. He told me that, too. I explained that you were a student here now, and he said he'd waive your last agreement. You got an eighty-three percent in the course. That's what I meant when I said you don't have to be here."

"I don't?"

"I don't even have you on the list. I already put you in the next class up. Now…" He cleared his throat, sliding his glasses to the top of his nose. "This means you'll be in class with actual nursing students. They took this course and got into the program, so in essence, you did, too, but not officially. Does that make sense?"

No.

He *knew*. He must've known.

He paused again, frowning at me. "Taylor?"

I nodded. He was saying something. I'd remember it later and figure it out. Class. The next one. Not this one. I nodded again, which was enough for him. He launched into the next part of his statement.

I wasn't listening. I couldn't.

"...tomorrow then?" He sounded so bright and cheery.

I forced a smile, and a weak "Okay."

"Great. Good. All right then," he said. "I have another class in here. What do you have next?"

I closed myself off, and my autopilot turned on. I was fine. I was great. I was so thankful to him for doing that.

And I almost convinced myself that was true as he followed me to the hallway and clapped me on the shoulder before turning toward the bathroom. He had to go before his next class, which he didn't teach, he explained. He was a normal student like me in that one. I nodded as he disappeared.

And my next class? I checked my schedule. I had enough time to grab a coffee. I was heading back with it when I realized that my next class was in the same building. My last class had been in Room 311...and the new one was 309. People were already going in, and I picked a seat in the back.

A bag dropped onto the desk next to me, and I looked up into the narrowed eyes of Logan Kade.

"You."

I straightened in my seat. "You."

"I recognize you from last night."

My chin went up, all my slight-panic fled, and it was on. I heard the challenge in his voice. "I recognize you from last night, too,"

I said. Challenge accepted. My body went from being numb to burning up. All the panic, pain, haunting memories—everything that Jeremy Fuller just brought up in me was wiped out by the mere presence of this guy. I should've been grateful, but I wasn't. I was hot. I was angry. And I knew it had nothing to do with Logan Kade, but like last night, I didn't care.

"You're friends with Jason Delray. I remember him now."

"You're friends—" I started, then caught myself. "Yes…he is my friend."

His top lip twitched into a smile. The rest of his gorgeous face was stoic. His eyes were alert, focused on me, but it was his mouth I couldn't pull my gaze away from. Some of my anger was melting into something else, something I didn't want to think about. For some reason Logan Kade had already wormed his way under my skin.

He stared back at me for a moment, a mask over his face, before he started laughing. "You are feisty."

"Is that a problem?"

"Do you not know me? Feisty women are my specialty."

"You're arrogant."

He was full-on laughing now. "Have you not met me? Nah." He waved that off as his smirk grew. He knew full well the effect he had on everyone. "I'm Logan Motherfucking Kade. I have my own hashtags, but," his eyes warmed, and he leaned closer, "I want to know more about you. I know your friend, but I don't know you. What's your name?"

I held my tongue. He'd find out my name during roll call. I wasn't concerned about that. No, I was holding my tongue because I was having a reaction to this guy that I'd never had before. Eric was a jackass. He proved that the day my mom died, but he'd been my constant before. He was sweet, popular, and always there. I had feelings for him, that was obvious, but nothing like this. I didn't quite know how to react to someone like Logan Kade.

The second he sat down next to me, others started glancing back at us, but now that he was laughing, more and more they were openly staring. A few girls down the row were almost glaring. Kade saw them too and raised a hand. "Hey."

Their stares morphed into smiles, and they waved back. One girl asked how the party was last night, and it clicked. These girls already knew Kade. I gave them a second look. They might really *know* him. A couple were giving him come-hither looks.

I muttered under my breath, "So this is what it feels like." *Huh.*

"What is?" He leaned back in his chair to rest against the wall behind us. His eyes pinned me down, but not in a bad way. He was curious—and amused. His mouth lifted in a grin. He *was* cocky. I hadn't lied about that, but maybe I'd gotten the other part wrong. The arrogance of a narcissist was lacking with him. He just seemed to be enjoying himself.

My eyebrows bunched together as I remembered the night before. He'd had the same look. That is, until those guys had gone after his girlfriend. Dark, brooding, and dangerous had taken over then. A shiver went down my spine as I remembered him hitting that guy.

Our professor entered the room, but Logan raised an eyebrow at me. "What *what* feels like?"

She cleared her throat and held up a stack of papers. "Here's your syllabus. We're going to hand these out and go through them before we start anything else."

I shifted back in my seat and shook my head. I was partly grateful for the interruption. Even though I'd just gotten to this college, I knew Kade was at the top of the social ladder. Hell, he probably defined the top tier.

He walked into a room and got attention.

Kade commanded this whole room. It was overwhelming, all of that power radiating from him, and having it directed at me? It was a whole new experience. I shifted in my seat, trying to get comfortable, but I felt torched.

"Welcome to Sociology 101, the scientific study of human society," our professor announced.

Logan leaned over and whispered, "Or as I like to call it, the tutorial guide on how to mindfuck entire groups."

CHAPTER 5

WANNA BET?
TAYLOR

"I have a bone to pick with your buddy Delray." Kade fell in step beside me as we left class. Hooking his arms through his bag, he pulled it onto his back and rested his hands on the straps. Somehow this made him seem even taller, or leaner.

"Yeah?"

He hurried around to walk in front of me, facing backward. I could've looked away before, but now there was no chance. I was locked in place. Not wanting him to fall down the stairs, which were ten feet away, I stopped walking. He did as well and smirked down at me, giving me the full impact of his six feet of height.

"I wanted him to do a gambling thing with some of my guys last year. He turned me down."

I frowned. "Okay?"

"You're going to get him to do a gambling thing for me."

I studied the amusement in those chocolate eyes of his. "Are you always like this?"

His smirk deepened. "Gorgeous?"

"Annoying." But that wasn't even true. I saw the amusement in his eyes. It was like he was laughing at me, but he glanced at the students filing past us and the look held firm. No. It wasn't just me. "Like you're laughing at the world."

He lifted a shoulder. "Because I am."

"It's annoying." It wasn't, though. It was something else. Logan made me feel like I was pushed off my chair and had to go through life lying sideways on the floor. It was disconcerting. "Not much bugs you."

He laughed. "Being called annoying? No. That doesn't register with me. I'm not being cocky when I say that girls like me—they really do like me. I'm funny, sarcastic, quick-witted, and enough of a bad boy to make girls wet. If I like you, I'm loyal to you. If I love you—and don't get ahead of yourself because that list is really short—I'll do *almost* anything to protect you. Girls drink that shit up like it's booze that makes you lose weight."

"You just likened yourself to a fat-free beverage."

"A fat-free alcoholic beverage, and yeah." His smirk was almost adorable now. "I know how chicks think. If something like that exists—where you lose weight while you get drunk—I'm buying all the stock I can. Don't tell me you wouldn't be all over that, too."

"What? The stock or the booze?"

"Both." His grin deepened. "Or just me."

I ignored the last statement, and began walking around him. I had to get lunch and figure out where my third class was, but he walked with me. He held the door open, so I ducked under his arm. I was just stepping outside, almost past him when I looked up. Claire was hurrying my way, her jaw clenched. When she saw me, her eyes slid to the arm I was ducking under and her eyes bulged.

I stepped past him, but I felt him moving with me. He was behind me, his breath on the back of my neck. I tried not to notice—I tried to shut my mind off. I failed. I'd been attuned to him since class started, but this went to a whole other level. He purposely moved so he was almost touching me, and my body went on high alert. My knees threatened to buckle. Sensations shot up and down my spine, and I had a full-on sauna effect going. I almost fanned myself to cool down, but Kade would've known instantly the effect he was having on me. I felt an ache between my legs that I hadn't felt in nine months.

Claire slowed as she approached us.

"Ah." His breath teased my skin. "Delray's friend number two. I can chat with both of you then."

"Hey," I murmured to Claire.

"Hey," she said, her gaze glued to him.

Logan chuckled. "You went here last year, right?"

Her gaze cut to mine, questioning.

I stepped to the side, away from Logan. I didn't want to move. No, actually *I* did, but my body didn't. I almost cursed myself, but I felt Logan's gaze on me. It was like he could see inside of me, right past the walls I erected.

"Uh, yeah, I did," Claire said.

"So you know Delray turned me down last year."

"Turned you down...?" She glanced at me again.

"The gambling circuit he used to run for Park," Logan prompted. "Is he still running it?"

"Uh..." Claire had become a statue. She was on the spot, particularly because I was present. Jason promised to quit gambling after we graduated. All three of us made a promise to each other, and that was his. I now knew that he lied, and so had Claire. She knew he hadn't quit.

"Yeah. He's still running it."

"This is what's going to happen." Logan clapped his hands together and rubbed them back and forth. His eyes were gleaming, but it wasn't malicious. He was being more mischievous, and that same expression of laughing at the world was there. "I'm going to take Taylor's number down." He pointed with both of his hands to me. "And yes, I'm using Delray to get your number. No shame in my game. I want your number *bad*, Bruce, but I have a message for Delray, too. He's gotta get in touch with me via my new sociology bud here." He put his arm around my shoulder, pulling me to his side.

A tingle shot through me at his touch.

He kept talking, "Tell him I want him to take some bets for me at a party I'm going to throw. And no, it's not negotiable. He has to do it. I let him off last year. I understood the conflict of interest, but Sebastian is gone. The numb nuts has been squashed. So, do we all know our roles now?" He looked at both of us.

Claire seemed wary. "You're going to call Taylor?"

"Yep." He held his hand out. "Phone please, Miss TayTay."

I handed it over, but tried to keep a firm scowl on my face. "I'm doing this under protest. I don't approve of Jason gambling."

Logan took the phone and paused, glancing at me. A slight smile flashed my way. "Why do you think I'm going through you for this?"

I didn't reply. My gut told me to let it go. Logan Kade was even more of a whirlwind than I'd realized he'd be, and I felt a little like I was in the damn Sahara. My mouth watered, and my lips were dry. I licked them, an unconscious habit, but when Kade's gaze lingered there, I realized what I'd done. I sank my teeth into my lip instead and forced my gaze away. It felt like I was fighting against a rubber band, stretched tight from me to him. The more I tried to break free, the stronger it became.

"Okay." He handed my phone back, and his eyes were laughing at me. A darker promise surfaced there too. My heart picked up. "I've got your number," he added. "I'll call you later, and I want Delray's answer through you."

"Why are we helping you?" Claire tucked a strand of her hair behind her ear. She was trying to be stern. She was failing. "Jason's our friend. Not you. Neither of us wants him to be part of the gambling world."

Logan smirked at her. "You're helping because I'm not one of those morally upstanding guys. I'm completely fine with blackmailing you, and you'll help because I may not know your name, but I remember the dudes you were flirting with last night. My friends can get to your friends, and when that happens? Well,

I won't take your friends away, but I *will* ban them from campus parties. And not to be a dick, but something tells me your guy friends are a little desperate when it comes to getting into parties."

"You're a dick." Claire gasped, her hand covering over her mouth. "I can't believe I said that."

He was, but he didn't seem to care. In fact, I think he was loving it.

He began walking away, backward again, that smug grin still on his face. He lifted both shoulders. "Like I said earlier, I've been called worse. I'll be calling later." He wasn't talking to Claire, and we both knew it.

He started to walk away, but his gaze held mine, and I was looking back. I shouldn't have been, but I was...and I didn't want to think about that either.

LOGAN

"What are you doing?"

I was walking to my next class, but swung around. Sam was standing there, her bag on her back with her hands holding on to the black straps around her shoulders. Her brown eyes were annoyed, and her mouth pressed into an irritated frown. She wasn't looking at me, though. Her gaze was trained on the two girls I just left.

"Hey there, sister soul of mine." I held a fist up. "How's it hanging yourself?"

She ignored the hand and shifted, one of her hands falling to her hip. "I mean it, Logan." She nodded to the girls. "What are you doing?"

"What?" I twisted around to look, too. The blonde seemed agitated, and the other one, Taylor, aka the hot one, looked...well, she didn't look like anything. I paused and frowned, focusing on her even more. That was surprising. Girls usually liked it when I said I'd call them. This one didn't seem too happy about it. "Huh." I scratched behind my ear.

"Huh?" Sam punched my arm. "Huh what? For the third time, what are you doing?"

"What?" My hand fell to where she hit me, and I rubbed there, absent-mindedly. Why didn't that girl seem to care? But then again, I remembered her at the party. There'd been something different, something dark about her. Something about why I sat next to her today.

"Logan!"

"Oh, yeah." I cleared my thoughts. "You remember Delray from last year?"

"No."

I shrugged. That didn't matter. "He was one of Sebastian's lackeys, and he turned me down for a job last year." I gestured to the girls. "They're his buddies."

"You're not."

"What?"

The ends of her mouth pinched together in disapproval. Sam cocked her head to the side, giving me that slanted look of when she was *really* disappointed in me. "Don't use them to get back at him."

"What?" I furrowed my eyebrows together. That was the farthest thing I was thinking. Well, maybe not. "No. That's not it. I'm using him to get the hot one's digits. That's all."

"Since when do you need to use manipulation to get someone's number?"

"Since it became fun, and besides…" I flashed her a grin. "Don't worry. I'm not planning on using that girl for anything. She won't get hurt. I promise. I'm just taking a few extra steps to make Delray squirm. That's it."

Her shoulders lifted up and slowly lowered. She continued to scrutinize me, but I saw the softening, and by the time her shoulders were all the way down, she was grinning back at me. She shook her head, rolling her eyes. "I like that girl."

"You remember her?"

She nodded, her eyes hardening. "She was going to step in and help me last night. I don't know her, but that's not normal, you know. Not many people would step in when it's one girl against three guys. People don't help like that anymore."

I nodded. I knew. We both knew how much I knew. Loyalty ran deep in our group for a reason. I held up my hands. "I'm not going to hurt her. I promise."

"Okay."

I smirked. "But I might bang her."

"Logan!"

"If she's down for it."

CHAPTER 6

LOGANISMS AND KAPOW!
TAYLOR

The house was dark when I walked inside with two bags of groceries. Hitting the lights with my elbow, I toed the door shut behind me.

"Dad? I got food."

He didn't answer, but he could've been in his office watching tapes. He always seemed to be there. Or else he was still on campus.

"Dad?"

I put a pot on the stove and put away the milk and orange juice. I unloaded meat for sandwiches, vegetables, fruit, and yogurt. After I pulled out the noodles and set them on the counter for dinner, I realized one thing: My coffee was still in the sink. I'd dumped it there this morning, and a small stain still sat around the drain. Dad hadn't been home all day.

He still wasn't home.

It was eight at night. Normal dads got home around six. My dad's last practice ended at three on Mondays. He'd spent last Thursday, Friday, and Saturday with the football team. Sunday was church, then he'd had his friends over, and I went out.

But today was my day. This was supposed to be my night with him.

I moved to turn off the stove, but I paused. I imagined flinging the not-yet-boiling water across the kitchen. For a moment, one moment, I considered it. Who cared if water got over everything? Who cared how hot the water was? Who cared, in general, about any of it?

I did, but the need to do something crazy was there—

"Taylor?"

My breath hissed, leaving me. That wasn't him, but I wanted it to be. Jason knocked on the door again as I turned.

He said, "Claire said I'm in deep shit with you."

"Yeah," I coughed out, my voice not quite working.

"Hey," Jason murmured when I appeared. His hand had been lifted for another knock, but he dropped it to his side. "You look, uh, a little…" He faltered and stepped inside when I opened the door. "What's wrong?"

I groaned. "Don't tell me I look like crap."

"You look sweaty and pale. You look good in most anything, but this ain't a good look for you."

He followed me back to the kitchen, and slid onto a stool, propping his elbows on the counter. "What happened today?"

Nothing.

"I mean, I heard about Kade," he added. "He remembered me after all?" He chewed on his bottom lip. "Claire said you both got the wham-bam-thank-you-and-maybe-I'll-call-you-later-ma'am vibe from him? That's called a Loganism, by the way. You got the drive-by version of it. He kapows people with whatever he wants to say, and they do what he wants— whether that's to get pissed at him or drop their pants for him." He quieted, cocking his head to the side. "I'm not getting that vibe from you. Taylor, what's wrong?"

My mom was dead.

My dad was absent.

My boyfriend left me.

I shook my head. "Nothing." Normal voice. *Be charming. Be… Remember why he's here in the first place. Use that.* I locked eyes on him and scowled. "Kade's going to ask you to do a gambling thing for him."

He shifted on his seat. "Yeah." He picked at a piece of invisible lint on his arm. "So?"

"Don't do it."

There it was. I'd meant it when I said I didn't want him to do it anymore, but judging from the way his shoulders slumped and he looked away, I knew he was going to do it anyway.

"You were beat up for it in high school," I added.

"Come on." He jerked in his seat. His hands fell to his lap, but he still didn't look at me.

"They threatened Claire," I reminded him.

"That's not fair." His eyes lifted to mine, and they were heated. He held a finger up between us. "That's so not fair, Taylor. It's different now too. I'm not doing the betting this time."

"You missed a payment, and they blackmailed me."

He snorted, folding his arms over his chest. "Yeah, well, Claire told me what Kade did. You must be familiar with being blackmailed by now." His eyes cut to the side again.

I'd never told him this next part. I waited. He had to be looking at me, and after a beat of silence, he did. "They were going to get their money no matter what—from you or from someone else."

"What are you talking about?" His voice hitched now. He was uncertain.

"They said either you give them their money or they'd get it from my dad."

His arms unfolded, and he leaned forward. "What are you talking about?"

"I never told you because you paid, but they were going to take me." A big ball landed in my throat. Oh well. What was new? "They called me on the phone one day. They were going to make my dad pay. I mean, it was just a phone call, but—"

"Wh—" He choked. The blood drained from his face. I wasn't

the only pale one in the room now. "You never—I didn't know that."

"It didn't happen." So I hadn't told anyone.

"Did Eric know?"

I snorted. "No way. He would've pissed his pants and run to the cops."

Jason quieted, tugging at one of his shirtsleeves. He looked ridiculous. It was a short-sleeved pink shirt —shave off a few more inches and he would've been wearing a tank top. But he kept tugging at it. For what? It wasn't going to cover his hand.

"Stop doing that." I pulled his hand away. "You're going to rip your shirt."

A rueful laugh left him, but his hand went to his hair. He still wore a stupefied expression. "I—I mean... My God, Taylor. You never told me."

"Why would I?" I needed something to do, something else to focus on. This was headed into territory I didn't want to visit: what Eric would've done, what I had done. All of that would spiral into other topics I'd been able to avoid for months. No, thank you.

"You want something to eat?" I turned the heat under the pot back on. "I was making this for my dad."

He glanced around. "I didn't think your dad was here."

"He's not."

"Oh..."

I had to ignore him. Ignore where this was going. That was my mantra.

"Uh, Taylor..."

"Do you want a beer?" I asked. "My dad has an entire fridge full. Trust me when I tell you he won't miss any. I have to go out to the garage to grab something anyway. You want one?"

"No." He watched me turn toward the garage, his mouth slightly open. "Thank you, though."

When I got back, I handed him a beer and opened the sauce.

"Taylor." Jason came over and took the jar from me. "Stop

making food. Stop it."

"No." I pulled it back out of his hands and nudged him aside. A gentle nudge, but still firm. "I was going to make this anyway. If we don't eat it, it'll be here for my dad. He'll be home any moment—"

Jason grabbed a note from the fridge and read aloud, "At Mike's house. Be back late. Hope your first day was great." He handed me the paper as he softened. "Signed, your dad."

I stopped for a moment. I didn't look at Jason. I didn't do anything. I just stared straight ahead. He'd said we'd have dinner, that he wanted to hear about my first day at Cain University…Nope. No way. I wasn't dealing with this.

I turned the burner off and took the note from Jason's hand, ripping it in two. "Okay." My chest was tight. "Let's go out, shall we?"

Jason said nothing, trailing after me. We went and ate, but if someone had asked me later where we went or what we had, I wouldn't have remembered. The storm was back. It'd been inside of me for nine months now. Jason knew what was going on, but he didn't push me. Thank God. During dinner we were nearly silent, each in our own thoughts and when we went back to the house, he broke the silence when I didn't move to leave the car. We sat in the driveway when he asked, "So did Kade call you yet?"

I frowned, but it was something *else* to talk about. "Why?" I wasn't asking why he was asking about Kade.

"I need the cash."

"We all need cash. Do something else."

He made a disgruntled sound.

"I mean it, Jason."

"And I mean it, too. Nothing will come back on you. Life's different now that we're in college. It's bigger." He held his hands in the air. "Grander. More freedom. More…I don't know. We're not so confined. I'm not tied to you and Claire. My problems won't come back to haunt you. I promise. And it's not the same either because

I'm not doing the betting. I'm taking the bets."

I stared at him, unmoving.

"Kade is rich. His friends are rich. I will lose out on a ton of money if I don't."

"Because you'll cheat them?"

"No, because most of Kade's friends are idiots. I mean, yeah, some of them aren't, and Kade usually isn't, but they don't care. This is their fun. They can afford to lose some bets. I couldn't in high school. That's the difference." He looked at me, pleading. "Just tell him I'll do it, and give him my number when he calls you."

"Maybe." I was mean.

"Taylor, come on!"

I rolled my eyes. I'd do it. I'd be the good friend to him.

Jason relaxed, sensing my surrender. He gave me a small smile. "Thanks, Taylor."

I nodded as he waved and climbed out to head for his car. When I went inside, I could feel that the house was still empty, but I checked the garage anyway. No car. No dad. I went to my room and read the two chapters for sociology class. They were due in two days, but good for me. I was being ambitious. When I'd finished, I watched the news.

No dad.

I was stupid for being worried. I mean, I moved back to be here for him. That was the plan, but it was obvious, and had been for so long, that he didn't want me here. Maybe I moved back for me? Maybe it would be too hard to go back to my old school. It'd be like I was leaving her behind, or maybe I still needed Jason and Claire? Or maybe I was here, hoping to be here for him because that was what she would've wanted me to do.

I sighed. I needed to let it go, let him go, but something was nagging me. I couldn't sleep so I checked my email and double-checked my class schedule for the next day. It was close to midnight.

No dad.

I read a book for another hour.

Still no dad.

That normal thing to do was to go to bed. My class was at nine in the morning. That'd be the *responsible* thing to do, but even when the clock told me it was after two in the morning, I was still wide awake.

My phone buzzed. It was on silent except for the alarm, but the screen lit up the entire room. My heart leaped to my chest as I rolled over, but no. Not dad. Instead I read, **Hey, hot girl. Forgot to call. This is Kade. You got an answer for me?**

I typed back, **Come pick me up. I'll give you your answer.**

My head fell back against my pillow once I'd hit send. I needed a ride. That was it. Kade could handle himself in a fight, and my dad was still gone. I needed to find out where he was—make sure he was fine and not at some strip club. That was all I was doing. That was it.

The next second my phone buzzed again. **Be there in twenty.**

CHAPTER 7

~~STRANGER PITY~~
TAYLOR

I was waiting in the living room with the lights off when his headlights swept across me. Everything lit up for a split second before his car faced the garage. Though it was the middle of the night—closer to early morning, actually—it was still humid. A small breeze wafted across my neck as I shut the door to the house behind me and hurried over to his car. Once inside, I didn't look at him.

Why I was here? Why had I texted? *My dad*, I reminded myself. His note had told me he'd be at Mike's house late, but this was ungodly late.

"Hot girl."

I looked up and immediately wished I hadn't. Logan hadn't gotten any less gorgeous since the day before. His dark eyes watched me, a hint of amusement still there—along with a hint of something darker. The darker element sent a rush through my veins. I ignored it, taking in the dark shirt he wore over jeans. The whites of his eyes stood out from his tanned complexion, and when he grinned, they matched his perfect white teeth.

He added, "Where to? I'm your personal driver for the night." He tapped the steering wheel. "I can be another type of driver for you, too, if you know what I mean."

I flushed, then scowled, regretting it. I ignored the fluttering in my stomach. "I have to run an errand."

A smooth chuckle came as he reversed the car. "Whatever you say. For real. Where we going? I didn't figure you really had to give me the answer in person." He started down the street, but slowed as we drew to the first intersection.

I pulled up my dad's GPS coordinates. "Turn right."

He nodded. "On it."

Thirty minutes later, we stopped outside Coach Mike's house. With one arm resting on the steering wheel, Logan faced me. "Want to tell me why we're outside my brother's head coach's house?"

"You know who lives here?"

His eyes seemed to be laughing at me. They always looked like that. "I do. I've spent time here with my brother. Been to your house, too, by the way. That's how I knew where to go tonight."

Oh, yeah. He never asked for my address. "You have?"

"There was a thing for your dad once, after your mom died. We all showed up with food. Sam made us make it ourselves. She wouldn't let us buy something, and she wouldn't listen to me when I said your dad wouldn't care."

He knew about my mom, but that shouldn't have surprised me. Of course, everyone on campus would know one of their beloved coaches had lost his wife. The corner of my mouth twitched. "That's funny."

"What is?"

I glanced up, holding his gaze. "Hearing that you knew about her. Usually it feels like having my insides ripped out with a spoon. This was...nice..." That was an odd sensation to me.

"Well, hey there, Hot Girl." His voice dropped low and sensual. He laughed under his breath. "If you're all about feeling nice, I'm chock-full of ideas." He waved his fingers at me. "You have my phone digits now, so anytime you want the use of my other digits, I'm just a button away." He lifted an eyebrow.

"I feel cheated, though," I told him, the edges of my mouth curving up. "I got the finger offer. I mean, seriously. Come on. If

I'm going to take you up on this, I want the full deal. I want to be tied up, stuffed from behind, and throw in a butt plug for you. How about that instead? I don't want a finger job. Not from the legendary Logan Kade."

I could have sworn I was joking, but as I sat back, a part of me was serious. Well, not about the butt plug. That was a joke...I think.

Logan flashed me a smirk. "Only if I'm the submissive. I like to be dominant outside the sheets, but every guy likes to have his softer side nursed." He winked. "Or whipped." He was damn near charming. "When do we start?"

I shook my head. It felt good to laugh. I sighed. "Thank you for that."

"For what? I was serious."

I gave him a look.

He cracked a grin. "I'm kidding, but I'm kinda serious about my first question. What are we doing here?"

"Oh." Craning my neck, I counted the cars. Four cars. Four coaches. And I lingered on the last Civic. "My dad."

"Your dad?"

"He's here." I pointed to the last car. "I just wanted to make sure."

"Ah, the old, 'I'm at my buddy's, but I'm really with my secret mistress'—or something worse..." Logan trailed off, watching me. "For what it's worth, Mason's never mentioned your dad having a proclivity for hookers or strippers, if that's where you thought we'd end up tonight."

The humor was gone, and I chewed the inside of my lip. What he didn't know... "Yeah, well, since my mom died, he's not really the same guy." My voice softened as I looked back at his car. "She wouldn't want him somewhere like that."

I expected Logan to defend him, but nothing came. I glanced over and saw him watching me, *only watching* me. No judgment. Nothing except mild curiosity.

"What? No comeback there?" I asked.

"I thought we were being serious." He lifted a shoulder. "Didn't seem in good taste." A wicked grin curled over his lips. "But if you want a comeback, speaking of good taste—"

"Stop." I held my hand up. "I already got the finger offer. I don't want to hear the next one."

"Okay, but I have to ask you something."

"Shoot."

"Why'd you want me for this? I asked around. You've been friends with that girl and Delray since high school, right? That means you must be tight with them."

"I am...or I was."

"Which is it?"

"I am." *One breath. Take one breath.* "A lot happened last year, but I'm still tight with them. They've been there for me."

He nodded. "So, why not them tonight? Why me? I know this wasn't about Delray's response."

"I—" I was going to lie, but no. He deserved the truth. "I didn't want to deal with their pity. It's worse than stranger pity." I gestured to him. My gut shifted, thinking about the other reason, which I shoved aside. "I didn't want to deal with their questions."

"Then you got the right guy. No pity here. Trust me. I get screwed-up parents."

I eyed him. "Yeah?"

He nodded.

Jason and Claire never pushed for answers, but the questions were there. I felt them. Every day. They wanted to know, and I couldn't blame them. They were concerned. I waited to see if he would ask more, but I didn't grit my teeth. My stomach wasn't clenched in knots. He didn't strike me as someone who would care. He wouldn't ask the invasive questions. He was easygoing with a joke at the ready all the time. There was also a darker side, but I don't know...maybe I was just lonely, and he was the only other person I knew.

That was it.

I was lonely. Good God. How pathetic.

Logan pulled back into the street and headed to the next intersection. "Now that I feel all close to you, you're stuck with me," he announced. "I'm hungry. You're going to keep me company." He rubbed his flat stomach. "The taco place by my house doesn't close for another half hour."

LOGAN

I whistled as I locked my car and headed for the house, bag of food in one hand and keys tossed in the air with the other.

I'd been at a party. Texted Hot Girl, picked her up for a random adventure, and now I was home after dropping her off. It was a few minutes till four in the morning on a Monday night, but this was college. This was life. This was what I was supposed to be doing: staying out, going where I wanted—not sleeping a solid eight hours a night and being wifed up.

Nothing against my brother's girlfriend, but the writing was on the wall. Mason and Sam had been through too much at an early age; they were going to be together forever. And that was the kicker. I don't even think they cared. They probably relished the idea of being only in each other's arms for the rest of their ninety years. I wasn't giving them an extra ten. Shit, Sam *might* endure that long—who knew if all that running she did was good for her body or was slowly killing her.

Nah, I guessed she'd tucker out around eighty-nine. My big brother? Seventy-five, and that was being generous. He was too cold, calculating, and disciplined. He'll have been under too much stress to make it longer than that.

Me, on the other hand, a solid eighty-three. And a horny eighty-three, too. I'd be doing the same shit as now. I'd get my tacos delivered to me in an old folks' home, preferably by some young thing. The idea had merit. I grinned as I headed inside, thinking of the sponge baths.

I stopped just inside. The kitchen light was on. We never kept that light on.

"Hello?" I walked inside and spotted Mason locking the back door. "Hey. What are you doing up?" I smiled again. "Had a fight with the wife?"

He scowled, scratching the top of his head as he walked past me to the hallway. "No, you asshole. I had to pick up Nate."

"Nate…" My voice trailed off, and I took in how my brother was dressed: Sweatshirt. Sweatpants. Bags under his eyes, his hair slightly messed up, and tired lines around his mouth—well, fuck. "I forgot him at the party, didn't I?" I looked around, but no one had come in behind Mason. "Where is he?"

"Yeah. You left him. I dropped him off at the hotel."

I groaned, grabbing on to the back of my neck. That was even worse. "His parents are in town." The pieces were coming back to me. Nate hadn't wanted to go to the party. But I did, so I talked him into it with the promise that we'd only be gone a few hours. His parents were arriving tonight—make that last night. "They were going to be jet-lagged, so he wanted to stay up and surprise them at the hotel. Shit. Shit. Shit."

Mason shook his head. "I hope the chick was worth it."

"The chick?" That's what they thought. I left him to have sex. I shook my head. "I'm not that shallow. I mean, come on."

Mason stood half in the dark hallway now, half still in the kitchen's light. His face was masked with shadows, but I caught the grin. "You didn't leave the party because of some girl?"

"I did, but—"

He snorted a laugh. "That's your problem. Whatever you did

and whoever it was with, I hope it was worth it. Nate is pissed." He walked backward toward his room. "And lucky for you, you sleep next door to him."

I hadn't left him to have sex. I knew that even when Taylor texted back. She wasn't that type of girl. But hearing it from my brother, I couldn't tell Nate the truth. It'd be even worse that I'd left him to *not* have sex. He wouldn't understand. I'd dropped the ball. Nate was my brother's best friend, but because all three of us grew up together, we were family. We all lived in the same house, along with Samantha, my future stepsister and Mason's "wife."

"'Night, little bro. You'll make it up to him. Don't stress about it." Mason paused before going into his bedroom. "Hey." His voice had softened.

"Yeah?"

"Did you have fun?"

"What?"

"With the girl. If you didn't have sex with her, did you have fun, at least?"

I scratched behind my ear. *Did I have fun?* "I thought you didn't want to know."

Mason lifted a shoulder. "You're a little different tonight."

I scowled. "I am?" I didn't want to hear crap like that. I was the same. "I was leaving to get food anyway. I forgot Nate was there because *he* was the one off with some girl. Not me. I've had a very asexual night."

"Logan."

"What?" My scowl didn't go away. That bothered me.

"I was joking. You're the same sarcastic jackass you always are."

"Oh thank God." I pressed a hand to my chest, giving him a watery grin. "That scared the living shit out of me. Don't do that." Sam called to him from inside the bedroom, and I waved him off. "Go back to Sam. Sleep tight, big brother. You've got a day full of twofers tomorrow." Which reminded me... "Oh hey," I added as he opened his door. He glanced back at me. "The coaches had a rough night. All four of them spent the night at the head coach's house tonight."

He cursed. "Are you sure?"

"Yep."

A second, third, and fourth curse. "That means we'll be doing sprints all practice."

I laughed. "Have a good night." I yelled past him, "You, too, Sam."

"Stop talking so we can go to bed!" she yelled back.

Mason closed the door behind him, and I went to the kitchen.

CHAPTER 8

MINDF'CKING PARTNER IN CRIME
TAYLOR

"What did you say to him?"

The sight of Jason waiting outside my classroom building hadn't registered before he saw me and pounced. Well, he didn't pounce, but it was almost the same thing. He straightened from the building, crushed out his cigarette, and flung a hand in the air as he rushed over to meet me. His hair stuck up all over, like he'd been running his hand through it.

"Uh…" *Wait a minute.* I frowned. "What are you doing here? You don't go to school here."

"I'm waiting for you." He glared and crossed his arms over his scrawny chest. "Kade turned me down. He asked for my competitor's number instead."

My mouth twitched. I wouldn't laugh. "He did?" I could feel myself smiling. I couldn't stop it.

"It's not funny. Do you know how much money I lost out on?"

I shrugged. "Look, I told him you'd do it. That was my job. I didn't say anything else about it."

"Then why'd he change his mind?"

"I don't know." A swarm of students headed inside—even the smokers were going in. "I have to go to class. Why don't you ask him yourself?"

"Because I can't."

I started for the door, but turned around to walk backward. "What do you mean?"

"He called me from a disposable phone. It's not in use anymore." I could see the wheels start to turn as he spoke. His gaze went to my hands, which were empty, then shifted to my book bag.

"No." I shook my head, stopping before I hit the door.

"You have his real number. He doesn't give that out."

I reached behind me, finding the door handle. "Apparently with good reason." My hand tightened around the handle. "And no, you can't use mine."

"Come on…"

I gave him a look.

He trailed off, his shoulders dropping in a sigh. "Fine. Okay."

"I have class. If you want, I'll brainstorm new jobs with you."

"New jobs?" He lifted a hand to scratch his head.

"You know, so you'll stop with the gambling stuff. Because you know I hate it."

"Uh…" He bit his lip and glanced around. "I think you're going to be late for class." He gestured behind me. "You should get going. We'll talk later, maybe this weekend." He began backing away.

I waited, watching him go. No matter which side he was on—taking the bets or making the bets—it was all the same to me. Same world. A dangerous world. I repressed a sigh. Jason would never stop. He'd just stop being honest with me about it.

But at the moment he was right. I needed to get to class. I was a few minutes late, but I slipped into one of the back chairs unnoticed. Or I thought I was unnoticed. I looked to the front of the room to find Jeremy Fuller, the TA from yesterday's class, leading this one as well. He had the syllabus projected on the wall and pointed at it as he ran through what was expected of students.

Without interrupting his speech, he grabbed a piece of paper and began walking toward me. He was explaining which textbooks were approved for the class when he placed the sheet of paper on my desk. *Glad to see you made it*, he'd written. My cheeks warmed, and I glanced up. He'd moved on to the criteria for an A grade, but he winked at me as he headed back to the front of the room. A couple of girls next to me witnessed the exchange, and I could feel their speculative gazes.

But whatever. I didn't think their attention was academically rooted. I looked over and one girl was still glaring at me. That was definitely not academic jealousy. Jeremy Fuller was good looking. I'd noticed it yesterday too, but he was the TA. I wasn't one of those girls who signed up to screw the TA for a better grade. Glaring Girl did not have to worry. At all.

I ignored her, and eventually she turned her heated looks back to the TA. When class was over, I grabbed my stuff to make a quick getaway. I felt like Jeremy might try to talk to me afterwards. Maybe I should've stayed and apologized for being late, but I didn't want to draw any more attention.

I was almost in the clear when I heard my name behind me. "Taylor."

I cringed and turned around, pushing back against the stream of students leaving around me. Jeremy waved me back into the class, and I could see the glaring girl waiting beside him. Of course. Gritting my teeth, I went back inside, but stood next to the wall. I didn't want to step any closer. I didn't want to fight. Not with her. Not with anyone. I just wanted to go to school and move on with my life.

"Glad you came today." Jeremy handed something to another student and spoke to me, reaching for his bag. He began putting his remaining papers and books in there.

The girl cleared her throat, slinking up right next to his table. "Jeremy?"

His eyes widened. "Oh, Sarah. I didn't see you there."

She didn't look amused. Her eyes grew flat, but her smile didn't slip a notch. "I was hoping to ask about the Honors Study Group. I heard you were leading it this year?"

"Oh." His eyes shifted to me, then back to her. "You know that's only open to students in the top two percent of their classes. You…" He faltered, letting out a small sigh. His hand curled around his bag strap. "You know you're not in that two percent."

She stepped back as if he'd hit her. Her sultry smile disappeared. I expected her to snap, but all she did was murmur, "Oh, okay." She hung her head and pulled her hands away from the table. "I'll just have to get there then."

"Yeah," he said, his voice cheery. He cleared his throat, glancing to me again. "We can see where you are after midterms. We add new students mid-semester anyway."

"Okay." She peeked back at him, a glimmer of a new smile wafting over her face. "Thank you, Jeremy."

"Uh, sure." He moved back from the table, holding his bag in front of him like a shield. "If you don't mind, Sarah…" He nodded in my direction. "I need to talk to the new transfer."

She looked at me, and the transformation was remarkable. Her eyes chilled. Her smile remained, but it became menacing. And I swear the room grew cold. A shiver moved up my arms, but I refused to cross them over my chest. I lifted my chin as she continued to look at me.

Her eyes narrowed.

So did mine.

Jeremy cleared his throat again. "Sarah, if you can go ahead? I'm going to lock the room behind me."

"Yeah. Sure." She cast one more glance over her shoulder before accepting defeat. She readjusted her backpack, gripping the strap where it lay over her shoulder, and scurried out the door. I stepped out behind her, with Jeremy bringing up the rear. I was cautious as I moved into the hallway. If she could've slung her bag to hit me, I think she would have, but she didn't.

My stomach relaxed as I saw her hurry down the hallway to the main entryway.

"Sorry about that." Jeremy closed the door and locked it. He stepped around me with a smile and extended his arm to lead the way. "Professor Gayle lets me use her office in between classes. We can go there."

I followed as he went to the back hallway where professors had their offices. He paused in front of the last one.

"Am I in trouble?" I asked.

He opened the door, but looked back, surprised. "Why would you be?"

"Because I was late."

"Oh." He laughed. "No, not at all. I want to talk to you about what that other student asked about."

I tilted my head. "The Honors thingy?"

He laughed a second time as he placed his bag on the cluttered desk and sat down in the chair. He motioned to the door. "If you don't mind, do you want to close that?" As I did, he pointed to the empty chair across from him. "You can take a seat."

Once I sat down, he leaned forward, his elbows on the desk. "We tell students that the Honors Study Group is only for those in the top two percent, but that's not entirely true. It's for whomever we choose. But more than likely the top two percent are among them. The group consists of the best students in the nursing program. We get together every other Thursday evening to do..." He shrugged, leaning back in his chair. "Just about anything. We study together, give each other pointers, help with papers and study guides, or just hang out. The last time we went bowling, and the time before that, one of the girls had us over to her house." He paused, a secretive smile on his face. "That was an interesting night indeed."

I felt like I was going to be inducted into a secret society of nerds—the kind who were entitled, self-righteous pricks who got off on how smart they were. If Claire were sitting where I was, she would be drooling at the exclusiveness. This guy was either going to invite me in or tell me how to apply. I bit my lip. I wasn't sure I wanted to deal with this, whatever it was, but a voice in my head kept me from outright saying no. It reminded me that sometimes it pays to put up, shut up, and see if there are benefits to being asked.

I kept quiet, hearing him out.

"Anyway." He clasped his hands together and rested them on the desk. "Gayle wanted me to ask if you'd be interested in joining us."

Gayle, as in Professor Gayle.

I frowned. He'd said the day before that she'd called in some favors because of my dad. Understanding flooded over me. This was because of my dad. "She's doing my dad a favor?"

His eyebrows lifted in surprise. "Uh…yeah, but it's not all because of your dad. Before your, uh, before what happened last year, you were in the top five percent of your class. Professor Gayle feels you'd fit in perfectly with the group, and…" He leaned closer and dropped his voice, though no one else was in the office. "Between you and me, it's worth it. Any extra time it might take, and even dealing with some of the egos, it's all worth it. We really do help each other, and you'll get to know the professors on more of a one-to-one basis. It's good to have a professor know your name and care about what happens with your future. It's really good."

I chewed on the inside of my lip. My eyes wandered around the room and found a picture of a stunning woman: Long, beautiful golden hair. White teeth. Perfect smile. Sparking blue eyes. She was slender with a heart-shaped face. I nodded to the photograph. "Is that Professor Gayle?"

He followed my gaze. "Yeah. That's her."

"Is she married?"

"No."

His answer was quick, quick enough that it seemed Mr. Fuller had a little crush himself. Professor Gayle looked to be in her thirties, and I got the same let-down feeling that filled me whenever someone used me to get to my dad. Maybe I shouldn't jump to conclusions, but I was betting Professor Gayle wanted to date my dad, or she already was and was looking out for his kid. Either way, I knew my answer.

I stood up, gathering my bag. "I can't."

He stood with me, looking surprised. "Are you sure?"

I nodded, going for the door. "Thanks for the invite, but I just can't right now."

"Oh."

I glanced back before opening the door. He stared at the desk, his mouth turned down.

My answer had stunned him. "Thank you again," I said.

"Yeah." His head bobbed up and down. "Uh, let me know if you ever change your mind."

People didn't turn chances like that down. That much was obvious. But I had to.

Women used to come to our house to see my father, and I was used to them fawning over me because they thought it would get them closer to him. My dad had a great job. We had money, and also an inheritance from my mother, which included money she'd received from her parents when they passed away five years ago. These more recent women could tell there was money somewhere, *and* my dad was handsome.

I resigned myself to the fact that he was going to date, but I didn't like it. I didn't have to like it, and I certainly didn't want it having an impact on my academic life.

My studies were mine alone. No dad. No wife wannabes. I wanted my dad's identity and mine to be separate. That meant keeping my head down, trying to keep quiet about my last name, and doing what I knew how to do: study my ass off and make my mom proud.

Thinking about living my own life reminded me of Jason, and I pulled out my phone to send him a text: **You still mad at me?**

I'm not replying to you.

You just did.

To tell you that I'm not replying to you.

So you're mad?

I waited a beat. No text came. But just as I slid my phone back into my bag, I heard it buzz again. I pulled it back out to see that Jason had replied, **Yes.**

I dropped it back in my bag with no reply. There was no point. When Jason got mad, I had to let him stew. He'd get over it, eventually. I was on my way to the food court for lunch before my next class when another text came. Jason again: **I won't be mad by the weekend. We should hang out.**

I replied with a smiley face, then really put my phone away.

The food court was set up like the ones at a mall. Fast-food booths lined the outside walls, and tables, chairs, and couches covered the middle. A large fountain filled the area next to the main entrance, and a river wound from it down through the center of the eating area. Potted trees and foliage added to the atmosphere. Doors to the side of the fountain led into the actual cafeteria for students with a meal plan. They just needed their ID card to get inside. I had a meal plan, but I still grabbed an empty table in the far corner of the food court, right next the windows. It was out of the way, and I could see all the students outside.

It was perfect.

Plopping down with my salad, an apple, and a water, I pulled out my laptop. I had an hour and a half before my next class. I'd just started checking my email when I heard a familiar voice. Claire came in through a side door near me. She was with a bunch of others, all of whom Jason would've rolled his eyes at.

Some of the guys wore pastel polo shirts over slim khaki shorts, their hair gelled and combed to the side. Other guys had their hair sticking up in a mess, but it was no doubt meticulously put together. Claire and a few of the other girls wore dresses, while two others wore jeans and T-shirts. Those two trailed behind, and I wondered if they were actually part of the group.

When they all found a table, those two girls sat at the end. Claire landed smack in the middle, right next to the guy who looked like the leader. He wasn't the tallest, but he had the most charisma and a wide smile. Everyone seemed to be talking to him, or waiting for whatever he had to say before continuing their conversation.

I could've called out or raised a hand, and she would've come over. Actually, seeing how snug she looked next to that guy, she probably would've called me over to join them. She sat with her back to me, so I knew she wasn't going to see me. I kept quiet. Sometimes being alone was too lonely, and sometimes—like now— it was a welcome break.

Then I heard, "It's my mindfucking partner in crime."

CHAPTER 9

REGULAR NICE GUY
LOGAN

Taylor wanted to be alone. That was obvious.

I saw her from outside before I came in. She was watching her friend, her cute face scrunched up. I could've done a play-by-play of her thoughts: *Should I call out to her? Do I want to? Then I'll have to deal with the douchebag pricks with her.*

Then her face cleared. She stopped nibbling on her bottom lip and shifted in her seat, turning away from the table with her friend. Yep. Taylor made the right decision.

And I made my grand entrance, dropping into the seat across from her. "It's my mindfucking partner in crime."

Her entire body went rigid, her apple frozen inches from her mouth.

I smirked. "Any time you spend with those sphincters is wasted time. Good call ignoring your friend."

Her cheeks flooded with color, and she straightened in her seat. "I'm not ignoring—" she started. She took a breath and looked around. "I didn't even see her over there."

I narrowed my eyes. "Don't lie." I waved at her face. "You turn purple when you try to bullshit. It's a bad look for you."

"I'm not purple." Her cheeks went from red to a lavender color.

"You are. It's kinda cute, if you want a guy that's into the whole

Barney look, but I'd assume those guys aren't going to be looking your way unless you're nine and like black, nondescript vans."

"What?"

"Okay. I'm stereotyping." I grabbed her water. "But I don't care."

"That's my water."

I opened it and took a drink. "It's mine now." I gestured to the coffee booth. "I have to get a latte for Sam." I lifted her bottle. "I'll grab you one of these. You want a coffee or something else, too?"

"No."

I stood, frowning down at her. "I'm not that big of an asshole, I swear," I told her, waving her water in the air as I walked away. "I'll buy you another one. I just need a little something while I wait in line. My throat's parched."

She eyed me with her usual look, a mix of wariness, curiosity, slight amusement, and something else. I hoped it was sexual attraction, but this girl was different than the others.

"Why'd you turn Jason down for the gambling thing?" Taylor asked when I returned to the table.

I sat down and slid a coffee over to her, along with her new water. I flashed her a grin. "See? I keep my word."

She scowled. "Answer me about Jason."

I snorted. "Impatient much?" I pointed to the water bottle. "I'd like you to note that I follow through on my word."

She looked down at the water and coffee. "What is that, and why are you making a big deal about it?"

I ignored one of her questions. "That's the stuff you drink, right? Or did I get the wrong kind? You had it in class, though I think you forgot it when we left."

"You got me coffee?"

"I told you I would."

"You didn't have to do that." She stared down at it, her hands around the cup.

I heard the wonderment in her voice and I frowned. "It's nothing.

It's coffee." I placed another cup on the table. "I have to take this to Sam anyway."

Her eyes lingered on Sam's cup before she murmured, "Oh, yeah." Then she shook her head and refocused on me. "Jason. Why did you turn him down? He's blaming me for it."

"He is?" The corner of my mouth lifted. I hadn't expected that. "Delray's some little shit, isn't he? I kinda like him."

The corners of her mouth were twitching, like she couldn't decide to laugh or glare. "You asked for his competitor's number?"

I remembered how Delray had sputtered over the phone. "Oh, yeah. Good times, but no worries. You're not to blame. I was never going to use him. I just wanted to make him jump through some hoops—revenge for turning me down last year."

"The whole thing was a lie?"

I nodded. "You weren't around last year, but your friend worked for a major piece of shit. When I saw him at the party last weekend, I was surprised. I didn't think he had the balls to come around one of my friend's parties, he or those other assholes. It was my way of sticking it to Sebastian, just a little bit, even though the guy is gone."

She still looked confused. I'd mentioned Sebastian before, and I was sure Delray had filled her in, but it was hard to explain the magnitude of the guy's asshole. He was a dark hole into the abyss.

I shrugged, standing back up. "But don't worry. Next time I see your friend, I'll let him know it wasn't because of you. I was being an asshole all on my own."

She looked out the window, frowning slightly. "Thank you for the coffee."

I studied her for a second and gave her one last parting grin. "See you in class tomorrow. Don't let some other douche sit next to you."

I heard her say "What?" as I headed out, but I didn't turn around.

I liked Taylor Bruce. I thought again about how she'd been ready to defend Sam. If another girl did that, I'd figure she had an angle—she wanted to use Sam to get to Mason, or even me, or use Sam herself for recognition and power on campus. My brother was a sports god, so his girlfriend was known, too. We all were. Just me sitting at Taylor's table had drawn attention. I don't think she was aware of it, but she would've realized it eventually and gotten uncomfortable.

Something happened that made Taylor avoid the limelight. I'd grown up in the spotlight around other people who wanted the spotlight too. Seeing someone like Taylor Bruce was refreshing. Hell, *she* was refreshing.

I wanted to bang her, but I wanted to bang a lot of girls. If the opportunity arose—I paused before pushing open the second door and stepping outside—, but there was something else in Taylor, something I didn't sense from other girls. I couldn't put my finger on what it was, but heading toward the communication building, I didn't think about it again. Sam waited for me outside and her eyes lit up when she saw the coffee. "Give me. Give me. Give me." After taking a sip, she closed her eyes with a contented smile. "Thank you, Logan."

I threw my arm around her shoulders. "See, that's how I'm supposed to be thanked for doing something nice. Getting coffee for someone—that's a nice thing to do."

"What?"

"Nothing." I squeezed her against me for a second. "Let's go to class."

See? I could be a nice guy. Sometimes.

TAYLOR

"You're friends with Logan Kade now?"

I'd been lost, still surprised by his generosity, when Claire's voice distracted me.

"Huh?" I looked up to find her standing in front of my table. Her bag hung from her hands, which were cupped together in front of her. Her eyes narrowed slightly, and she glanced back over her shoulder. I followed her gaze. Her entire table watched us with mixed expressions. The girls' eyes were big. One had a dreamy smile on her face, and most of the guys looked mystified. Their leader seemed stoic, his face unreadable, but I caught a flash of hardness in his eyes before it shifted. When he caught me studying him, a warm smile transformed his features. His eyes grew friendly and welcoming. It was such an abrupt change that I didn't know how to process it. Instead, I shifted back to Claire.

She sat across from me, grabbing a water from her bag and placing it on the table. "So, are you?"

"What?"

"Friends with Logan Kade now?" She turned to look through the window, where Logan had gone.

As we watched, he handed the other coffee to that girl, the one from the party. Her eyes lit up, and she inhaled it, a blissful expression on her face. She said something, and he threw his arm over her shoulders as they went into the building. Whether she was his girlfriend or not, his utter devotion was evident.

My stomach churned slightly. I wanted that. But as soon as I had the thought I stopped myself. It wasn't the devotion I wanted from Logan Kade. I wasn't jealous about that; it was the loyalty. Eric hadn't been loyal. He'd left me, literally. And my dad... No. I wasn't thinking about my crap right now.

I forced a smile. "Has Jason texted you today?"

"You're not going to talk about Logan Kade?"

I shrugged, glancing to the side. "I have no idea. I think he just likes to mess with me or something."

"Oh." Her eyebrows pulled together. "That's all?"

I focused on her again. "I didn't think you liked him." I glanced over at her table. The guy she'd been sitting with was still watching. "What's his story?"

She cast another look over her shoulder. "That's Ben, and before you ask, I have no clue what's going on with him."

"But you want something to go on with him?"

Her head did another little shake. "I have no clue, like I said, and I'm over thinking about it. He pays all this attention—sits next to me, calls me, wants to study together, go get food together. But then when we get around other people? Nothing. I have such a hard time reading him. I don't know what he wants, or if he even wants anything." She began picking at the edge of the table. "You were here before, right?" She tilted her head and looked at me. "That's what Malia said. She saw you first. Well…" She rolled her eyes. "She saw Logan first, but she said the girl was already there when we got our table." She paused, her eyes flicking down to the table and back to me. "Why didn't you say anything? You could've sat with us."

I inclined my head toward her. "I thought about saying something, but you were with your friends. You know me. I've not been the most social creature lately."

Her eyes grew sad.

"I didn't want to bring you down," I murmured. "Me and lots of people don't mix well."

Her eyes lowered, and she began picking at the table again. "I could've come over to sit with you. You didn't have to sit here alone."

I gestured to the empty seat next to her. "I wasn't alone, remember?" Logan had occupied that seat. "Unfortunately."

Her lips pinched inwards, giving her a thoughtful and almost disgusted look at the same time. She moved to the edge of her seat, her hand now weaving figure eights on the table. "Yeah. That's… weird, huh?"

I sat back.

"Logan Kade's kinda taken a liking to you or something." She jerked up a shoulder. "I mean, that's what it looks like to me…" Her voice trailed off, like she wanted to say something else.

I sat still as the realization hit me. Claire was jealous, and her friends were, too—the girls anyway. I scanned the food court. There were more than a handful of girls watching us, watching me. This wasn't a normal reaction. I didn't know what it was, but I knew it wasn't normal. If Eric had come to Cain University and become popular, I wouldn't have gotten this reaction from people. Others might've noticed me, but I couldn't imagine this envious, suspicious, and somewhat guarded scrutiny. It's like they were trying to decide if I was a threat or not.

Shit. I let out an abrupt laugh. "Does this guy have semen made of gold or something?"

"What?"

"Nothing." I started gathering my stuff. Staying here meant another girl might come over with questions. I didn't want to chat. So I stood, hoisting my bag onto my back. "I have to go to class."

CHAPTER 10

YOU'RE BAD
TAYLOR

The rest of the week passed without drama. Thankfully. Classes ran on a Tuesday/Thursday or a Monday/Wednesday/Friday schedule, so I had to see Logan one more time. I expected debauchery, lecherous jokes, or a crapload of innuendos, but when he dropped into his seat Friday morning, I got none of that.

I tried to tell myself the feeling of being let down had nothing to do with him, but it did. I was disappointed. In just a few days, I'd grown accustomed to Logan's...well, to *Logan* and how he was. There wasn't a word to describe him perfectly, so I went with *Loganisms* to explain encounters with him. And I didn't get any of them that morning, and I missed them. Somehow, Logan made me forget the things I needed to forget.

When class was over and he offered me a nice "see you later" as he got up to go, I almost called him out. He looked tired. He'd run his hand over his face a few times during class, and his eyes seemed heavy. Something was wrong.... But I couldn't handle my own stuff, so how could I take on someone else's? And Logan was gone before I could ask if he was okay or not.

In class, Jeremy, who I now tried to call Mr. Fuller because using his first name made me uncomfortable, mentioned the Honors Study Group one more time. And as I opened my mouth to tell him again that I couldn't, he interrupted. He placed a hand on my shoulder and said, "Just think about it. It helps to have friends in high places sometimes."

It did. I couldn't deny that, but my dad... Finally, I nodded. "I'll think about it."

"Great."

After that I ducked out of the room, and now here I was, filling out my third job application. The first had been for the university library, the second for the coffee shop on campus. This one was for a small pub a couple of miles from my house. It was off-campus, had nothing to do with Cain University, and though the owner said she knew my dad, she didn't seem to care one iota about him. It was perfect.

Then Logan walked in.

I looked up, my pen poised in my hand, and stared at him.

He came in with another guy, throwing the door open wide, and they sauntered like they owned the place. A week ago I would've hated that cockiness and the smug smirk that adorned his face, but today? I swallowed over a small ball forming in my throat.

I was *not* excited to see him, and I ignored the little flutter in my stomach. I was just glad to see that whatever had been bothering him was gone now. His normal flair had returned, and I held still as he scanned the room.

He found me in the corner eventually and did a little double take. His smirk grew as his eyes took on a mischievous twinkle. He said something to his friend, who nodded and headed for the bar. Then Logan came my way, sliding onto the bar stool across from me. He didn't ask what I was doing there. He pulled the application away from me and began reading it out loud.

I grabbed it back, glaring. "That's private."

"Bruce." He shook his head with a playful *tsk*ing sound. "Nothing's private about my friends."

I frowned. "We're friends?"

"We haven't had sex, and you haven't called me an asshole or slapped me yet, so yeah." He winked at me. "That classifies us as friends in my book."

There had to be some retort for that, but it wasn't coming to me. I just stared at him. He scooted his barstool over so he could lean against the wall and brought his legs up to rest on another stool in front of him. Everything about him was relaxed, and for a moment, a warm surge rose in me. I liked this side of him. I got the sense that Logan didn't classify a lot of people as friends. Or maybe he had a thousand friends, and I was just one of them, but it didn't stop the flutter inside me.

I felt included.

I had Jason and Claire, but this was different. I didn't know what it was, and I didn't want to analyze it. I just wanted to enjoy the feeling.

Logan signaled for the guy he'd come in with and caught me staring at him. His eyes narrowed briefly. "What?"

"What?"

"You're giving me a weird look."

His friend placed a pitcher of beer onto the table. Logan moved his feet so the guy could sit. As he did, he nodded to me in silent greeting.

Logan snapped his fingers. "Nate Monson. Taylor Bruce. You've been introduced."

Nate nodded again, asking Logan, "Bruce?"

"Mason's coach."

I tensed. Some guys flipped out when they found out who my dad was, but not this one. I knew Logan didn't care either. So I relaxed. Nate had jet-black hair and features that would've looked at home on a runway. He wasn't as lean as Logan, but he was a little taller. As he got comfortable and poured some beer in a glass, I glanced back and forth between the two. Nate seemed reserved, quiet, and very unlike Logan, who watched me as I sized them up.

"Bruce," Logan started, leaning closer to me over the table, his hand wrapped around the beer. "What are you doing applying for a job here?"

I glanced at Nate. Was he going to chime in? But he just lifted his beer to take a sip and turned to watch the bar. He didn't seem to care about Logan's question.

I shrugged. "I need a job."

"Bullshit. I've seen that house you live in. You guys have money."

Nate glanced at Logan then, a small smile on his face. Logan saw it, and his own lips curved, but neither said a word to the other.

Logan arched an eyebrow at me.

I shook my head. "I don't know what you want me to say. I need a job. That's it."

I needed something to do outside of school and my studies. I didn't want to depend on Jason and Claire to always be there to entertain me, and I didn't want any other friends. I wasn't ready to wade into the drama friendships sometimes brought.

Logan leaned back, raising his beer again. "I call bullshit, but whatever." He glanced around. "This is a good place to work. Beer isn't too watered down. We get free snacks." He gestured to the popcorn machine. "And good tunes." He nodded to the stage where a band was setting up, then to the jukebox.

Nate chimed in, a low, smooth baritone, "It's far enough from school that you don't get a lot of sorority chicks either."

Logan nodded in agreement.

"Is that normally a problem?"

Both guys looked at me.

I shrugged, feeling a little intimidated. "I mean, don't guys want drunk sorority girls at a bar?"

Nate grunted. "Sure, if you want a cheap lay. I'd rather have a sober girl at the end of the night, or at least one who knows who she is, not someone so insecure she'll do anything I ask of her."

"You guys are reverse snobs."

They both frowned at me, confused.

"What do you mean?" Logan asked.

"Guys like wasted girls."

Logan shook his head. "Insecure guys want wasted girls. I've got a rep. I know that. But none of those girls were wasted. No way."

Eric always liked getting me tipsy. He didn't care if I was drunk or not. This made me look at Logan a little differently. Something close to respect had started to form in me.

I needed to go. That was dangerous. I already looked forward to his jokes, but if I respected him, too? That was just bad all around. Those things could lead to something more, something deep, so I had to go.

I grabbed my purse and slid off my stool.

"Where are you going?"

"I, uh..."

Nate wasn't paying any attention. He watched the band setting up on the stage. But Logan almost seemed disappointed. I grabbed the application, crinkling it into a ball.

"I have to go home."

"You're not going to apply now?"

"No." My tongue lay heavy on the bottom of my mouth. I turned to go. My hand rested on the table.

"Hey." Logan scooted off his stool and came around to me. He crowded in, moving closer so I could feel his body heat. He rested his hand next to mine and his finger grazed against mine. He barred me from slipping out and asked, "What's wrong?"

He cared. I didn't expect that from him. I reminded myself that I didn't really know him. A week ago, I hadn't known him at all.

"Taylor?"

"Use my last name." I moved him back a little so I had some breathing room. I tried not to notice how good he felt, or how strong his arm was under my touch. "It's more appropriate."

"What?"

There it was again. Genuine confusion. He wasn't angry. He wasn't getting defensive. He was just confused.

"What's going on here?" He edged back one more step. "You okay?"

"No." I waved my hand at him. "It's you."

"Me?"

"Because you're bad."

He smirked. "I know I am."

I gave him a dark look. "You're bad news. I can't handle you."

He groaned, throwing his head back and closing his eyes. "Do you know how many directions I could take that? Seriously, Tay— Bruce. Watch your words if you don't want me hitting you with one-liners."

I paused. "What?"

"Nothing." He forced out a breath. "Go on. I'm bad news. Why?"

"Because I can't hand—" I started to repeat my words, but Logan let out a closed-mouth half growl. "I can't deal with the attention that follows you around," I offered instead.

He let out a breath he'd been holding. "Thank you. I didn't think I could hold back anymore if you didn't stop."

I pressed my lips together. I was trying to ditch him, and he was crafting his Loganisms, even if he wasn't delivering them. Of course he was, and he was amused by the whole thing. The more his smile grew, the more I wanted to forget that I needed to stay away. Part of me *wanted* to stay. I wanted to hang out with him and Nate. They didn't care. I didn't understand, but I liked it, whatever it was they didn't care about. I needed it.

Logan studied me, and it was like he could read my mind. He threw an arm around my shoulders, and a rush of warm emotions swept over me. He turned me back to the stool and patted my hip. "Okay. Hop up there."

I ignored how good his hand felt, touching my hip. And once I was back on the stool, I didn't think about how I missed the weight of him and how safe I'd felt, tucked into his side.

He sat on the empty stool next to me, across from Nate, and turned to face me. I thought he was going to put his arm around me again, and I wanted it, though I shouldn't have. I held my breath, but he didn't.

Logan filled the third glass Nate had brought to the table and nudged the beer toward me. "Come on, Bruce." He touched the rim of his cup to mine. "I don't like drunk girls to screw, but I do like drunk friends to hang out with." His eyes peered right into mine.

I licked my lips. That damn flutter was back in my stomach. "Friends?"

He grinned down at me, his eyes darkening with promise. "To friends, Bruce."

Still watching each other, we lifted our glasses and took a sip. That was when I knew it.

Logan Kade had really become my friend. God help me.

LOGAN

Shit.

I wanted to fuck her. No. I wanted to do a whole lot more to her, but she wasn't ready. She wanted a friend, so fine. I'd be the best fucking kind of friend there was. I scanned her up and down, and I grew hard, looking at the cut of her jeans, how her shirt shifted and I could see the side of her breast. How soft her skin looked, how soft her hand felt.

Nope. I'd put on a hat I rarely wore and do what she wanted, and with that thought I glanced up. Two girls had been eyeing our table. I moved so I was facing them, and then I stared. That was all it took.

They shared a look between themselves, then grabbed their purses and their drinks. They came over. And I could sit next to the girl I wanted, hit on the girl I didn't want, and be a friend.

Fucking hell.

TAYLOR

Three hours later I stared at my empty pitcher of beer. No, I wasn't just staring at it. I was clutching it in my hands and inspecting the hell out of it—turning it over, looking inside, sniffing inside, and then placing it back on the table. All that beer. Was gone. Consumed by me.

I was drunk.

The first hour had gone by fast. It was fun being Logan's friend. His one-liners turned from sexual to just wickedly smart. He liked to rile Nate up. I learned that real quick. A few choice words from Logan and he would stiffen, glare, then finally roll his eyes at himself and shoot back an insult. Logan lapped that up, usually turning the insult back on him.

The girls had come at hour two. That was when I learned I really was Logan's *friend*. He still sat beside me, but he had turned toward the two girls standing at the end of our table. Nate had disappeared from the table with another girl. I nudged Logan and asked who she was. He said he had no clue, just that Nate liked to get some mouth-on-dick action when he could. He said it so casually, like he was telling me the time. That was the beginning of my solo journey with this pitcher of beer.

It had taken me an hour to drink it.

That wasn't counting the three beers Logan had poured for me before, or the shots Nate brought over for all of us, or my empty stomach. I'd stopped here on the way home to fill out the application.

Nate and Logan had both ordered food earlier, but I hadn't been hungry then.

My stomach growled.

I looked down at it. I was hungry now.

"Logan." I tugged on his sleeve.

He glanced over his shoulder, but didn't turn away from the girls. "Hmmm?"

See? I was one of the guys now. It sucked.

"I have to eat, or I have to go home." I tried to give him my most serious face. "What do you propose we do?"

The corner of his mouth twitched, like he was trying to hold back a grin. "Well, *friend*." He emphasized that word.

I winked at him, shooting him with my finger. "Good one."

He shrugged, looking proud of himself. "I'm being good. I haven't hit on you once tonight, have I? I held back. I was being a good friend."

I nodded, then stopped. I don't think I wanted to encourage that, did I? Then my stomach rumbled again. If I could feel it when I was this drunk, I knew I would've been starving if I were sober. "How do you propose we get home? Or get food? The grill closed an hour ago, right after dinner, didn't it?"

His chuckle slipped over and caressed me. I wanted to close my eyes to savor it, but instead, a goofy grin came to my face.

Logan straightened from the table and scanned the bar. Then he rotated on his stool to face me. This put his back to the two girls, and both seemed irritated, but this was Motherfucking Logan Kade—his words two hours earlier, not mine. They weren't going to argue.

Grinning at my thoughts, my body jerked awake as Logan placed his hands on my knees. He leaned forward and murmured, "I'm not being such a good friend now. I should apologize, but I'm not going to."

I almost closed my eyes, letting his words slide over me. They warmed me, and I was fast not caring if we were friends or not. His knees also rested against mine, trapping me between his legs. Then his hands started a slow slide. They left my knees and progressed to my thighs at a snail's pace. All I could do was hang my head and watch them. They stopped right before touching my stomach, and his fingers splayed out. His thumbs rested very close to my happy spot.

I held my breath. "I'm a bit inebriated, Logan."

He grinned and good God, my heart leapt into my chest. My body was burning up. It was a fucking Sahara in here, then he said, "Me, too." His forehead rested on mine, and he was right there, like *right there*. Our eyes were looking into each other. His breath was teasing me, acting likes its own seductive caress. This guy was dangerous, with a capital D. I needed to start fanning myself because I was losing all senses here.

I glanced down. I had to do something, or my lips would be on his and that'd be trouble, so much trouble, but I felt Logan's attention was fully focused on me. My body was still burning. I was on fire. I gulped, and I started to lick my lips, but I heard his groan. I stopped, or I tried to stop. My body leaned forward. It was edging just a centimeter toward him.

No! Stop, Taylor. I tried to command myself, but I felt my body going. He wanted me, too, but he was waiting for me. He'd made the first move, and now it was my turn. One move from me, and it was game on.

I'd never had sex in a bar, but Logan made me wonder why not.

"I got the hail." Nate came to the table, interrupting whatever the hell had been going on.

I jerked back from Logan's hands, those delicious hands, and he laughed. Lifting his head, he asked Nate, "Can you drive?" His eyes remained on me.

"Fuck, no."

Logan's mouth dipped in a rueful expression. "Neither can I."

Both turned to me.

Inside I was swimming in my beer, and all the gloriousness from my hormones. They were screaming Logan's name. I gave them a smile.

Nate shook his head, pulling out his phone. He shot Logan a look. "Mason's going to be pissed."

"We could cab it?"

"My friend is sober," one of the girls piped up. "She can give you guys a ride home." The girls hadn't gone anywhere. Nope. They were now being helpful, eavesdropping on our conversation.

Evidently my top lip lifted in a slight snarl, but I wasn't aware until Logan smoothed it down with his finger. He turned, hiding me from their view as he asked, "You can fit all three of us?"

"Oh, yeah. Plenty of room." The girl who'd offered the ride was damned cheery.

"Well..." Her friend sounded more cautious. "Someone will have to sit on a lap. It could be a tight fit."

"That's no problem." She elbowed her reluctant friend.

I rolled my eyes.

The girl's enthusiasm grated on my nerves. She loved the idea of sitting on a lap, and I had one guess whose lap she was hoping for.

But when we got to the car, Logan's hand found my waist. A tingle broke out over me, giving me a shiver, one of the delicious kinds. He stood right behind me, and I had a hard time concentrating on what was going on. His touch was almost possessive, like he was claiming me, but I knew that wasn't what he was doing. That wouldn't have made any sense.

The car doors opened, and his hold tightened as he said, "Taylor can sit on my lap."

Good gracious. My body heated. Hearing him say those words, an ache formed between my legs.

Friends. Friends. I started reciting that to myself. Friends only...I looked up and caught his gaze. He wasn't looking at me in a friends-only way.

I gulped.

Nate had rounded the other side of the car. He paused now,

hearing Logan's offer, and looked at us. He snorted, shaking his head before he got inside.

The first girl had looked ready to say something, but her mouth formed an O. "Oh. Okay then."

Logan moved around me, and his hand trailed across my back, sending a fresh wave of sensations through my body. That same hand lingered on my hip before he got into the backseat. It was a small car. He pushed a bag and blanket to the middle between him and Nate, then held his hand out to me.

This was...I didn't think.

The way he looked at me, it was hypnotic. My legs worked on their own, and I went to him. Somehow I perched on one of his legs, turned toward the inside of the car. I tried to sit up so all of my weight wasn't on him, but he tugged me down. His arm lifted around my back to rest on his leg. I was cupped in his arms. I could've laid my head on his shoulder and curled into a ball.

Maybe it was the booze. Maybe it was the fact that I'd survived my first week at Cain University, or maybe—I didn't know what it was. But what should've been the most awkward situation ever just wasn't. I tensed as both Nate and Logan gave directions to my house, but Logan tugged me back down. His hand went from his leg to my leg and anchored me in place.

I couldn't deny it felt good. To be there in his arms, and that both of them were giving directions for me. The same feeling from before trickled in again. I felt included—by Nate, too. I was drunk, but I knew this sort of inclusion was a rarity.

The envious looks I'd been getting all night at the bar, the ones at the food court this week, in sociology, and even now from the two girls in the car—they wanted to be where I was. Now, where that was I had no real idea. But for now, I wasn't going to question it. I was going with the flow, a very Logan thing to do.

"Your girl have a hot date she stood up?"

My eyes were closed, but Nate's voice grew clear as he must've looked in my direction. Logan shifted underneath me and leaned forward. His voice sounded from right above my forehead. "Is that Delray's car?"

My eyes opened in a flash. Thoughts whirled in my head. I tried to remember...then I did.

I was supposed to watch movies with Jason tonight. I'd just stood up my best friend.

I groaned, falling back against Logan's chest.

CHAPTER 11

STILL BAD
TAYLOR

Logan's hand tightened over my leg. "You want me to come in with you?" he asked, right next to my ear.

Oh God. The idea of someone else taking care of my business was so welcome. I wanted to say yes. I'd done so much in the last nine months: arranging all the funeral plans, picking out the casket, burying my mother, being the hostess when people brought food to the house, transferring to Cain U, registering for classes, getting my books, going to school, and even today, looking for a job. It was just life, but it was exhausting. I wanted someone to help me, but it couldn't be Logan.

I shook my head, feeling weak but determined. "No. I messed up."

Jason would've had a conniption if I sent someone in my place, particularly Logan. I owed him an explanation. He was my best friend.

The girls' smiles were brighter when they realized Logan wasn't getting out with me. Both Logan and Nate offered a wave as I stepped back and the car took off. The little flirtation I'd just had with Logan was nice. Hell, it was like dancing with the devil for a moment. It was tempting—the promise of something great—but in the end that was all it was. A dance with the devil. I'd be blind not to see how many girls wanted him. I was also not deaf. I'd heard him at the bar when he said we were friends because we hadn't had sex. *Yet.* Sex seemed inevitable when it came to Logan.

"We haven't had sex, and you haven't called me an asshole or slapped me yet, so yeah." He'd winked at me. *"That classifies us as friends in my book."*

Logan slept with girls. They got emotionally attached. He didn't. Then he was called an asshole and slapped. That was likely the story of so many, and maybe if there'd been no Eric, or maybe if my mother hadn't died in front of me, maybe I would've turned off my rational side and let myself go down the same path as those other girls.

But there was an Eric who left me, and I lost my mom on the same day. I couldn't fall for Logan Kade. I understood why girls did, but I just couldn't. I wouldn't come back from that if I let myself go. I wasn't special. I was just like any other girl, and Logan Kade didn't love. He'd told me that as well.

"If I love you—and don't get ahead of yourself because that list is really short—then I'll do almost *anything to protect you. Girls drink that shit up..."*

The writing was on the wall. *"I'm not being cocky when I say that girls like me, they really do like me. I'm funny, sarcastic, quick-witted, and enough of a bad boy to make girls wet. If I like you, I'm loyal to you."*

For whatever reason, Logan liked me. I would take that. I could make do with his loyalty. I remembered how it felt when he'd touched me, how his hands held me and I wanted to close my eyes, sink into him, and let his strength wash over me. *That* was the dangerous side of him.

I shook my head. The car was long gone, but I was still standing on my front lawn. I had to reset myself, pull out the hooks Logan had put in me. I couldn't walk in like this with an angry Jason waiting for me. He'd see right through, and when Jason was mad, he didn't hold back. I needed to wall myself back up so I could handle whatever he threw at me.

I heard the door to my house open behind me. "Taylor?" Jason called.

I felt like I was zipping myself up, pushing all the raw and exposed feelings back inside. I could feel it pulling me together, closing over my head. When it was done, I was okay. I was ready to go.

"Hey. Yeah," I called. "It's me." I started for the door.

Jason gestured inside the house, moving back so I could get through the doorway. His eyes were worried. His face looked strained, and his hands had pulled inside his sleeves. When he did that, he was anxious.

"I used the extra key," he told me. "Your dad isn't here."

I wasn't sure if that was a question or a statement. I ignored it, going to the kitchen. I expected a note, but there was none.

"There's no note," I said.

His eyebrow lifted. "Is there usually?"

No. Not very often. "He's been trying."

Jason folded his arms over his chest and sat down at the table. He snorted in disbelief.

"He has been."

"Not to be an insensitive dickhead, but I've only seen one note from your dad." His elbows rested on the table. He propped his chin on his hands, still inside his sleeves. He watched me.

"Well." I fell back against the counter, hitting it hard enough that I'd find a bruise there later. I grimaced. "You are being an insensitive dickhead."

His other eyebrow arched, and he pursed his lips together briefly. "You stood me up tonight."

I flushed.

"But I don't think we should be throwing words around," he added. His eyes went to the window, and an angry glower came over him. It didn't last long—appearing, then vanishing—but I readied myself. When Jason looked back at me, his face filled with something akin to disappointment. He leaned back in his chair, his eyes locked on me. His hands fell to rest on his lap. "You know..."

Here it came.

"Claire told me you and Logan Kade are buds now. Is that who dropped you off?"

And there it was.

"I was applying for a job at Pete's Pub. He came in with a friend."

"Because that makes sense."

I sighed. "You don't have to be sarcastic."

He shot forward in his seat. "Why are you applying for a job? Your mom was loaded. I know you're getting that inheritance."

He didn't get it. I shrugged. "Because."

"Because why?"

"Just because." My jaw hardened. "I can't study all the time."

"Who's asking you to study all the time?" He shook his head. "Taylor, I get it. You need to keep busy. And I'm assuming you don't want to burden me and Claire with your presence."

A lump formed in the back of my throat. Maybe he did get it?

His voice softened. "But you're not a burden, honey. You're my best friend."

"You have lives." My voice came out as a whisper. "You and Claire. You have other friends."

"You're our friend. You're family."

The more he spoke, the more emotion rose in me. "I can't handle people."

He gave me a look. "And getting a job at a bar is going to help that?"

"It's not the same." There I'd be expected to do a job. Get a drink. Bring them their bill. Be nice. "Being around people and working around people are different." They wouldn't know or care about my name. "I saw Claire with her friends today, and the thought of sitting with them..." My voice faded. A pressure was pushing down on my chest. "I can't do that, Jason. I just can't."

"Okay." He stood, his chair scraping against the floor as he approached me. "I get it. I do. I'm a loser, remember?"

I frowned. "You're not."

He shook his head and came to stand right in front of me. His hands came out of his sleeves to cup my arms. His touch was soft. "I am. I always have been. I'm gay, Taylor. People still hate people like me."

I wanted to shake my head. I wanted to protest, but he was right. So many didn't care, but so many still did. A tear fell down my cheek. "Those people are assholes."

He laughed softly. "Yeah. Those people are assholes, but this isn't about that. I'm trying to remind you that I understand what it's like."

I was on the outside at the moment, but he'd grown up on the outside. My hands turned to grasp his arms in return. I squeezed. "You're not a loser, and you're not on the outside anymore." He shook his head. The old pain I always saw in high school bloomed over his face. I squeezed his arms harder. My voice rose. "You're not. I hate the gambling stuff, but I know you have some good friends."

He began to protest.

I cut him off again. "I know you do. People are always calling you." I frowned. "Unless those are clients."

"No." He laughed. "They aren't. You're right. I do have a circle of friends at school."

"I'd like to meet your friends sometime," I told him.

His head moved back an inch. "You would?"

Then I thought about it, and my cheeks grew red again. "Maybe later, or maybe one of your friends. Just one at a time," I added.

"My friends are better than Claire's anyway. Her friends have their heads up their asses, smelling their own gas fumes and getting high."

"Say it like you mean it."

A half-grin formed, and he rolled his eyes, letting my arms go. He scooted back to lean against the counter across from me. "Claire's lucky we deemed her our friend. If we didn't, she'd lose herself. She's drawn to those types of people because that's who her family is. They all just think about how special and important they are. They're like plastic—fake and breakable, honey."

I relaxed. When Jason started throwing out the *honeys*, he was being himself. I didn't hear that word too often anymore. "Don't hold back," I urged him. "Tell me what you think of Claire's family and friends."

He'd been staring off into the distance, but his eyes moved back to mine, and we shared a smile. Jason had always thought Claire's choice of friends was poor. We were the exceptions, and in his head this was because we'd chosen Claire. That was the truth, sort of. Jason chose me. He saw me in seventh grade and told me I didn't need too much makeup, as I was just what the guys liked. Then he saw Claire beside me, took in her heavy makeup, and raised his nose in the air. He sniffed at her. "You look just fine, too."

Her mouth dropped. She wasn't confrontational, but that day she sputtered out, "Fuck you."

Jason had paused, stared at her, and a slow grin formed. It had been best friendship at first sight.

"We all know how Claire's life is going to end up," he told me, looking around the kitchen. "She's going to marry a politician who'll cheat on her in some public scandal, and she'll divorce him but not his money. Or she'll marry some up-and-coming entrepreneur. If he loves her more, she'll end up cheating on him. If she loves him more, he'll cheat on her. That's how it always goes with her. Either way, she'll divorce him, end up with all his money, and have us over for margaritas."

That sounded accurate. "I look forward to the margaritas."

He laughed. "You and me both."

We got mad. We got sad. Now we were laughing. All in all, this had gone better than I expected.

Then Jason sighed. "Don't fall in love with him." His eyes were solemn, almost sad again. "Don't, Taylor."

"I'm not—" I started to argue.

"You're hurting." He waved my words away. "I don't know what happened with Eric, but you were with him for years, and then you weren't, and you still won't talk about it. I know you're trying to put on a brave face and march on, like you always do, but I know you. I see you." His voice softened once more. "A guy like Logan Kade is very dangerous to a girl like you."

My eyes closed. Everything he'd said was true.

CHAPTER 12

#CHEFLOGAN
LOGAN

Cheese—check.

Eggs—check.

Vegetables—check.

I stood back and perused the ingredients on the counter. I had everything...wait, I didn't. Bacon—and double-check. We were good to go. Mission To-Build-The-Best-Omelet-Ever was about to commence.

"What are you doing?" Nate came in behind me, opening the fridge.

I blocked him and swatted his arm. "No juice for you."

He moved back, sending me a frown. "I was reaching for the milk."

"No milk for you." I pointed the spatula at him and motioned to the table. "Sit. I am Chef Logan this morning."

"Oh God." He groaned, but sat. "What the hell is that?"

He was looking at the pile of fruit sitting next to the juicer. "That's for the wide receiver when he wakes up."

"Since no one else in this house plays football, I'm assuming you're talking about me, and yes, *he's* awake," Mason said, coming into the kitchen. He stopped, gave the pile of fruit a lifted eyebrow, then ran a hand through his hair. "Shit, Logan. I said to grab a few pieces of fruit. You got the entire produce section."

I smirked. "You don't know. That could be my new pet name for Nate's asshole. Wide receiver—"

Nate yelled, "Shut the fuck up!"

Laughing, I waved the spatula at both of them. "Calm your tits, Monson. I'm fooling, and yes, I meant my big badass brother, but no hate, Mase, on the fruit. I'm following Mama Malinda's rules: Go big or go home."

"My stepmother would not buy the entire fruit section at the grocery store," Sam said as she followed Mason into the kitchen. But when she saw the fruit piled high on a platter, she sighed. "Never mind. She'd totally do that."

I raised my finger and pretended to add a number to the air. "Score one for me and a big fat zero for the rest of you. As it should be in Logan Land." I turned to my brother. "For real, though. I got all that shit for you. Don't make me regret it."

Today was Mason's first home game. He asked the night before if I could get the fruit and juicer for him. Mason was always one for training, but since he decided to stay at school the last two years and get his degree before going pro, he was extra careful about his body—what he put into it and avoiding injury for the next two years. It was becoming rare to go to college all four years before the NFL. I knew Mason wanted to get a college degree no matter what, but as he started the juicer, I watched him glance over his shoulder at Sam. She was the other reason he had stayed.

I thought I loved Tate. That ended horribly. Then Sam came into our lives, literally moving in with us with her psychotic mother, and now Sam was family. Then there was my last girlfriend, Kris. She'd been young, with some of her own problems and an overprotective sister. I cared about Kris. I was with her for almost a year, and I was faithful. A lot of people assumed I was unfaithful, but fuck that. I wasn't a weak-ass coward—not like my dad. I cared about Kris, but I knew I didn't *love* her. Maybe that's why Mason and Sam's love was a bit much for me sometimes.

I loved vagina. That was what I loved, and I knew it would be a long-lasting relationship. No matter what, I would never stray from pussy. That sweetest part of the female anatomy was my soulmate.

"What are you thinking about, Logan?"

Nate had been watching me. "If I could marry vagina—not a particular person's, but vagina in general—I think I could call myself happy in love."

There was silence.

Nate coughed. "I'm not even touching that one." He lifted his hand. "Can I get a glass of juice, Mason?"

"Oh, yeah."

Mason made the juice. I did the omelets, and everyone got one, even Sam. Hers was double-stuffed with everything. She started to protest when I gave it to her, but I fixed her with a firm look. "You're going to have all of that worked off within an hour when you go running. Deal with it, and eat it."

No one else jumped in to support her, so she lowered her head, lifted her fork, and dug in. After a bite, she gave me a warm smile. Around a mouthful, she said, "Stho goo, Loganth."

I grabbed my own plate and sat in the last open spot at the table. "Damn straight it's good. I made it. It's Logan approved."

"When did you get all this stuff?" Nate reached for his glass. "It wasn't in the fridge last night. I would've eaten it if it were, and I came in after you."

After dropping Taylor off, the two chicks took us home. There was a lot of flirting, but for once, I wasn't into it. I went inside, and Nate left with both of them.

"I got it this morning. I was well-rested." I grinned at him. "Did you have a twofer last night?"

He laughed. "Uh…" He put his glass down, concentrating on it more than he needed to. "Let's say the one girl was a little hurt you rejected her." His smile grew more prominent. "I tried to make her feel better."

Sam's nose wrinkled. "I'm eating here."

Mason laughed. "I think the big news is that Logan turned a chick down."

All three gazed at me. I frowned. "What?"

Sam asked, "You turned a girl down?"

"I can be selective."

"Not normally," my brother responded. "With who you date, yes. Not with who you screw. You screw a lot of girls."

"Shut up." I scowled. "I went through all this to get your fruit and your juicer, and I became Chef Logan this morning." I waved at the table. "Most of your plates are already empty."

"No one's saying anything negative, and you know I appreciate you doing all this. I really do."

I could hear the *but* coming from my brother. He shared a look with Nate before continuing. "We've all noticed a decline in your female activities over the last week."

Sam shot her hand up in the air. "I'm okay with it. I love that I'm not coming home and finding a new random in the kitchen or wandering around the house." She pointed her fork at Mason. "I didn't enjoy that one girl in our bed last week."

He stiffened and pointed to me. "That was him. I had nothing to do with her."

"I know." Her fork rotated to me. "We have a lock on our door, but I'd never used it till that day."

"That was the redhead, right?" I grinned, remembering her. "She was a spitfire. I liked her."

Nate grunted, tucking a napkin under his plate. "Not enough to date her."

I shrugged. That was normal.

"I was just wondering if it had anything to do with Coach Bruce's daughter." Nate's eyes were narrowed, but he showed no other reaction as he spoke.

I leveled him with a look. He held firm.

Nate was Mason's best friend. He'd been our neighbor growing up until his family deemed Mason a bad influence and moved away, taking their son with him. He came back at the end of his senior year of high school because he'd finished all his classes and turned eighteen. His parents had no say anymore.

He'd been with us since then, but dynamics changed. I was Mason's best friend. Nate was the second-best friend. Well, that wasn't counting Sam who was more than Mason's best friend, so I still claimed the spot. Nate didn't handle the shift in friendships well. He was a weasel for a little bit, doing some shady shit and had a full-blown rebellion when he and Mason came to Cain University for their freshman year.

He was the reason Park Sebastian had even come into our lives.

A brooding feeling came over me. My thoughts were too intense. I could play an asshole. I could be the asshole, but no matter what brought it on, I didn't enjoy feeling like the asshole.

I studied Nate for a moment. "What's your problem?"

"You like her."

The table grew silent again. That wasn't a question from him. It was a statement. And for some reason, it didn't sit right with me. I scowled. "Back off of this, Monson."

Sam looked up at me. It meant something when we used last names. But she didn't say anything. Neither did Mason.

Nate's hands lifted in the air. "I'm not trying to be a dick here."

"But you are. You're inferring shit that's not there. I didn't want to screw a sidechick. So what?"

"You're getting upset over one question."

"I'm not." I leaned over the table. "Coach Bruce's daughter is a friend. That's it."

"I'm not saying anything otherwise."

"Yes, you were." I gestured around the table. "No one here is an idiot. I'm not going to sit here and let you lay the groundwork to what? Tease me? Cause trouble? If I like a girl, I'll date her. If I want to screw a girl, I'll bang the hell out of her. If I want to piss on someone, I'll do that too, but what I'm not going to do is let you steer things around so I'm on the defense and you're on the offense. Never going to fucking happen with me."

"Logan." Nate moved to the edge of his seat. His eyes were wide and clear, not narrowed or cagey. He placed his palms flat on the table. "I know how that shit happens, and that's not what I was doing. I swear. The girl was hot last night, and you seemed into her until the ride home. Then you were all about Bruce's daughter. I was just trying to bring it up in a nice way to see if there was something more there. I'm not trying to fuck with you."

My pulse pounded in my veins. I felt it through my jawline as I stared him down. *Fuuuuck.* He wasn't holding anything back. I thought he was coming for me, but he wasn't. "Sorry. I misread you." I felt like a dipshit.

"I wasn't trying to stir anything up," Nate murmured. "But a week ago, you would've taken that girl up on what she was offering last night. Plus, you wanted to hang out with Bruce's daughter. That's not normal. You don't hang out with chicks unless you're banging 'em."

Nate cast Mason a look. He'd been quiet, observing the entire exchange.

"Nothing's there," I told them. "Yes, I want to bang her. She's hot. But I don't know." I glanced at Sam. "She reminds me of you somehow. Maybe that's it."

She cocked her head to the side, growing thoughtful. "Because both our dads are football coaches?"

"No. I mean, yeah, but there's something else—"

"There's trauma there." Mason stood and took his plate to the sink. He turned and rested his hands against the counter as he leaned his back on it. "His wife died a few weeks before Christmas break last year. Coach Bruce was a mess the rest of the year."

"There was a thing at his house, right?" Sam asked. "We took food over there?"

He nodded. "I heard rumors, but I didn't say anything because we were dealing with Sebastian then. It was all around the same time."

"What do you mean he was a mess?" I moved my chair back from the table, folding my arms over my chest.

"He was always in the fieldhouse. I didn't notice it much during off-season training, but I heard rumors. His wife didn't die from cancer or anything medical."

Sam inhaled softly. "Did she kill herself?"

A sick feeling started in me. I didn't like my parents most days, but I loved them. If they ever took their lives—I locked gazes with my brother—that would gut me. How could a parent choose not to be there anymore? I thought about Sam. Her parents weren't dead, but they'd left her. David, Garrett, Analise—all three of her parents had left her at one point or another. Shit, I guess our mom was half gone most of the time, but that was different. One phone call and she'd be here. She'd be annoying and acting all pretentious, but she'd be here. Sam didn't have that, and go a step beyond that to where the mother actually offed herself?

Is that what had happened to Taylor? Did she see it?

It felt wrong to be talking about it. "Let's shelve this, can we?"

Mason and Nate nodded.

"You like her?" Sam asked me.

My eyes went to hers. She wasn't inferring anything like Nate had been, so I nodded. "Yeah. I like her."

Resolve firmed her features. She nodded, and her eyes grew serious. "Then I will, too." There was one last piece of omelet on her plate, and she speared it with her fork, eating it quickly. She gave me another small smile. "Sounds like she could use a few friends."

CHAPTER 13

MERLOT AVOIDANCE
TAYLOR

Monday morning I went to the registrar's office and switched to a different session of Sociology 101. I felt ridiculous—switching a class because of a guy? I was *that* girl? But I had to face facts. Even if Logan and I were friends, as he'd said we were, I couldn't be stupid. I was already damaged.

After changing my schedule, I went to my class. Mr. Fuller, Jeremy—I still didn't know what to call him—asked me to wait after class and walk with him to Professor Gayle's office. Maybe it was the empty feeling I got when my dad and I crossed paths during the weekend. We stopped and stared at each other. There'd been no easy words between us, or maybe it was even because I knew I wouldn't be running into Logan anymore, but when he invited me again to the Honors Study Group that Thursday night, I said I'd go.

The small party was at Jeremy's apartment. No professors would be there, but each student could bring a date. After he said the last part, he waited, and an awkward silence settled between us.

I frowned, but nodded. "Okay. Sounds good."

"Great." He smiled, but it seemed forced. "In case I don't remember to give you the details during Wednesday's class, here you go." He scribbled directions to his apartment on a piece of paper. "Uh, just remember to let me know if you're bringing a date.

I need a head count for ordering food. Oh—" His smile softened. "And there'll be wine, and I know some students aren't twenty-one yet, so if you could keep quiet about the party…yeah…"

I pretended to zip my lips. "Consider the key thrown away. I won't be narcing on an Honors Study Group party."

"Great." He pointed at a number on the piece of paper now in my hand. "You can buzz that apartment, but if it's really loud—oh, hold on." He took the paper back and wrote his phone number on it. "You can call me, too. I'll keep my phone in my pocket. If I can't hear it, I'll still feel it vibrating, so no worries. People will probably be outside anyway, so the door will be open. You shouldn't have a problem getting in."

"Okay." I tucked the piece of paper into my textbook. "I'll see you Wednesday for class."

"Yeah." He followed me to the door. "And then Thursday for the party."

I nodded. Yeah, the party.

The week was uneventful. I hated to admit it, but I missed the Loganisms. My new sociology class wasn't fun. There were no comments about mindfucking. No one made me feel awkward with sexual innuendos, or made me feel something I really shouldn't be feeling yet. But that was why I switched. Logan was too much, too soon. And on Thursday night as I was headed to Jeremy's apartment, I had a feeling I wouldn't have that problem at this event.

A group of students were standing on the front steps of Jeremy's building. I recognized a few of them from around the science building, but I faltered. Did I really want to do this? Go up there and be social? But no. This was why I came to this party, I reminded myself. It couldn't only be Claire and Jason. It was the same reason I was getting a job—which I still needed to do. But until then… I looked up to an opened window on the third floor. Music and laughter drifted down.

Okay, Honors Study Group party, here I come.

Jeremy didn't answer when I knocked on the door. A girl was there instead. Her cheeks were red, along with her neck, and her eyes glazed over. She held a huge glass in her hand, filled to the rim with red liquid, and she almost fell over from the force of opening the door. "Whoa." She skidded a little. Keeping a firm grip on the doorknob, she nudged some of her hair from her face with her arm and squinted at me. "Do I know you?"

"Uh—"

She pointed at me. "You're Claire's friend."

I frowned. Claire was here?

"Hold up." She turned around and hollered, "Claire! Your high school bestie is here."

I didn't hear a response, but when I stepped inside, the girl shut the door behind me and took off. She held her glass high above her head and weaved through the crowd standing in the living room.

"Taylor?"

Claire's head appeared, popping up from the kitchen. She wedged her way past a guy and two of his buddies, circling the table covered in fruit trays, cheese trays, platters of meat, and bowls of crackers. There was popcorn too, next to little clear plastic plates and a bowl filled with toothpicks. A pile of napkins sat next to the plates, but no silverware.

"What are you doing here?" Claire had a similar glass of red liquid, and I leaned forward, taking a sniff.

I didn't have to get too close. "Is that Merlot?"

She nodded. Her cheeks were flushed like the other girl's. "You want a glass? One of the chemistry guys brought an entire case from his family's winery. It's potent stuff, but it's so good."

I was a beer girl, and from what I remembered, Claire had been a shot girl in high school. I shook my head. She didn't seem to care though, a goofy grin on her face. She linked our elbows and moved us around to a hallway, where we could spy on the kitchen, but the people packed in there couldn't see us.

She leaned close and whispered loudly in my ear. "You remember Ben, right?"

There were three guys and a girl in the kitchen now. "Malia?" Then I remembered the guys, too. It was the same group from the food court. Ben was the leader, and the guy Claire was crushing on. "I remember."

A good whiff of Merlot mixed with something citrusy overwhelmed me as she sidled in close, her body almost pressing me into the wall. Her arm clamped around mine.

"So Ben's the one who was invited to this party," she said. "He's friends with the guy who lives here, who runs the Honors Study Group, but I can give you the four-one-one on that guy another day. Ben wasn't supposed to bring all of us because we're not in the group. He's allowed one date, and he asked me to go, but then Malia found out and threw a fit, so now all of us crashed the party." She glanced around. "I think a lot of people crashed the party, but back to Ben. He made a move earlier," she squealed.

"Really?"

Her eyes lit up with excitement, and her head bobbed up and down. "Can you believe it? I've been hoping for so long, and I didn't know when it would happen, or even if it would happen, but it did." She bounced up and down with her toes still on the floor. "I've liked him for so long, Taylor."

"How long?"

Her eyes sparkled. "Since last year, since…" Someone turned off the lights inside her. The sparkle vanished, replaced by a dull, blank stare, and her hand lost its grip on mine. "Since a month after you came back."

Eight months then. I felt a pang in my chest. "So, a long time, huh?" I squeezed her hand. "That's great, Claire."

"Oh, Taylor."

I winced. Her pity slapped me in the face. "No, stop. I wasn't really present even though I was here after it happened. I'm good. I mean it. I just wish I thought to ask you earlier than now."

"You had other things going on." Her fingers interlaced with mine. "And I've been a little absent this last week. I'm sorry."

I waved off her apology. "Don't worry. You and Jason checked in on me so much after I came back. I think I took you both for granted." I moved to face her and squeezed both her hands. "I'm happy you have a guy to crush on, and I'm happy he kissed you tonight. I really am."

Her eyes closed. A tear trekked down her cheek. This was how we used to share our secrets. If we were bursting with news, we'd link our hands together. The last time we stood like this was when my mom was buried. I cried that night, and Claire held my hands. Jason stood behind me, pressing his forehead into my back.

"Taylor—" she started.

I rocked my head back and forth. It was my turn to be there for her. "Nope. No apologies. I want to hear all about Ben."

"I *will* tell you all about him, but not tonight." Her hands grasped my arms, and she laughed, pretending to shake me. "What are you doing here?"

I opened my mouth, but it was then that I realized I really shouldn't be there. They weren't my crowd. An image of being at a certain bar, filling out an employment application flashed in my head. I didn't want to think about that, but I knew this wasn't right either. "You know, I'm actually going to go."

"You sure?"

I nodded. "Yeah. I'll see you later, though?"

"Sure. Yeah. Let's do lunch."

Lunch sounded great, and I slipped out of the apartment. Maybe I should've sought out Jeremy, said my goodbye, but as I headed down the sidewalk, my thoughts weren't on my professor's assistant. In fact, they were on someone that I really didn't want to think about at all. So, of course, when I first heard him, I thought my mind was playing a trick on me.

Nearing my car, I pulled my keys out, and that was when I heard him again. "You were at that party?"

I stopped. Was it—yes, it was.

Logan Kade stood with his hands in his jeans pockets, looking back to where I'd just come from. When his eyes met mine, I saw a touch of hurt.

He added, "You've been avoiding me."

CHAPTER 14

THE BAD'S BACK
TAYLOR

"What are you doing here?"

Logan gestured to the side where a taco shop was. "It's the closest one to school." He twisted back around again and looked at the group on the steps. "Whose party was that?"

"No one's."

Then I heard my name being called. Jeremy was hurrying toward us. When he saw Logan, he paused a few feet away. I couldn't help to compare the two. Logan was taller, leaner, and his shoulders were wider. He wore a black T-shirt and jeans, and with his hands in his pockets, his jeans slipped down to offer a peek at his obliques, the defined ridge where his stomach muscles and hips met in a downward V. It was tantalizing, a temptation I was already feeling. Though he was handsome, next to Logan, Jeremy looked drab in his jeans and polo shirt. He couldn't compete.

Logan was confident, with a hint of darkness. Jeremy was academic, with a hint of snobbery.

"Jeremy," I said. "You didn't have to come after me."

"Claire said you left…" He trailed off, glancing to the side at Logan.

Logan lifted an eyebrow and turned to sit on the trunk of the car next to him. He looked comfortable and almost carefree. I caught a spark of interest in his gaze and knew he was anything but, and his attention was fully directed at Jeremy.

"Hello." Jeremy held out his hand. "You are?"

Logan looked at his hand, but made no move to shake it. He gave Jeremy a half-grin. "Like you don't know who I am."

A flush wound its way up Jeremy's neck, reddening his cheeks. "You know Taylor?" He withdrew his hand, stuffing it into his pocket.

Logan nodded. He didn't speak, just watched.

Jeremy cast a quick glance at me. "Well, huh." He ran a hand through his hair, upending the strands. They'd been perfectly combed to the side, but the slightly messy look suited him better, made him less stuffy. "Taylor." He moved toward me, angling away from Logan with the same movement. "I wanted to make sure you were okay, and to thank you for coming even if it was for a short while."

Logan scooted over on the car, moving closer. He looked between us like he was a spectator enjoying the show.

I fought against rolling my eyes. He was trying to get underneath Jeremy's skin, and it was working. I suddenly felt sorry for Jeremy. "I'm fine. I just wasn't up for a party after all. I'd thought maybe I was."

"Oh." His head lifted and moved down again. "That's good then. I'm glad you're not sick or anything."

"I'm fine."

Jeremy was still giving Logan the side-eye. Logan stared back at him without reservation. My pulse quickened. I'd never seen Logan in action, and I didn't think this would come to fighting, but I still felt something dangerous in the air. Logan almost reveled in making him nervous. Instinct told me to remove Jeremy from the situation or he was going to be humiliated, so I gestured to my car.

"I'm—uh. I'm actually going to my car—"

"I was hoping to talk to you," Logan said, his eyes meeting mine.

And there it was. I couldn't leave now, and there was no doubt about Logan's purpose here. Jeremy straightened.

"Oh," he said. His face twitched, then cleared. He gave me a smile. "I'll, uh, I guess I'll see you in class tomorrow."

"Yeah."

He nodded to Logan, then headed back, his shoulders slumped a bit. I felt a twinge of sympathy for him.

"Don't do that."

I turned to Logan. He shook his head.

"Do what?" I asked.

"Feel sorry for that pretentious prick."

I pressed my lips into a disapproving line. "You don't know he's like that."

He scoffed. "You do." He gestured to my face. "It's written all over you. And you feel sorry for him because of what? I'm the big, bad asshole, and he came off looking like a regular nice guy next to me? Please."

He stood up and ran a hand through his hair. His hadn't been combed perfectly like Jeremy's. It was already messy, and when his hand dropped back to his side, it was even messier, which added to his already dangerous allure.

"Don't be fooled by that guy," he said. "If you were in a bad spot, a guy like that wouldn't save you. He'd save his own ass. But me?" He stepped closer, softening his voice. "I'll always save you."

"Eric!" Someone was screaming in my ear. I didn't know who it was, but as Eric looked at me, I realized it was me. I reached out. He could pull me to safety. I looked for my mom again. I didn't know where she was.

A gunshot boomed from down the hallway.

A second scream started in my throat, but I slammed a hand over my mouth. I couldn't let it out. They'd find me...

The flashback ripped through me. Everything lurched inside me and I clenched my eyes shut, lowering my head. I didn't want memories. I couldn't handle them. Even now, I was trembling, my teeth rattling against each other.

"Hey." Logan's voice was low and soothing. He stepped even closer. I could feel his body heat, and his hand touched my arm. "What just happened?"

I reached up to move his hand off me, but found myself holding it instead.

"Taylor?"

I concentrated on breathing. That was what the counselor had said to do. One breath. Hold. Five, four, three—I counted down and exhaled, repeating the countdown. In through the stomach, out through the lungs. I cycled through the process, and when I was done, my forehead rested on Logan's chest. His free hand held the back of my head, keeping me in place. His other hand tangled with mine, our fingers laced together.

When the pressure began to ease, I looked up to blink at him, clearing the tears that had come with the panic. I felt ridiculous.

He shook his head. "Don't."

"What?"

"Don't be embarrassed by that. I can see it on your face. You had a small panic attack just now?"

It was a flashback, but I nodded. It was easier to let him think it was a panic attack. "You get them?" I asked.

"I used to, when I was little. I had a few."

"Someone helped you through them?"

"My brother." His eyes lowered, shielding him. I couldn't see into him anymore. He'd put up a wall.

I stepped back, and his hand fell from my neck. The shield he'd projected brought me back to reality. I didn't know him—not like I knew Claire, not like Jason.

I lifted a shoulder. "I'm sorry."

His jaw hardened, and he looked past me. "Don't be. Shit happens."

Apparently. I wanted to ask what shit happened to him, but held my tongue. He didn't want to tell me. That was obvious. Still, if he hadn't held me, I'd still be stuck in the flashbacks. When they came, they were like a tornado, circling through me over and over again. Instead, Logan eased me out of it. The tornado only came through once this time.

"Okay." I looked to my car. "I should get going."

"Wait," he said. "I wanted to ask you something."

"Yeah?"

The wall fell away. "Why'd you stop going to class?" he asked softly.

Oh. This. I should've had an excuse at the ready. I didn't. "I switched sections."

His eyes narrowed. "Why?"

I shrugged, looking away. "It just worked better with my schedule."

"Nope." He laughed quietly. "I don't buy it. I think you're avoiding me."

"Really?" My lip twitched. "I'd change my entire schedule around because of one guy? Who I've only known for a couple of weeks?"

His smile appeared, stretching to show the dimple in his cheek. "I'm Logan Motherfucking Kade. I'd switch classes, too. I mean, shit. If I were a chick? I'd be all over me. I couldn't keep myself away from me." He let out a whistle. "Bring out the handcuffs and bullwhips. We're going the BDSM route."

I grinned, feeling some relief. "You don't have a self-esteem problem. That's for sure."

He grunted, his eyes growing serious again. "Why would I?" He gestured up and down himself. "I'm awesome. No one can forget it."

I laughed out loud, shaking my head.

His grin dimmed, and he gazed back toward where Jeremy went. "Are you really not in the party mood?"

"Why?"

"You answer first."

I thought for a moment. I hadn't felt like being at that party tonight. I went because—I couldn't remember anymore. It had been nice to talk to Claire, though. I smiled at that thought, and then I knew he had me.

"Come on." Logan's eyes darkened, a promise there. I felt it pulling me in.

I shouldn't...but I heard myself saying, "I might be—in a party mood, that is."

A grin stretched on his face, and he reached for my hand. "Leave your car and come with me."

"Where are we going?"

"I'm going to take you to a real party." He led me across the road to his Escalade. Once we sat inside, he pointed over his shoulder to Jeremy's apartment. "It's not going to be like that, I promise you."

"No wine?"

"More like kegs." He started his vehicle and pulled onto the road.

I shouldn't be going with him, but I heard myself talking again. "No cheese trays?"

"Only for holidays and when I'm in my thirties." He grinned at me. "Expect lots of beer, pool, beer pong, maybe some nudity." He winked at me. "If you're lucky."

Resting my head back against the seat, I laughed with him. "Sounds wonderful."

And it did, which surprised me. That should've been a nightmare, but I was going with Logan. Everything was different with him. Everything would always be different with him. I felt that realization deep in my core, and something fluttered inside of me, but I couldn't identify it.

I didn't want to.

CHAPTER 15

HE'S A GOD.
NO, REALLY.
TAYLOR

I was in trouble.

As soon as Logan pulled into the driveway, I realized this was the same house as the first college party I came to with Jason and Claire—the one where I'd seen Logan for the first time. Unlike last time, when a large crowd had formed in the backyard, tonight almost everyone was inside. When we stepped through the front door, I felt all eyes on us. They went to Logan first, as if they'd been waiting for him. Then they noticed he was with someone, and when it registered that I was a girl, I really felt their attention.

None of this was blatant and obvious, but it was in the air. I could feel a shift in the atmosphere. Logan must've felt it, too, as he reached behind him to grab my hand, tangling our fingers together. He didn't look back at me, and my heart pounded. I pressed a hand to my chest, hoping to soothe myself, but there was nothing I could do.

The hairs on the back of my neck stood up as we went through the living room and into the kitchen. Once we stepped through the doorway, my hand tightened in Logan's for a split second. I wasn't sure if this party was any better. The girl I recognized from last time was here. Samantha. She leaned against the counter, surrounded by a couple other girls. She was laughing at something, but the two girls next to her wore different expressions. One was a little heavier with red hair curling freely over her shoulders. She wore a scowl. The girl on Sam's other side was much more petite with almost white-blonde hair. She wasn't scowling, but she seemed confused, as if trying to figure out the world's most important riddle. I noticed all of this before they noticed me.

When they did, Sam looked surprised, and suddenly the other two wore matching frowns. They did not seem to be fans of me.

"Hey!" A guy saw Logan across the room and raised his arms in the air. "Kade is here. Hell yeah, buddy."

Logan let go of my hand and moved forward to bump fists with the guy. Then they pounded each other on the shoulders. After that guy, it was like a line formed. Logan stayed in place as guy after guy moved past him to do the same fist-bump-shoulder-pound thing. When I realized the line wasn't going to end anytime soon, I sank back against the doorframe and folded my arms to half-brace and half-shield myself. I felt like I needed it.

"Hi."

My muscles were rigid, but the soft voice soothed them a little. Samantha, the only girl I knew Logan cared about, had moved to stand in front of me. I looked down, and she held her hand out. Damn. She was nice. I swallowed a knot in my throat. I put my hand in hers and felt how she closed her hand over mine.

"Hi," I said.

She smiled, and it lit up her entire heart-shaped face. She had dark brown eyes, beautiful plush lips, eyelashes that couldn't be manufactured, and the long black hair that had helped me recognize her. I'd known she was stunning, but she was even more so up-close. Add the genuine kindness I sensed, and I was forming a girl crush on her.

After letting my hand go, she gestured to herself. "I'm Sam. I don't know if Logan's said anything about me."

He hadn't, but I already knew. "You're dating his brother?"

She nodded. "There's a whole long story that goes with that, but yeah. I'm dating Mason, and my mom is going to marry their dad, so I'm the future stepsister, too." Her lips curved into an impish smile, and she rolled her eyes. "It's all one big fuck-up, but Logan—"

She stopped as Logan sidled up next to her and placed his arm around her shoulders. He pulled her close and grinned down at me. "She's family." The fondness in his eyes was clear. He genuinely loved this girl. A sensation I hadn't felt in a long time seized my heart, squeezing it in a painful grip.

I was jealous.

Completely.

Utterly.

I wanted what she had.

My throat was suddenly parched, and I let out a quiet cough to clear it. "It's nice to meet you." I nodded at her, and she smiled, a knowing look in her eyes. She'd seen my reaction and knew what it was. She grinned up at Logan. Her hand found his on her shoulder, and she squeezed it before removing his arm.

"We should all go downstairs," she said. "Nate's down there."

"He is?" Logan moved back, his eyebrows bunching together slightly.

She nodded. "Yep, and he seems happy." Her finger rested on Logan's chest. "Don't take that away from him."

"Why would I?"

"Because the two of you bicker like you're married. You're either loving each other or you're at each other's throats. Stop it." She meant business. "I'm getting flashbacks of Analise versus David 2.0."

A look of horror flashed in Logan's eyes. He stopped in his tracks. "Don't insult me like that. At least tell me I'm David, not Analise. Anything but Analise."

Sam shook her head, moving ahead of him. "Then stop the

bickering." She led the way out of the kitchen, and the two girls who'd been at her side earlier fell into place again.

Logan remained a step behind with me. He shook his head, muttering under his breath. "That's the worst thing she could've called me. I'm not Analise. No way in hell. I'd be David all the way." He cringed. "I don't even want to be that."

"Who are David and Analise?"

Logan was still shaking his head, but his arm lifted around my shoulders, like it'd been around Sam's moments ago. The whole motion seemed so natural, like I'd stepped close to him thousands of times before and my shoulders were always where he rested his arm.

I didn't register it until it was done, and I was tucked close to his chest. I faced him, staring right into his collar where it rested against his neck and chest. I blinked a few times, then my body caught on to where I was standing and grew heated. It bloomed up inside of me, sending my pulse on a race, and I tried to calm down. I didn't want him to feel my heartbeat. His arm lay so close to the veins in my neck.

If he could feel it, he didn't seem to care. He rested his forehead to mine. "Do me a favor."

Anything. "Yeah?"

His arm tightened a fraction, and he gazed into my depths. "Never insinuate that I'm being like someone's parents, especially ones that are super fucked up."

I frowned. "Okay."

"Thank God," he breathed out.

I thought he was going to remove his arm then, and I waited for it, knowing I would miss it, but he didn't. He just turned so we could walk beside each other. I followed his lead as we left the kitchen and went to the basement. When we reached the bottom of the stairs, Nate stood at the pool table, aiming to take a shot.

Logan stopped, watching in silence until Nate's pool cue connected with the white ball. It shot forward, hitting a red ball that bounced off the side of the table and hit a blue striped ball. That ball sank into the pocket, and the red ball ricocheted to a far corner of the table.

"Hey!" Nate's opponent protested. "Thanks, asshole. That was going to be my next shot."

Nate straightened and gave the guy a smirk. "Why do you think I used it? I had a straight shot if I wanted."

The guy grumbled, stepping back as Nate circled the table for another shot. The guy muttered something, but it was lost as Logan's arm left my shoulders. He caught my hand and led me around a group of girls to a table in the corner where Samantha, her two friends, and a few guys had gathered. All were watching the game, but as we approached, their focus shifted to Logan and me.

Particularly to our joined hands.

I pulled away, and Logan moved forward, a smirk already on his face. He went over to where Nate stood.

"Taylor?" Sam gestured to the empty seat across from her. As I slid into it, she leaned forward so I could hear her. The music and conversation in the basement were loud. "Logan's talked about you."

"He has?"

She nodded. "Just to say that he likes you. That's high praise from him. He acts like he's everyone's good friend, but he doesn't actually like a lot of people."

Her two friends groaned.

Sam shot them a look. "This is Kitty and Nina. They lived on my floor last year," Sam added. "When we were freshmen."

I nodded to both. "Hello."

Each gave me a polite, forced smile.

Sam laughed and leaned in. "Don't take that personally. They're both a little in love with Logan, even though I've told them not to be." She gave them a pointed look, her eyebrows arching up.

Kitty, the redhead, wrinkled her nose and turned away to watch the pool game. Nina, the petite one, didn't react. She didn't scowl and pointedly look away.

Sam sighed, shaking her head. "They'll warm up to you. Don't worry. They're actually really great and loyal *friends*." She threw that last word toward them with another pointed look.

Kitty didn't look at her, but the scowl lessened on her face. Nina met my eyes for a moment, and I caught the slightest glimmer of a smile before it vanished.

Sam gave me one more reassuring smile before turning toward the pool table. "Logan, you and Taylor want something to drink?"

Logan was saying something to Nate, but he turned to see the empty space in front of me. "I was going to grab something upstairs. Taylor, you want something?"

Sam stood, waving for him to stay. "Taylor and I will go grab something for both of you. What do you want?"

He shrugged. "A beer is fine." He met my gaze again. "You want me to come with you?"

Sam blocked his view of me. "She's fine. I got her." She started toward the stairs and Logan opened his mouth, but she waved at him again. "I swear, Logan. She's fine. I'll take care of her."

I didn't know what was going on, but they seemed to be having a more involved conversation with their looks and words.

I gave Logan a smile as I passed by. He shifted so our arms grazed each other and I could feel his eyes following me all the way upstairs. It felt good. I couldn't deny that. It felt damn good, and then Sam was there, waiting for me when I stepped through the door.

"Sorry to strong-arm you away from Logan. I wanted to give him some time with Nate before he got distracted and remembered you were here."

I nodded. "Oh, yeah. No problem."

She spoke over her shoulder. "Those two really do bicker like a married couple, but there's more to it."

"Did something happen?"

"Uh…" She hesitated as she gestured toward the kitchen. "Let's get something to drink."

She glanced over her shoulder with another smile, but I got the message. It wasn't for me to know. When I saw this group at the first party, I'd been on the outside. Everyone looked tight, but now I could sense the layers. Logan was closest to Sam, then Nate, and then—I had no idea. Suddenly and so completely, I wanted in.

I wanted to be on the other side of whatever wall he kept between him and most people. I wanted it almost desperately.

I followed Sam as she waded through the crowd to the booze. Hers wasn't exactly like Logan's reception, but a lot of the same guys moved aside and greeted her. They called out hellos. A few offered to get drinks for her.

With her hands full of vodka, beer, and some other bottles, she smiled as she took in the look on my face. "It's because of Logan."

"I'm gathering that."

"They like him."

They respected him.

Sam glanced around as the guys took the drinks from her arms and headed downstairs. She ran a hand through her hair, a rueful expression on her face. "I'd forgotten what it's like."

"What what's like?"

She grinned at me. "You. Your face." She looked around the room. "Seeing all of this for the first time. It's overwhelming. That's how I remember it."

"They act like he's a god." *That wasn't normal, was it?*

"Logan would have their backs in a heartbeat. That's what he does. He's actually a lot nicer now than he was in high school."

"What?"

She laughed at my surprise. "He was meaner in high school, but I think he was just more protective of his brother." She stopped, her lips pursed together. "Or maybe that was Mason bringing out the mean side of him?" She shrugged and patted my arm. "You'll get used to it."

What did she mean by that?

She read the question in my eyes. "Logan likes you. If he likes you, everyone else will, too."

"Your friends didn't."

She waved that off. "They'll come around."

"How do you know?"

She started forward, turning back over her shoulder as she headed downstairs and said, so simply, "Because Logan said you're a friend."

CHAPTER 16

#CHICKSHOWDOWN
TAYLOR

I was having fun. I was laughing. I was joking.

I was drunk.

Logan came back with another beer for me, and I stopped counting how many I'd had. It had been this way for the past two hours. Logan spent time with Nate and the guys, but he kept coming over to check on me. If I hadn't been smart, I'd have let it go to my head. But nope. Logan and I were friends. Samantha had said it earlier. Logan had said it on a couple of occasions, and with a decisive bob of my head, I reminded myself of it, too.

Friends. Nothing else. But as I watched him line up a shot—his eyes narrowing so he could focus, ignoring the guys trying to distract him—there was a little pitter-patter in my heart. I wasn't just in trouble. I was firmly in deep shit.

"I don't want to be intrusive," Sam said, leaning across the table. She cast a look over to her two friends, but both seemed oblivious.

She said they'd warm up to me, and they had. They were now past warming up and were drunk right along with me. Well, I still bordered between really tipsy and drunk. Both had glazed eyes and open mouths as they watched Logan. His ass was right in front of us as he bent over for a shot. I tore my gaze away and refocused on Sam.

She continued, "How did you and Logan get to know each other?"

I shrugged, shaking my head. "I was in a sociology class with him, and…" I frowned. There'd been something else. I snapped my fingers. "Jason."

"Jason?'

Logan must have heard me, and when he finished his shot, and came over to stand next to the table. He leaned on his pool cue as Nate took the next shot. His eyes lingered on me.

"Delray," he said to Sam, switching his gaze to her. "That little shit is one of her friends. He turned me down last year because of Sebastian, so I used Taylor to get a little revenge on him."

"You used her?" Sam glanced at me, questioning.

I shook my head. "It wasn't like that."

"Come to think of it…" Logan lifted a hand to scratch behind his ear. "I used *him* to get her phone number." He winked at me. "Best move I've made in a long time, that is until she abandoned me in my quest to mindfuck entire groups."

"She abandoned you?"

I touched my cheeks. I should've been blushing, but the alcohol had already given me perma-blush. "I had to switch sections."

"She couldn't handle me anymore, Sam. I must've broken her heart without even realizing it."

"Logan!" The guys called him for the game again.

He gazed down at me as if we had our own private joke. "Actually she broke *my* heart. She left me all alone. I've got no one to plot evil schemes with now."

I couldn't keep from grinning. "I don't think you have a shortage of people who'd love to do that with you."

"Logan!"

He ignored them, leaning down to grab my beer. He took a drink, his eyes on me the entire time, before he put it back down and murmured so only I could hear, "But no one like you."

"Logan!"

He gave me another wink before going back to the pool table. He rolled his shoulders and lifted his cue in the air. "Chill, fuckers. I'm going to win now or five minutes from now. Why do you need to hasten my victory?"

Nate started laughing, but the others grumbled. My eyes lingered on Logan a moment longer than they should've as he leaned over and sank one more ball. I turned back into the table, only to realize Samantha had been watching me the whole time. She had a knowing expression in her eyes.

I coughed and stood up. I didn't want to see the pity that would come next. She didn't know me, even though in that moment, she probably knew me on a level no one else did. She saw feelings I was still trying to lie to myself about.

"Excuse me," I said. Her friends gazed up with similar, owl-like dazed looks. I kept my eyes averted from Samantha as I pointed over my shoulder. "I, uh, I have to go to the bathroom. Be back in a bit."

"Taylor." Logan came around the pool table as I was heading for the stairs. He caught my hand.

A tingle raced up my arm, burning all through my body. I looked down at our joined hands before I forced myself to pull mine free.

"I have to go to the bathroom, and I should call my dad, let him know I'm safe. You know, just in case." My lie sounded stupid, even to me. I needed to compose myself.

"You okay?"

I nodded, not meeting his gaze. I could feel the weight of his eyes. "Yeah," I mumbled. "I'll be back."

"I'll win this game, and then we can go," he told me. "Nate talked about heading back to the house and doing a bonfire. Sam will probably go to bed, but he and I don't have an early class tomorrow. We were going to stay up and have a few more beers. I thought maybe if you wanted, you could come, but if you need to get home—"

"No." I looked up to meet his eyes. "I want to do that."

"Yeah?"

I nodded. A bonfire with him and Nate and no one else? I couldn't pass that up. After tonight, I'd stay away from Logan, I promised myself. Hell, I'd even go on a date with Jeremy Fuller if I needed to—anything to erase Logan Kade from my mind. But first, one night.

One *more* night.

"I should still call my dad." I held up my hand. I thought my phone was there, but it was a beer instead.

Logan grinned. "I'll be up in a bit."

I nodded. "Okay."

I made no phone call, but I did use the bathroom. Then I sat outside on a picnic table that had been carried to the front of the house. It was almost in the same place I'd been the first time I was here with Jason and Claire. Only this time I was sitting alone, and it wasn't Jason I was waiting for, it was Logan.

"Logan's coming in a minute," said a voice behind me. "He said you were up here waiting for us."

I closed my eyes and didn't look at Samantha as she slid onto the bench a few feet away. There were no other sounds so I knew she'd come alone. I sensed she wanted to say something, but I didn't want to hear it. She didn't know me. She didn't know anything about me. She hadn't earned the right to tell me what to do, or warn me away from Logan, or whatever she felt the need to share. I had this under control... Mostly... But I didn't need a thing from her, no matter how nice she seemed.

"You know..." she started. Her voice faded, and when I looked over, she stared down at the table. "Logan's hurt a lot of gir—"

"How many times have we met?" I interrupted her.

She looked up, slightly surprised. "Logan told me you were here the last time Blaze had a party."

So she'd been asking about me. I could tell she was full of wisdom about Logan. Maybe I should hear what she had to say. She didn't strike me as someone malicious, but she was too much for me right now.

"We've only officially met tonight." I held her gaze, making sure she couldn't look away. "When you meet people for the first time, do you usually force a heart-to-heart with them?"

I didn't want to be confrontational, but I needed to push her back, get some breathing room.

Her mouth opened. She had a response, but she held it. No sound came from her until a rueful laugh slipped out. She hung her head, her eyes closing for a beat before she looked back up at me. Her cheeks were pink now. "You're right. I'm out of line. But just so you know, it's not because of you. I don't know you. You're right about that, too, and I have no place telling you what to do. It's just..." She trailed off, shifting to look out at the street. The moonlight lit up her face, and I was reminded once more how beautiful she was. An ache dug its way inside my chest, making a hole there. Logan cared for her in a way that I wanted him to care for me.

I had feelings for Logan. There it was. I admitted it to myself.

"You're different," Sam said quietly. "Logan's never acted this way around a girl, and I'm sorry, but that's why I'm acting like a pushy mother, or a pushy big sister." She swung her dark eyes over to me and I was surprised to find a haunting quality in them.

My irritation with her melted. Whatever haunted her, my own pain responded. I was looking at myself, then she blinked, and it was gone. The connection we'd had broke.

"I told Logan I'd be a friend to you," she continued. "So I'd like to do that, and I'd like to do it the way I'd want it done for me: No opinions. No judgments. Just an easy acceptance."

That sounded wonderful.

She ducked her head and gave me a half-smile. "If you'd like that?"

"I would." A rueful laugh followed my words. "Being friends with people is work. You have to give, and you have to be okay with not getting back. I've been friends with Claire and Jason since seventh grade, and we've all had times when we haven't been the best. The last nine months have been my selfish time. I only took from them. I didn't give back because I didn't have it in me *to* give back, but since starting school…"

I shrugged and looked down. We sat side by side, both turned toward the street. "I was going to *only* be friends with them and make a point of giving them whatever they needed. But all that went out the door when Logan sat next to me in sociology. Somehow, and I truly have no idea how, he's become my friend." I gazed over at her. "And having said all of that, yes; I'd love to have one more friend this year."

People didn't usually proclaim that they were going to be friends. But this felt like the most natural thing in the world.

"That's great." Sam smiled so warmly at me, then said, "And if you hurt him, I'll become your worst enemy."

My grin faltered. "Oh."

Her smile grew and she never looked away, and just then, Logan came around the house. He lifted his arms in the air. "There you are. Let's go get our bonfire going."

Nate was behind him, and Sam stood up to meet them. Logan's arm came down around her shoulders. He paused, waiting for me to stand. I still sat at the table, blinking for a moment. Sam's threat wasn't a threat. It was a promise, and as I looked up at her, an eerie shiver went down my spine.

"Come on, Sam," Nate said. He touched her arm, pointing to the street. She broke away to go with him. "We'll meet you guys back at the house," Nate called as they left.

Logan nodded before turning back to me. "You okay?"

"Yeah." I stood. "I'm good. The bonfire's still a go?"

"Yep."

I watched Nate getting into his car. Sam rounded to the passenger side. "Can you guys even drive?"

"Nate and I didn't drink tonight. We just let the others think we were." He winked. "It's easier to win that way."

I shook my head, not really surprised at all, and stepped into his side. His arm came over my shoulders as naturally as breathing. As we walked to Logan's vehicle, Nate drove past. Both he and Sam waved.

When we got in, Logan asked, "What was going on with you and Sam?"

I paused. "What do you mean?"

The corner of his mouth lifted. "I know when Sam's just delivered a bomb. I can recognize the look by now. #Chickshowdown. It's hot, but seriously, I know she said something. What was it?" All his joking and teasing vanished. "I don't want you to get the wrong idea about her. Mason, Sam, and me—the three of us have been through a lot. She's been put in the hospital because of us, stuff like that. I could tell she was paying more attention to you than she normally does to girls I bring around, but it's just because she's protective of me. That's it. I'm the same way with her."

"Yeah." I willed the tension in me to dissipate. "You guys all love each other. That's obvious."

He didn't let up. His eyes only narrowed. "What'd she say?"

I shook my head, my hands lifted from my lap. "Nothing. She just said that if I hurt you, she'd become my worst enemy."

His head back moved an inch. "That was it?"

I nodded. "Yeah. That was it."

"Oh." He shrugged that off, starting his Escalade. "That's nothing then."

"That's normal for you guys?"

He pulled away from the curb. The glow from Nate's rear lights was still visible, and he headed toward them. "Oh, yeah. Hospital visits. Car wrecks. Car explosions. Fights. Lots of fights. You'd be surprised what our normal is." He smiled to himself. "Good times."

I sat back, stunned, and then I remembered—I still hadn't met his brother.

CHAPTER 17

#RIPROARINGDRUNK
TAYLOR

Nate was in the back building a fire when we got to the house. I knew it was late, and I could have checked my phone to find out the time, but I didn't want to. I didn't want to think about anything. I just wanted to be. Reminding myself to focus on the moment, I looked around at Logan's place. They had a nice setup, an *impressive* setup. The house was big, so I knew the back would be nice, but when I stepped out there, I was still taken aback.

In the corner of a massive porch was a fireplace made of all different colored rocks. Around it were a bunch of padded benches, but Nate had started our bonfire in the yard, farther down from the porch. They had a huge circular bricked area with an oversized metal container right in the middle. Nate piled wood there, and as Logan shut the door behind me, Nate lit a match. He flicked it on the pile and *oomph!* Just like that, the entire south section of their backyard was bathed in light.

When it settled, Nate spread his arms wide, grinning from ear to ear. "We got ourselves a bonfire."

Logan's hand rested on the small of my back, and his other held two beers for us. "We're coming. Where's Sam?"

Nate waved at the house. "Mason was awake when we got home, so she went with him."

"You want anything to eat?"

I glanced up. Food hadn't entered my mind all night, but at Logan's question, I realized I was ravenous. "Yes, please," I told him. "Can I help with something?"

He nodded in Nate's direction. "Head on down. There are blankets down there and more beer, if you need either. Nate will set you up."

"What are you going to do?"

"I'm going to make some food for us. Be down in a few."

It felt a little weird. I associated bonfires with party atmospheres. With only a few people, it seemed intimate. Nate was rummaging in a storage bin a few feet from the bonfire. I didn't want to feel an intimate vibe with him. Logan now represented my comfort zone, and that in itself should've been an alarm signal. Instead, I focused on making it until he returned..

"Hey," Nate said as I approached. "Blankets are in here if you get cold."

I looked at the raging fire. "Don't think that'll be a problem."

He laughed, sitting down on one of the benches. "Yeah, but you'd be surprised how chilly it can get when the fire fades."

I frowned at him. Was he trying to tell me something?

He noticed my look. "What?"

I shrugged, sitting down on one of the farthest benches from him. "Nothing." I shoved my hands into my pockets and hunched over. "Logan's making us food?"

"Yep. He does that. Chef Logan. That's all we've been hearing lately. It's annoying."

Oh. "Do all of you guys live here?"

"Yeah." Nate hunched forward too and poked the fire with a stick. "We had a different house closer to campus last year. Since Sam's living with us now, Mason wanted something more private and secure." He used the stick to wave over the backyard. "You can't see it, but there's a perimeter around the house. Anyone we don't know steps over it, and we all get alarms sent to our phones."

I looked around, but this was the outskirts of town. The backyard was trees, and that was what filled up the front yard, too. "Who are you guys?"

Nate grinned. "We've had our fair share of enemies; I guess I can say that much."

"You can say that and more." Logan joined the conversation as he arrived, holding a pan in front of him with an oven mitt on his hand. He set the pan down on a brick near the fire, taking the bench between us. "I made quesadillas. And see?" He pointed to a platter with three smaller cups. "Dip."

"You made the dip?" Nate sounded impressed.

"No." Logan shook his head. "But I put it in those little things. Chef Logan always makes it right for my man-husband." He winked at Nate.

"I've told you..." Nate rolled his eyes, but grinned as he reached for a quesadilla. "You need to stop trying to get into my pants, Logan. Mason's made it clear. Our romance is strictly forbidden."

Logan gave a low, smooth chuckle.

Even his laugh was infectious. It slid into me, warming and relaxing me all at the same time.

Logan mirrored Nate, kicking his legs up on the corner of my seat, and the two began talking. I tuned them out to stare at the fire, but I couldn't tune out Logan's feet so close to me. I felt the stirrings of things I shouldn't be feeling. Images of going to Logan, sinking next to his side, feeling his arm around me, or—I closed my eyes; the images were vivid now. Kissing him. Touching his face. I held my breath. It was so temping to go over and sit next to him. His arm would go around my shoulders. I could lean in. Then...

I was burning up, an ache building between my legs.

Logan and Nate talked and laughed. I was holding myself back from jumping Logan. And then I was somewhere else. Eric and I had been laughing together in bed that morning...

"Come on." He'd poked me in the side as he lay next to me, our naked limbs tangled together. His mouth rested on my shoulder, and his lips had

grazed my skin as he added, "We should get up if we're going to stop and see your mom when we get home."

I didn't have a chance to respond.

The poke had turned into a tickle, and soon Eric was on top of me. All the laughter and shrieks soon transformed to moaning. He'd slid back inside me, and we'd stayed in bed for another hour.

I gripped my plate on my lap and stared into the fire, but I was back there. I remembered when we'd pulled up to the hospital. Eric held my hand as we walked in. We didn't stop at the front desk. I'd grown up visiting my mom at work. The receptionist waved as she saw us go past, down the hallway. That was when we heard the first gunshot.

"Taylor?"

I started. My hands jerked, and the plate went flying. "Shit." I reached for it, but Logan got there first, his eyes on me.

"Bruce, you okay?"

I relaxed instantly. It was stupid, but my last name put distance between us. It gave me space to think, feel, breathe. I wouldn't do anything stupid. I nodded, relaxing the rest of my body as best I could. "Yeah. I'm good."

It was probably obvious I wasn't. After a brief moment of silence, Nate coughed and stood up, his plate in his hand. "Think I'll head to bed for the night." He picked up the empty quesadilla platter and his beer, as well as the one Logan had emptied. I had a beer in front of me, but I hadn't touched it.

He paused, looking down at it, but moved past. "'Night, guys."

I wanted to disappear.

If Logan waved or any silent messages passed between the two, I didn't see it. My head was firmly folded down, my chin against my chest. Once I heard the patio door slide open, then closed, Logan adjusted his legs. His feet rested next to mine, and he tapped my shoe with his.

"Hey," he said. "What's your damage?"

My head flew up, and I was ready to fight. But I stopped as soon as my eyes found his. He'd delivered no derision with that phrase. I'd reacted too soon. He was steady, calm, and waiting for me to answer. He'd just been trying to lighten the mood.

"Sorry." Even my jaw was tight. Goddamn. My hands had balled into fists. I forced them open. "I have these moments where…" *I go insane.* "I remember things…from before."

"Yeah?"

God. A storm of everything ravaged me. Guilt. Shame. Anger. Betrayal. And, I swallowed tightly, even relief. I survived. My mom hadn't. And I was sitting here, trying not to kiss this guy because he could break me.

What the hell was I doing?

"Hey." Logan leaned closer. His elbows rested on his knees. His head came close to mine, and his fingers tapped my leg. "Look." He straightened. "I know some shit went down last year with your mom. I've got no idea what, just that something happened. If you think I care what it is, you're wrong. I can see it's hurting you. That's the only thing I care about. So if you want to talk, I'm here. If you don't, I don't either."

The more he said, the more tension left me.

His voice softened. "We've all got shit in our past." He gestured to the house. "Those people in there? Mason, Sam, even Nate— they're my family because we've had our own battles go down. I love my parents, but I didn't grow up because of them. I grew up because of Mason. So whatever went down with you last year—I don't know what I'm saying. I guess you can hold on to it if you want, if that does something for you. Fuck." He expelled a breath. "I don't say shit to anyone either, so who am I to encourage all the sharing?" He stood, holding his beer bottle so tightly his knuckles were almost white. "I suddenly want to get rip-roaring drunk."

I expected him to pass by, head for the house, and my gaze went back to the ground. But his feet never moved away. I looked back up, and he held his hand out to me. "You coming?"

I couldn't look away. "To get drunk?"

He shrugged. "For whatever, but yes, I'd prefer if booze was involved."

I looked up into his eyes then. The storm that raged in me was there too. The joking, playing side of him was gone. This was the real Logan, and there was a whole lot of darkness there. I took his hand, felt myself standing with him, and I followed him inside. Everything said yes to me. Yes, I wanted to hold his hand. Yes, I wanted to get drunk with him. Yes, I wanted to tell him what happened. Yes, I wanted to go wherever he was taking me.

I stopped thinking. I would probably regret it, but I was done thinking, analyzing, worrying. I was done being afraid. I was going with the feels, and as Logan went inside, he grabbed a bottle of Jack. The feels would be dangerous to me that night. I embraced them.

Logan went upstairs, then up a second flight of stairs. He had the entire third level as his bedroom. He'd set up a small living room in the corner with a massive television screen mounted on the wall. A video game console sat halfway between the television and the couch. Logan nudged it back toward the wall and sank down on the couch.

I stood in front of him. He gazed up at me, our hands still laced together. My heart beat so fast.

Nothing was said, but I felt him. I felt that he wanted me. I wanted him, too. The air was thick. I felt it pressing down, but it didn't bother me. All I could feel was the desire to touch him, to taste him.

I wanted to forget everything.

My voice was raspy as I said, "What are we doing?"

"Honestly?" He opened his legs and tugged me forward. "Anything you want."

I was trapped between his thighs, and I loved it. I started to lower myself to rest on one of his knees, but Logan set the bottle aside and found my waist. He lifted me, only to pull me back down, straddling him. My hand still held one of his hands, and they rested between us as he leaned back against the couch. Reaching for the bottle again, he unscrewed the top with his free hand, then thumbed the cap off, tossing it to the floor. His eyes found mine again.

His hand left mine and moved to my waist. It slid under my shirt and inside my jeans to grip my hip. "What do you want to do?"

He asked so much with that question. My eyelids were heavy. I just wanted him. That was it. "I don't want to think tonight."

His hand tightened over my hip. He took a long pull from the bottle, then passed it to me. I held it in front of me. I closed my eyes and tipped my head back, feeling the burn as the liquid slid down my throat. It warmed me. I took a second pull, then a third. Logan did the same.

"What's the verdict, Bruce?"

I grinned at my last name. "What do you mean?"

His hand slid up, curving around my back. He leaned toward me as his hand stopped right at my bra. I closed my eyes to savor the feeling of his fingers there. I wanted my shirt off. I wanted my bra off. I wanted the touch of his fingers, but I bit my lip and waited for his answer.

"You know."

I did. My eyes opened, I gazed right down into him. Our foreheads were so close. Everything was so close. His eyes darted to my lips, darkening, and I thought, *Screw it*. I closed the distance, but once my lips touched his, he took over. He'd been waiting for me, holding off, and once I gave my answer, he was ready. Sweeping me up in his arms, he carried me to the bed.

He skimmed a hand up my back, leaving a trail of tingles in his wake. He lifted my shirt as he went until he could pull it clear. As my hair fell back down, it gave me a slow caress as well. I shivered a delicious and intoxicating shiver as Logan tilted my head up to meet his gaze.

Hunger. Need. His eyes darkened before his lips fell to mine. That slight pressure sent a mass of sensations through me, and my toes curled at the tantalizing touch of his lips. I wound my arms around his neck, pressing against him as I burned, yet goose bumps ran up and down my bare back.

"Taylor," Logan murmured, one of his hands falling to my jeans. A gentle touch there, and he guided me backward.

I moved down onto the bed, his arms locked around me. He rolled with me and held himself above me. When he undid my jeans, the ache that had been building turned into a throb. I was wet, already wanting him there. I wanted the feel of him sliding into me, how tight that would be, how connected and intimate. I stretched slowly, savoring the smooth, soft feeling of his sheets on my back as he started to pull my jeans down.

"Logan." I reached for his face. I wanted to kiss him again. I wanted the touch only lovers could relish, and as his lips moved back to mine, I kicked at my pants.

Logan pulled back, and I moaned at the separation, but his smooth chuckle calmed me. I felt his breath moving down my body, a ministration in its own right as he pressed kisses along the way and lingered before he pulled my jeans off, then my underwear. He paused, lifting his head.

I opened my eyes to see him studying the inside of my thigh. I bit my lip, knowing what he saw, and I prepared myself. But when he looked back at me, there was no judgment. He smoothed over my skin and asked, his voice husky, "You have a tattoo?"

I nodded, my throat full with emotion and praying he wouldn't ask more. "It's a sparkler."

"It's beautiful, Taylor." He bent and pressed his lips there. "It's a Goddamn firecracker. Perfect."

I gasped, my back arching at the shock of his touch. Then he turned his head, moving his mouth to where I ached. As he began to stroke me–kissing, nibbling, licking, and rubbing–his hand grazed over my body from my shoulder to my arm. The side of his hand then brushed against my breast and came to rest on my stomach.

The pleasure was building. The longer he caressed me, the higher my back arched. "Logan!"

He still didn't stop. A smooth chuckle came from him, sending vibrations through my body, but I was so far gone. I reached down, my fingers sliding into his hair and grabbing hold. He used his tongue now, and I felt a scream building in the back of my throat. It was going to rip from me, so

I sank my teeth into my lip. Then he moved away, and I gasped at the sudden break. But then his lips were on mine as his fingers sank inside of me.

I moaned, unable to keep it in. I'd never been loud during sex, but Logan brought out something new in me. It had never been like this with Eric. There'd been a touch here and there, a hand on the boob, a quick finger pump, and then he'd fill me. He didn't stretch me, not the way Logan was doing. His finger slid deep before pulling back to go in again. Then a second finger moved with the first, and he kept going. He went deeper than Eric had ever gone, and I was panting.

I grabbed his shoulders, and my nails sank in. He stiffened above me, and I laid my head back on the pillow.

"Oh, no, no, no." Logan grinned down at me, desire almost palpable on his face. He shook his head, *tsk*ing. "If you think you can lay back and just enjoy this, you're mistaken."

I stopped biting my lip to grin back up at him. This was new too—laughing, teasing. I was used to silence until Eric was done. I'd get a quick pop of relief, followed by a short, trembling climax, but that was it. Tonight my body glistened with sweat, and I held back from climaxing right now.

Logan looked rested and ready to go all night. "I've got a feeling I'm going to be sore tomorrow," I told him.

"Tomorrow?" He pulled his fingers out and rested, gazing down at me. "You're going to be sore tonight. I'm going to ride you long and hard until you think the world is only made of sex." He smirked, arching an eyebrow. "How's that sound?"

He stole my breath. The way he looked at me—cocky, his eyes full of arousal, and his sole focus on me—he was breathtaking.

I lifted a hand to cup the side of his face, and my finger traced his mouth. "You're beautiful," I said.

He didn't respond, but surprise bloomed over his face. He gazed down as I looked up, and in that moment, a wall slid away. He let me in. I saw the little boy in him, the younger brother, the friend. I saw the protective family member. I already knew the player, joker, and fighter, but this was once again the real Logan.

A wave of emotion rose up in me. I was thankful. I was moved. I felt inspired, followed by a sense of desperation. He'd let me in. He didn't let anyone in. I needed to prove I was loyal, that I would respect him as he had given me respect, that I was worthy of this gift. I blinked back tears. "Logan," I said softly.

A different look appeared in his eyes, making them bright and clear, almost awestruck. His eyes fluttered closed, and he bent his head once more. This time the kiss wasn't just to give pleasure. It was more. It was a message from him to me, and as my lips moved under his, I answered.

What the message was, I wasn't ready to understand. I just knew it was deep, it was primal, and I had never experienced it in my life.

As Logan slid inside of me a little later, condom in place, he filled me to the fullest. Tomorrow, he would find claw marks on his back. Tomorrow, I wouldn't be able to walk. Tomorrow, I might be overwhelmed by how raw and exposed I felt tonight. But tomorrow would be tomorrow. I'd deal with that then.

For now, I clasped on to Logan and moved my hips with his.

CHAPTER 18

LOGAN SEX MACHINE KADE
TAYLOR

Logan was still sleeping when I woke up. He was curled toward me, one hand resting on my hip and the other under his head. Our legs were tangled, and I took a minute to look over him.

He was cocky and so full of life when awake. When he slept, he looked almost angelic. Eyes closed, his chest moved in a quiet, steady rhythm. Once he woke up, he'd have a smart-ass comment on his lips, and in that moment, I didn't want it. I wanted this serene feeling I had now.

He was peaceful, and almost pure. Then my eyes fell to the tattoo on his side, reminding me he wasn't. I'd seen it last night and wanted to ask him about it, but his lips had twisted as I touched it, a flash of anger in his eyes. I'd guided him back to me without a word, but he paused, looking at his tattoo and then at me. The moment had been brief, and I knew he wasn't angry with me. It was that tattoo. I'd ask him about it one day.

Hearing a small buzzing sound from the floor, I held my breath and eased out of Logan's bed, scooting to the edge. All my clothes were in a pile, and my phone had fallen out of my jeans. It kept buzzing, so I grabbed where it landed, right underneath my bra.

It was my alarm for class, and raking a hand through my hair, I cursed under my breath. I was almost an hour late. I wouldn't make my morning classes. After turning my alarm off, I saw a text message from Claire and grimaced. We said lunch yesterday. I checked the message; she needed to move the time back twenty minutes. That was not a problem.

Gathering as much of my clothing as I could, I slipped into Logan's bathroom and dressed. I texted Claire back, letting her know the change of time was good for me, and decided to order an Uber. And…I was stuck. I wasn't sure where I was. Operation Sneak-Back-Ignore-The-Gorgeous-Guy-In-The-Bed-And-Find-His-Mail was a go.

I tried to be quiet in the bathroom, but when I edged the door open, I peeked around it and saw Logan on the edge of his bed, sitting right where I'd been earlier. He had pulled on his jeans, but they weren't zipped up. He frowned, his hair sticking up, and he rubbed a hand over one of his eyes.

"You look like a hot cat burglar right now," he said. "Why is that, and why do I want to be your sidekick?"

I smiled. I couldn't stop myself, and I came the rest of the way into the room. I didn't dare get any closer, though. I wasn't stupid. We'd end up back in bed. Even now, my eyes skimmed all over him, taking in his wide, strong shoulders, remembering how they'd lifted me. And his stomach. He was lean, sculpted, and cut. I remembered how he'd held himself above me, watching me as I climaxed. Those muscles had rippled under my hands as I explored him in turn.

I fanned myself. "You got a window? We should open it."

He smirked. "Round two." He patted the space next to him. "I'm ready when you are, Firecracker."

That name… I looked down. It felt good. It felt really good, not to mention the rest of what he'd said. I almost groaned. The idea was tempting, but no—Claire. I could not forget Claire. I waved my phone at him. "I have a lunch date. Round two will have to be postponed."

The smirk vanished. "Don't tell me you're meeting that douche for lunch."

"What?"

"The guy from the party last night."

"Oh…Oh!" He meant Jeremy. "No. It's Claire. We set it up last night before I even saw you. And speaking of, what's your address? I was going to call a driver."

Logan snorted. He stood up, gesturing to my phone. "Put that thing away. I'll give you a ride wherever you need."

"My car's still outside that douche's apartment."

He grunted, stretching at the same time. All his muscles flattened. I couldn't stop watching. When his arms dropped back to his side, my eyes were pulled lower, lower, all the way to the V that dipped beneath his jeans.

After a moment, I realized Logan was watching me watch him. Another burst of heat came to my cheeks, and I turned away. "It's like you're a machine or something," I mumbled. "Just get dressed, please."

Logan chuckled, disappearing inside his closet. His voice carried out, "A sex machine."

I heard the gloating in his voice.

He came back out, and I looked up. The smirk was back in place, as was a simple shirt that fit him nicely and didn't hide what was underneath at all.

"I do believe that's the best compliment I've heard the morning after." He winked at me, grabbing a baseball cap. "Just call me Logan Sex Machine Kade from now on."

"You looked so angelic when you were sleeping."

"No, Taylor." Logan went to the bathroom, but stuck his head back out. His grin turned wicked. "I looked *fucking* angelic." He paused. "That doesn't make sense. Carry on." He disappeared again, but his voice echoed out to me. "Keep telling me how you were watching me in my sleep. I want to hear all about how gorgeous I was."

I groaned, sitting down on the bed to wait. "You're not hurting for humility. That's for sure."

The water ran for a minute, then he turned it off. He returned, drying his hands, and smiled down at me. "Confidence is sexy, and speaking of sex..." He leaned down, suddenly in my space.

I stayed firm. A tingle shot through me at how close he came, but he stopped a few inches away. His eyes raked over my face, going to my lips, then back up to my eyes.

He grinned, slowly, deliciously. "When's round two going to happen?"

I tried to ignore the adrenaline that shot through my body and the fact that if he lowered his face another two inches, his mouth would be on mine again. I gulped. "Technically, round two already happened."

And round three. He'd bent me into a position I never knew existed. My mind started to wander, remembering that moment and instantly, my body was getting hotter. I cleared my throat and fixed a smile on my face. "Can you take me to my car now?"

He chuckled, moving back, and, good gracious, I didn't want him to leave. I almost sagged forward at his abrupt absence.

"Come on, Firecracker." Grabbing his wallet and keys, he opened his door and pointed to the hallway. "You're lucky you have a lunch thing, or I'd make you get some food with me. I never did get those tacos last night."

As I moved past him, he gave me one firm little swat on the butt, then fell in line beside me. The door shut, and his arm came around my shoulders. We walked down to the main floor like that, and I liked how it made me feel, like I was his.

At that thought, my veins filled with ice.

His.

No, no, no. That was wrong. What was I doing? His arm fell from my shoulders as we reached the front door, and he told me to wait a minute for him. He went to the kitchen, and I heard him talking to someone. I didn't want to go in there, especially after I heard Sam respond. She would take one look and instantly know.

A lump the size of a baseball formed at the bottom of my throat. I had feelings for Logan. What was I going to do about them?

He came back out, his eyes meeting mine, and a genuine smile appeared. He liked me. I could see it in his eyes, but that was known. He'd told me that. Sam had told me that. Even Claire had mentioned it, but this was Logan Sex Machine Kade.

"He's all about sex, fighting, and having his brother's back." Jason's words filtered through my haze. He'd warned me about Logan. Hell, I'd warned myself, but it was too late now. This must be about Eric, I reasoned. Logan brought up emotions in me that were really about Eric. But even so, as Logan came toward me, I felt a flutter in my stomach.

I was falling for Logan Sex Machine Kade.

"You okay?" He frowned, his eyes on mine as he reached for the front door. "You look a little pale."

I caught movement in the kitchen from the corner of my eye. I knew it was Sam. I could almost feel her judgment—or worse, her pity. I didn't look. I didn't want to see that look. I'd dealt with enough of those looks in the last nine months, so I nodded to Logan and said, "I'm fine." And before anything else could happen, I stepped outside and hurried to his car.

Logan stopped once on the drive. He bought coffee for both of us, and it still seemed like the trip to my car went way too fast. He pulled up next to it and left the engine running. I glanced over as I undid my seatbelt. Last night had been…I was assaulted by images of us in bed, my legs around his waist as he went deep into me.

I let out a small cough. "Well, that was—"

Logan laughed, his head falling back to rest against his seat. "Save your words, Bruce. You and me, we're going Night 2.0 in a few."

My hand let go of the seatbelt. My heart moved up into my throat at that promise.

He leaned over, his body brushing against mine as he opened the door for me. Before he moved back, his head turned and planted a kiss on my lips. It was quick, but firm and authoritative. "Stop thinking about it," he whispered, his lips still on mine. "I'm not ready to let you go yet."

His words pounded through me. Feeling dazed by everything, I nodded, my lips brushing over his. "Just fun," I whispered.

His eyes darkened. "Hell, yeah."

Yeah. Fun. That was what it was, but his words still lodged in me. He wasn't ready to let me go, and I wasn't ready to let go of him yet either. Still, I pressed my lips to his and slid from the car. My knees were unsteady as I shut the door and turned toward my vehicle. Glancing over my shoulder, I saw that Logan was waiting for me. Once I started the engine, he lifted his hand in a wave and drove off.

I slumped forward, resting my forehead on the steering wheel. Good God. Logan Kade was going to be the death of me.

But you're alive, a voice that sounded a lot like my mother's said in my head.

I took a deep breath, feeling my pulse thumping and tingling sensations sizzling all through me. The voice was right. No matter the ending, Logan Kade would be worth it.

I was alive.

I was nervous when I met Claire for lunch. I hadn't been a virgin yesterday, but I was different now. There was an extra glow to my face. I was the one wearing it, but even I could see it. I could practically feel my eyes sparkling, but she didn't seem to notice. I was relieved, then bored as I sat back and spent an entire hour hearing about Ben. Apparently, Claire had been right, and Malia did have a thing for him too. Anytime he and Claire had been alone on the patio, she kept intruding. She was drunk, and all she could do was hang all over him. That had pissed Claire off, but the end of the night made up for everything.

He kissed her. Again.

And it hadn't stopped there. They had a full make-out session when he walked her to her apartment door—even though Malia and another guy were waiting in the car. After a little while, Ben had said *screw it*. He'd gone inside the apartment with her and texted their friends to leave without him. He stayed the night, and today Claire was falling all over herself, giddy and giggling.

I couldn't remember her this happy since…was it high school? Since… I could feel the glow drain from my face. Since before my mother died and Eric left. Claire started to describe Ben's girth, and I focused on numbing the feeling away. Only it wouldn't go.

Logan.

I remembered how his hand had skimmed up my back. I remembered how his lips had grazed over mine, how he'd cupped the side of my face as he slid inside. I remembered arching my back, feeling his lips trail down my throat. I remembered the way he'd held me through the night, how he'd cradled my face to his chest and brushed his fingers through my hair, rubbing the back of my neck.

I remembered how he'd called himself Logan Sex Machine Kade this morning.

"What's funny?"

"Huh?"

I looked up. Claire had stopped talking and the corners of her lips were pinched; she looked in pain. She pointed at me with a fork. "You were smiling."

"Oh." I cleared my throat. "Just hearing you talk about Ben, it—uh—reminded me of high school. I was thinking about the last time I saw you this happy."

Her frown disappeared. She seemed to melt, her shoulders relaxing dramatically. "Oh, Taylor." She blinked and pressed a hand to her chest. "You're right. I haven't been this happy in a long time. I mean, last year was—" She froze. She reached for her glass of water, but even her eyes stopped. They were trained on a spot on the table.

I didn't want the mood to shift, so I asked, "Does Jason know Ben?"

That launched her on a whole other discussion. When they should meet? But, wait, she didn't know if there was even a reason for Jason to be introduced. Were they a couple or not? She didn't know, and over the next half hour, Claire questioned every comment Ben had ever made. When we finished lunch, she was still glowing, but the light had dimmed a little bit, and an anxious look formed in her eyes. She gripped her phone tightly as we walked out of the campus café together. I was about to ask her about her weekend plans when she threw a distracted "see you later" over her shoulder to me and headed off.

Well. Okay, then.

CHAPTER 19

#LOGANSDICK
LOGAN

Last night was the best sex I'd ever had, and we continued to have great sex the next night, and the night after. The week after. The week after that, too. In fact, we had great sex for an entire fucking month, and I was in a glorious mood. The only thing not glorious had been my time spent away from the family. I'd been selfish, keeping Taylor to myself. We did the parties, but we spent a lot of those nights in either my bedroom or hers, and standing in front of the refrigerator, I couldn't stop thinking about the upcoming weekend. Mason's game was away and we were going to road trip to it, and by 'we', I meant the family. I owed them that time, but there'd been no mention of Taylor coming along. I knew that hadn't happened by accident.

I wanted her to come. Shit. I think I was starting to need her to come, but then Sam snuffed that idea out.

"You're going to hurt her," she said, coming to stand behind me.

I was reaching for the juice, but I stopped and straightened up. She was in the kitchen doorway. Her eyes were troubled, and she crossed her arms over her chest.

I shook my head, letting the fridge door shut. "Don't, Sam."

"I didn't like Kris in the beginning, and I know you really cared for her…" She trailed off, frowning, and looking at the floor.

I cared, but I hadn't loved Kris. That was where Sam was going. I knew she'd started to care about Kris at the end. Was that what this was about? Sam didn't want to start liking another girl and hurt for her when things ended with me? I propped a shoulder against the wall by the fridge and folded my arms over my chest as well. "Where are you coming from with this?"

She shook her head, but didn't look up. "I don't know," she murmured. She uncrossed her arms, and her hands clasped together at her waist. "I like Taylor."

"So do I."

Sam looked up. I saw the surprise. This would've been the perfect time for a smart-ass remark, but this was serious. I narrowed my eyes. "I didn't get the feeling you really liked her the first night."

"That's not true. I just—" She bit her lip and looked away.

"Sam." I waited till her eyes met mine, and then waited another beat. I didn't want her to look away. "You've never warned me off of a girl before."

"You're going to hurt her," she repeated.

I frowned. Sam looked away again, and I got the sense she wasn't talking about Taylor at all. "Okay. Well… Noted." I kept frowning at her, but she was lost in her thoughts. "I disagree, and I'm still going to hang out with her."

She let out a breath. "Don't invite her this weekend, okay?"

I shook my head. "What the hell? You're not like this."

"I know. I just—it's too soon. If you don't want to fuck things up, like you say, go slow. You're just sleeping together, right?" Her eyes met mine again, finally.

My head jerked back. I hadn't been prepared for the haunted expression on her face. What was going on with her? I gentled my voice. "You okay, Sam?"

She nodded. "Yeah." Her voice was equally soft. "I just...don't want to see *her* hurt. That's all."

Bullshit. I wanted to say that, to interrogate her, but I held back.

She wasn't talking about Taylor. "You're not talking about Taylor at all, are you?"

There it was. I put it out there. We'd been through too much shit not to be honest. I waited, and got my answer when she hung her head. I was right. I murmured softly, "She's not going to hurt me, Sam."

"That's what you say now." She shook her head, grimacing. "You're the glue of us. Did you know that?"

I smirked. "When am I *not* the glue?"

"No. I mean it." The haunted look was back. She didn't even hide it now. "Things have changed even since I joined the group, but the glue's not Mason. Not anymore. It's you. Mason doesn't seem to care. I think he likes Taylor, but I know Nate and I are worried. And we...just...we don't want you hurt. That's all."

"I'm good, Strattan." I winked for good measure. "I'm always good. You know that."

Her shoulders lifted up in a slow and deep breath. "Yeah, well." She bit down on her lip before looking away again. "You're like me, Logan."

"What do you mean?"

"You grew up being hurt, just like me."

I felt her words in my gut, and I didn't like it. I frowned. "Well—" A flippant remark was on my tongue, but she shook her head, saying over me, "Don't. Okay? Mason got to see his parents happy at some point. I know you didn't. Neither did I, and if I did, I can't remember it anymore. I know that kind of hurt goes deep, tunnels inside of you like a cancer. You mask it, just like I did."

Fuck. She went deep, but sorry, Sam. I wasn't going to go there. Not yet, anyway. I changed the subject, trying for a smile, "You haven't been running as much lately."

A wry laugh came from her throat. She looked away again, then nodded to herself before finding my gaze once more. "Surprising, huh?" I relaxed. She was going with the topic change. She was a sister to me, but I wasn't ready. I didn't want to go there with anyone. I hadn't, except Mason. Then she was saying, "Considering my mom's been back all summer."

"Well, since you brought her up, yeah." My lip twitched up. What a fucking psycho.

Sam's mom, Analise, came back into our lives last Christmas, but Sam had stayed away from her. She'd refused to go home for holidays, and when summer break arrived, Sam spent a month at her dad's house. She'd been back here, staying at the house with Mason, once he started early training. He told me Analise had been calling Sam more lately, pushing to spend time with her, so I had a feeling the old days when Sam would run for hours would be happening again, and soon.

"You know..." Sam gave me a forced smile. The corners of her mouth lifted, but it didn't extend to her eyes. They still looked dead. "Never mind about what I said before. I love you, but you know what you're doing."

"You sure?"

She nodded, turning back to the hallway. Her head lowered, and her voice trailed off. "Yeah…" She looked over her shoulder one last time before going back to her bedroom. "Fuck her brains out."

I smirked. "That's the plan. As often as I can."

TAYLOR

I'd been staying mostly at Logan's house over the last month. I hated to say it, but most everything and everyone went to the backburner. It wasn't that I wanted to do that. It just happened. Jason was busy with friends. So was Claire. I saw them every now and then, and Claire for lunch a few times a week, but that was it. Logan was the same. We saw Nate at parties, sometimes going with him, but we always left on our own earlier. And for whatever reason, we hadn't crossed paths with Logan's brother and Sam that often. There'd been a few times, but nothing where we spent a lot of quality time together.

Last night had been one of those times, and like the other mornings, I headed to class before Logan without a plan for the weekend. I overheard other students talking about the away game. They hadn't had one yet, which wasn't normal. People were excited, planning on road tripping for the event. I wondered if Logan was going to go, and what that meant about us, but I got my answer later.

Hey! Sex Machine here. How's your day? Can we meet up Sunday night? We're going to the game this weekend so we won't be around.

We. He said *we.* My grin faltered. What did that mean? *We.*

Not *me,* as in *he* wouldn't be around, but *we,* as in he and others, like they were all going to hang out together, like they were friends. Hearing my own thoughts, I rolled my eyes. I was being an idiot. I replied, **Sounds good. Have a fun weekend!**

Sweet. Talk to you later, Bruce.

I sighed and scooted lower on the couch. I had to ask myself the same question again: What the hell was I doing? I typed back, **Will do. See you Sunday.**

Figuring the conversation was done, I started to put my phone back on the table, but it buzzed again.

You're probably going to get drunk text messages from me. Be prepared.

My grin returned. **They better be good.**

Only dick pics.

I laughed out loud. **Promise?**

I can send you one right now.

If you do, I can't promise what I'll do with it.

I suggest banners, maybe even fliers. Everyone should know it by sight. ;)

I typed back: **It should have its own fan group.**

#Logansdick I'll get Nate to be the admin for it.

We kept going back and forth, and it was late when we finally stopped, and my sides hurt from laughing, and my cheeks hurt from smiling.

And they didn't really hurt, not at all.

Logan texted a few times during the next day. Cain won, he wanted to share with me. The rest were jokes throughout the day. I was drifting off to sleep when my phone lit up. When I saw the first text, I laid back, already smiling.

If I weren't in a hotel with Nate, three hours away, this would be a booty text.

I typed back, **Are you drunk?**

Yes. If I weren't, I'd probably be driving to your house instead.

That'd be good with me. My dad's gone tonight.

Shit. Because of the game, right? Fuck. See? I should've asked you to come after all.

I paused. He had thought about asking me? I sat there surprised for a moment. **That's okay. I needed to get a lot of stuff done. I applied at Pete's Pub after all.**

You did? Did you get the job?

Trained tonight already.

Fuck yeah! Wait. Are you a server?

A bartender.

Even better. Shit, I gotta go. Nate's going to take my phone away. I'll call you tomorrow.

I typed out a goodnight and left the phone on the nightstand. Sinking into my covers, I didn't even try to hold back the smile on my face. It felt good to have that excited feeling in my belly.

# #

"Eric!" I would've screamed, but I couldn't. Another gunshot sounded from farther down the hallway. I crouched on the floor and looked down the corridor, holding my breath. They hadn't come around the corner. There was still time. I reached out my hand. Eric stood frozen over me. He'd started to bend down to help me up, but then that shot went off. He couldn't move. He just stared right where they were going to come from.

"Eric," I whispered. My hand reached for his.

He still didn't move.

I was growing panicked. "Eric! Please."

One more gunshot.

"Eri—" I started again, but he looked down. The fear in his eyes was stark.

I knew. Even before he started to shake his head, I knew. I felt it in my bones, and it chilled me. He was going to leave me here.

I tried to push myself up from the floor, but I couldn't. My knee wouldn't work. "Eric. Please."

His eyes went flat. His head shook from right to left, and he began to move backward. He almost melted away from me. He moved so softly, like a ghost. I barely heard him when he said, "I can't. I...I can't, Taylor."

"Eric!" I hissed, sitting up as much as I could. "Help me!"

He was my first kiss.

He still shook his head. He was so far away now, almost to the front desk.

He took my virginity.

He was the first guy to hold my hand, the first guy to take me to a dance, the first everything. He was the first one I'd loved.

"I'm sorry, Taylor." His hand trembled. He paused at the door, just before slipping outside. "Please forgive me."

He was the first guy to abandon me.

I woke up screaming. I'd thrown off my covers, and my entire body was drenched in sweat. I jerked up to a sitting position and grabbed my knee. I could still feel the pain there. But no, I was in my bedroom. I forced myself to look around. The window was open. A soft breeze whooshed through the room. I drew a shuddering breath as my heart pounded in my ears.

It was a dream.

My mind felt jumbled. It hadn't been just a nightmare this time. There were other thoughts mixed in I rubbed my hands on my face and rocked back and forth for a moment. I needed to calm down. Pressing my forehead to the backs of my knees, I drew in air. I felt something cool against the backs of my hands. It wasn't sweat. It was tears; I'd been crying.

No one was home. It was just me.

"Mom," I whispered to myself. I wanted her here. I wanted to feel her arms around me. I closed my eyes, imagining the touch of her lips to my forehead. No matter the nightmare, no matter my age, she always took care of me. I turned to my side and grabbed the blanket. My hand formed a fist around it, and I imagined it was her hand. She sat next to me. She was still my mom.

But she wasn't here. She was gone.

CHAPTER 20

ALREADY?
LOGAN

I glanced at my phone on the way home and frowned at the blank screen. Well, it wasn't completely blank. There were texts there, but none from Taylor. I texted her that morning and a few more times since we started home.

My dick was hard just thinking about her.

If I were someone like Nate, I'd be insecure—worried she must've changed her mind or there was another dude. He thought things like that, but that wasn't me. I glanced down at my man and felt him nod in agreement. We were both confident. It wasn't me.

Something was wrong.

"What's wrong?"

I looked over at Nate in the driver's seat. He volunteered to do the last leg because Sam was sleeping in the back, all curled up with Mason. Both Nate and I knew Mase wasn't going to drive. It was only three hours, but he was tired, and he should be. He kicked ass on the field. I should know. We coordinated a drinking game that corresponded with anything he did. If he scored a touchdown? Two shots. If he blocked another guy? One shot. It was our fucking luck that he'd had the best damned game of his life.

I was hungover, as well as worried about Taylor.

I put my phone away. "Nothing."

Nate's gaze fell to the console between us, where my phone was. "Mmm-hmmm."

I let out a sigh, leaning back in my chair. "For fuck's sake, what's your problem?"

"You texting that chick?"

"The chick has a name, and yes, I was."

"You falling for her?"

I glared at him, and Nate went back to paying attention to the road. That was when it hit me—fuck, maybe I was. Who gave a shit? I dated Kris, and nothing happened. I could date another girl. It was no big deal.

"Yo," Mason said as he shifted up toward the front seat from behind us. "Sam's out cold." He propped his arms on the backs of our seats and leaned forward so he was almost sitting between us. "What are you guys talking about?"

Nate grinned. "Logan's girlfriend."

"She's not my girlfriend."

"Been in a month now." Nate glanced sideways at me. "We've hardly seen you for that month."

I frowned at him. I'd had longer flings, but what was up his asshole? Then I remembered Sam saying he was worried, too. Still. My frown switched to something darker. I was the glue, whatever. That was nice. He still needed to mind his own business. I shot back, "And what of it?"

Nate didn't answer. He kept driving, his jaw clenching.

Mason looked between the two, then turned to me. "My coach's daughter? Right?"

I leaned forward, then turned so I could see both of them. "So what? Yeah. Her. I like her."

Mason held up his hands. "Dude, I'm not raining on your parade. I'm fine with it. I was just making sure you hadn't moved to someone new." His eyes shifted to Nate. "I'm thinking Nate hasn't been completely honest about his thoughts."

There it was. Mason laid it out. It was Nate's problem. But Mase had been the one to bring up Taylor a few times, like he had trouble with the situation. I needed to make sure. "You don't have a problem with it?" I asked him.

He appraised me carefully. "You guys are dating, like a couple dating?"

I shrugged. "I don't know. We're just going with the flow for now."

"Would you want to date her in that way?"

I shrugged. "I like what we're doing. We're not thinking. We just are, right now. That's enough for me. We're still getting started."

"Then that's enough for me. Who gives a shit what I think?"

If anyone should've been bothered, it was Mason. Taylor's dad was his coach, and though Coach didn't seem to be the best father to Taylor, he was a damn good coach to the team.

I nodded my thanks, and Mason turned to Nate. "And why should we give a shit what you think?"

Nate didn't say anything.

And I blew up. "What the fuck, Nate? Or is that it? You want to fuck her or something?" Enough with the bullshit. I wanted to hear his problem.

"No." His jaw clenched as he watched the road. His hands were tight on the wheel.

He was going to play the silent card? I didn't think so. "Nate, come on."

Mason folded his arms over his chest. "It's truth time, Nate. If you have a problem, you should speak now."

"Or what?" He glared at Mason through the rearview mirror.

"Or stop dropping little baits. You've tried it before, too, but Logan blew that up in your face."

"When?"

"The juicer."

Mason was right. I remembered that morning. "You tried teasing me like I was a little bitch. No way am I letting that happen. If I like a chick, I'm going to bang her. When the hell have any of us needed permission to get it in?"

"Is that what you think she is? Some piece of ass?" Nate's voice was like gravel.

His response was quick, too quick to have been a random thought he threw out. I straightened in my seat and shared a look with my brother. That was it. That was what was eating Nate.

"Is that what you think? I'm not valuing her enough?"

Nate didn't reply. He only jerked up a shoulder.

I was floored. "When have you ever cared about a girl I was seeing?"

"So, you *are* seeing her?" He threw me a side look.

"No—I don't know. I don't know. I just went over this. Maybe." I looked from him to Mason, and spared Sam a glance in the back. She was lying down, so I could only see her feet. "I've never gotten so much grief about a girl. Sam got in my face the other day about her, too."

"Look," Nate started. "I don't know what Sam said, but I'm just bringing it up because this girl is different."

"Because she's Mason's coach's daughter?"

"No." He rolled his eyes, his jaw tightening again. "Because she's not like other girls. She's different. You had her programmed in your phone as Hot Girl before."

"Nate."

He added, "Now she's programmed in as Firecracker. You have your own nickname for her, and it's not like others. She's not Girl from Grocery Store, or Call After 2, or even Could Be Stalker."

"I don't use girls. You're making it sound like that."

"No." He shook his head. "You don't, but you don't smile when you text them, like you do when you're texting her. Logan, I—"

I was growing tired of the questioning. "You better be real careful about where you go with this."

"Loga—"

"Real. Careful." My hand jerked, forming a fist on my leg.

Nate glanced at me out of the corner of his eye. He looked back to the road and sighed. His shoulders relaxed a bit. "I'm not trying to be a nosy pain in the ass, but this girl is hurting. And if I can see it, I know you can, too."

"You think I'm going to hurt her more?"

"No. I'm wondering if you're falling for her *because* she's hurting."

Huh? I cocked my head to the side. "Say again?"

"Oh, boy." Nate adjusted his hold on the wheel and rolled his shoulders back. He looked in the rearview mirror at Mason for a moment. He spoke as his gaze returned forward. "You fall for girls that are hurting. Tate—"

I interrupted, "—wasn't hurting."

"Yeah, she was. She had that thing going on with her parents. She was hurting back then, and so was Kris."

"Kris." I frowned. She hadn't acted like it, but he was right. She'd been messed up because of her parents, too. "Okay, I'll give you Kris."

"And…" Nate softened his voice. "Sam."

Oh, fuck. He went there. I shook my head. "There was a brief moment of attraction with Sam, but that was snuffed a long time ago."

"You're an asshole for bringing that up," I said.

Mason was the giant elephant in the van at that moment. The whole question of Sam and me had been dealt with. It wasn't a problem, yet Nate went there.

"I know." Nate's hands jerked on the wheel. "I'm sorry, but there's a pattern. That's my whole point. I'm worried that you're going to fall for her because she fits some pattern for you, but your feelings won't hold long-term. They didn't with any of the others."

The fuck? "I dated Tate for two years, and I was with Kris for one."

"But you didn't love them. And this girl, I can see you thinking you're in love. That's the problem."

"That I'm going to fall for her and date her? *God* forbid."

Mason started laughing, and hearing it, I relaxed a little. The question of Sam and me had been dealt with two years ago. I didn't want Nate to spark that back up, judging from Mason's laugh, he seemed fine.

"No, I'm talking how you think you fall for them, start dating them, and realize later you don't love them. You hurt Kris a lot."

I rolled my eyes. "And Tate hurt me. It's part of dating, Nate. I'm still figuring out why you're being a nosy punk-ass bitch right now. Do you want to date her? Is that the real issue here?"

"No." His voice was firm, and he reached up to press his eye before returning his hand to the steering wheel. "I'm just worried about you."

"Then tell me what you're really worried about. Stop dancing around the issue."

"Okay. This is what I think is going to happen: You like this girl. I can tell, and yes, you're whatever right now. You care for her. It's obvious the sex is good, and I can see it going somewhere deeper. But I'm worried you'll do what you've been doing. You'll date her, thinking you love her, and then you won't. You'll get sick of her. I'm worried you'll shatter this girl, and I'm worried that'll make you even more jaded." His tone softened. "I'm worried about you. It's not really the girl."

"What. The. Fuck?" I stared right at him. "You on crack? Should you be driving right now?"

"You're jaded." Nate threw me a hard look. "I'm the one who goes out with you all the time. I see how you talk about girls, how you act around them. You're hard inside when it comes to relationships. Tate damaged you."

"Shut up, Nate."

"Liking Sam, and then realizing she was Mason's soulmate? That bothered you, too."

"I mean it, Nate. Shut up."

"Then Kris. You dated her, and you almost broke her. That girl straight up loved you. I'm talking real love."

"Nate!" My hands formed fists in my lap, but I pressed them against my leg.

He didn't stop. "I know it bothers you that you hurt her. You've not dated another girl since. You screw 'em, and you discard 'em. I'm wondering how that's hurting you, too. I think this girl, if you do date her—it's going to happen again. You're going to think you love her, but not actually let yourself love her because you've got some fucking hard walls up to girls right now. I'm worried about the long-term effects."

We were nearing the house. If we hadn't been, I would've made him pull over. Nate didn't know anything. I focused on keeping my hands on my lap because if they came up, I'd hit him. I felt it in me— the need to fight, to lash out. It was like a demon. That motherfucker wanted out of me. He wanted to act up, do some damage.

"Logan—" Nate wasn't paying attention to me. I could hear it in his voice. He was going to keep going, keep dishing his shit.

"Stop," Mason cut him off. His voice was soft. I could feel my brother's eyes on me. He added, "Drop it, Nate."

"What?" Nate's voice grew clearer. He must've looked over at me. "Oh."

We drove the last few blocks in silence, but I kept hearing Nate's words in my head. As soon as he wheeled into our driveway, I was out and rounding the vehicle. Nate just opened his door when I reached in, grabbed him. I yanked him out. No words were spoken. He knew what was coming, and I hit him. I hit him as hard as I could, and after the one hit, I let him go. I turned around, not giving a damn if he fell to the ground or if he was just dazed. If I looked, I'd want to hit him again, and maybe a third time.

Mason came after me. "He's wrong."

"No." I shook my head, acknowledging what Nate said. Some of my anger melted, but it was replaced with bitterness. "He's not."

"He's wrong, Logan. He is." My brother's voice quieted. "Tate did this shit to you. Kris and Sam, they didn't. Don't let him make you think that."

"No." Mason was wrong, too. "Don't you get it? It's not them. It's not even Tate." That was the problem. "I *wish* it was them."

"Then what is it? Are you hardened?"

"Yeah." I drew in a sharp breath. That stung, even just admitting that. "But it's not because of any of them. That's not why I'm like this."

"Then why?"

I had to laugh. The sound was sad and bitter. It came from a dark place in me. My brother, who knew everything, who'd raised me since we were little, didn't know. But it wasn't his problem. He had someone who'd never leave him. He'd never leave her. He never had to have this problem.

I backed up toward the house, shaking my head. "No, Mase."

"Logan." He started to come with me.

"No." I shot my hands up, stopping him. "I need space."

TAYLOR

Last night's nightmare kept me awake for a while, so when I went back to sleep, it was late. I woke up late, and when I checked my phone, there were no texts from Jason or Claire. There were a few from Logan. I was already grinning when I clicked on the first one.

Drunk. 3 am. That means one thing. I'm missing my taco. ;) Are you my taco?

That was followed with, **All jokes aside, I want to take you to that place. Your DoucheCanoe lives right next to it, but it's good food. It's worth the risk of murky douche waters.**

I laughed and clicked on another message. It had arrived earlier this morning. **Escaped unscathed. A little bit of a hangover headache. That's it. Reading over my texts to you last night. No wonder I dreamed about fucking tacos. I thought I watched some weird porn last night.**

And the last one was sent an hour ago. **Heading home. If you don't text back, I'm going to be that guy. I'm coming over. Don't call the cops on me. I don't have a record with them. Yet.**

I got a five-second warning. I read that text, heard a car door shut, and my doorbell was ringing in the next breath. And it kept going. He was holding his finger to it. I cursed, made sure I was wearing a bra, and hurried to answer the door.

Logan stepped back, but kept his finger on the doorbell as I opened the door. "You didn't answer my messages," he said over the noise.

"Stop." I grabbed his arm, pulled it away. Finally, the air was silent. My ears were not. They were still ringing. "I'm going to hear that damn thing for the next hour."

"Give me an hour." Logan passed me, heading inside and swatting my butt on the way. "I'll make you come so hard, you'll be hearing your own climax for the next week, Firecracker."

Oh dear God. I stopped in the doorway. His words and the casual way he spoke them burst a dam inside of me. I was instantly wet, and I groaned under my breath.

"You coming?" he asked.

I rolled my eyes as I shut the door. "Did you have to use that word?"

He'd disappeared around the corner to the kitchen, but he came back now, a wicked glint in his eyes. "We can skip the formalities and head right for your bedroom, if that's what you want?" he drawled.

My heart pounded against my chest like it wanted out. "Can you lay off and at least let me have a cup of coffee?"

I stopped as soon as I started. *I* used the wrong word this time.

"What was that about laying you?" Logan's grin went up a notch. "You want me to stop, and you say that to me?"

I held up a hand, shaking my head. "Just…leave it alone for now." I walked around him, giving him a wide berth. If he touched my ass again, I didn't trust myself. We might end up in my bedroom sooner than I wanted. Logan followed me, and I snuck a look at him from underneath my eyelashes. He was poking around the kitchen and dining room, and for once, his hawk-like attention wasn't on me.

I had to get real with myself, and I had to do it fast. Logan Kade was a tornado. When he showed up, he took over, and everything was swept up in his wake. Yes, as soon as I'd seen him on the doorstep, I knew it was going to happen. It always did, but this time, I hoped to prolong it. I wanted more time with him, outside of the bedroom. I poured myself some coffee and put the pot back. My hand tightened around the handle. I had to manage some semblance of control, or he would talk me into bending over the table.

Logan was hot and charming. He had charisma coming out of his asshole, but things needed to simmer. I looked at him and gulped. He was giving me bedroom eyes, like he could see through me, see my thoughts, and why the hell weren't we already up there?

"You okay?" he asked.

"What?" I hadn't expected that question.

He moved a step closer to me. "Your hand is shaking a little bit."

I crossed my arms. "I'm fine."

"You sure?" His tone ceased oozing sex and switched to concern. "You never did respond to my texts, you know."

"Oh, yeah. I—" I glanced to the clock on the microwave. It was almost eleven. "Whoa. I slept late this morning."

"You've been sleeping this whole time?"

"Yeah." A chill went through me as I remembered the nightmare. "I couldn't sleep very well last night."

"Because you're alone?" He glanced around the place. "The

team should be back. We had breakfast with them before we took off. Mason rode back with us."

My heart sank. "My dad will probably..." *Fuck it.* "I have no idea where my dad is. He's been absent the last year."

His voice softened. "I know."

"That's right." He would know. He drove me that one night. A sad laugh wrung itself out of me. I leaned back against the counter and held my coffee cup with both hands. That had been back when I knew he wouldn't care. If I saw pity or judgment in his eyes, it wouldn't cut me deep—not that I'd expected to see that from him.

Things were different now. There were feelings involved. What type of feelings, I had no idea, but they were there. The lines had blurred.

"If he comes home, it won't be till late." My chest burned. "And that's *if* he comes home. He could stay out all night...somewhere else..." With someone else, someone who wasn't my mother. The burning grew stronger.

"Okay." Logan took the coffee cup from my hands.

"What are you doing?" I asked as he put it on the counter and took my hand.

He led me out of the kitchen. "Go to your bedroom."

"Already?" I blurted, then cringed.

He gave me a smug smirk, but stopped at the stairs and pointed up. "Go up there."

"And do what?"

"Change."

I looked down. "My oversized sweater and yoga pants aren't working for you?"

He shook his head. "Those are period clothes. I know a thing or two about females. That's the stuff you put on when you're feeling like shit." He held his hands up, palms toward me. "Not that I'm saying you're on your period, but—" He gestured to my face with a finger. "I can tell something's wrong. So go up and change clothes."

He turned me around and urged me toward the steps with a gentle push.

"Where are we going?"

"Does it matter? We're going to have fun."

"Fun?"

"Yeah. Go." He made a shooing motion. "I'll be in the car waiting."

And with that, the decision was made. Logan went outside to the car. I went upstairs to change.

A few minutes later, I stopped in front of the mirror before I went outside. I smoothed a hand down my form-fitting black shirt and jeans. My mother had bought this shirt for me. It was the last time we'd gone on a shopping spree together.

I sucked in my breath, expecting a wave of sadness. It didn't come... *Why didn't it come?* Logan was waiting for me. I didn't have time to wonder. Releasing the breath, I held my head up and went out to the car.

We had sex.

We had fun.

That was it.

Why was this feeling like more?

CHAPTER 21

ABANDONED ROLLER COASTER HAVEN
TAYLOR

I didn't know what to expect, but the entire day was different—a good different. We went to a few different places, and he had the normal one-liners and pick-up jokes, but he was different, a little more withdrawn and a little quieter than normal. Every time we left a place, I expected him to take me home. But he never did. It was a movie first, then the arcade across the street, then Pete's Pub for a meal, and by the time we left my place of employment, it was evening.

I considered asking him back to my house, but I didn't, and he drove to an old part of town. We pulled up outside a large door, and he put the vehicle in park to text someone.

"What is this place?"

The walls were high. It was a gated entrance to something, but I couldn't get any idea what was on the inside. I glanced around at the abandoned houses and saw one of the street signs. "Is this the old amusement park?"

Logan nodded, sending another text before putting his phone away. "Yep."

"This place went bankrupt years ago. I remember coming here when I was kid." I twisted back around, lingering over some of the houses. They were rotting. The front porches were half falling off.

Paint had peeled off, replaced with graffiti. "I haven't been back in so long. I knew this place went downhill, but I didn't know it was this bad."

"My dad saw this place last year and bought it."

"Your dad?" I settled back in my seat. Logan wasn't looking at me. His gaze was trained on the dashboard, and I had a faint sense that he wasn't even in the vehicle.

"He came to buy me out of a sticky situation last year."

My mouth went dry. "What happened?"

A dry laugh slipped from him before he glanced over at me. His eyes weren't laughing. "I got the shit beat out of me, that's what happened."

"What?"

He nodded, looking forward again. His head rested back against his seat. "I swung first, so there was a meeting about me. They were going to kick me out, but my dad came in and did what he always does. He paid big for them to keep me. The assholes got off scot-free. It was five on one, but they got it twisted around on me."

"Who?" My heart pounded at the thought of five guys going against Logan. I wanted to find them and beat their asses back.

His head still rested against his seat, but he turned to grin at me. "You going to take them on?"

I shrugged. "Maybe. I could hire someone. If I could get away with it."

He laughed, but the sound was almost sad. "It was the guy your buddy worked for, Park Sebastian. He's gone now. Mason ran him off."

"Oh." I frowned.

Logan gestured to the gate. "My dad was on the way out of town after that when he got lost. He drove himself that day, for some reason, and he ended up here. He had visions of a new factory or business or fuck if I know, and two months later he told us he'd bought this place." He pointed to the houses. "Those too. I have no clue what he's going to do with it, but it's empty and abandoned for the next couple of months until all the permits are approved. I think he's going to demo the whole place."

All of this told me one thing: Logan was rich. Not just rich. He was *rich* rich, super-wealthy rich. He never acted like it. I'd thought I was the one with an inheritance, but it was nothing compared to what he described. I wasn't sure what to say.

"Oh."

That was it from me.

Logan laughed again. "I'm waiting for the guy to come let us in."

"You come here?"

"Sometimes. It's kinda cool in there, actually, and there's one place I like to go. I usually just climb up and over, but I figured I'd be the gentleman this time and legally enter." His eyes warmed as they lingered on me. "Do I get points for this? Being all nice and shit? Or do you want me to go badass and break into the place? Either's good with me."

Yep. I felt a flutter in my chest. Oh boy. But I only smiled. I'd been feeling those flutters all month now. "A badass and a gentleman. Suppose I should just answer that with, 'you're too kind, *sir*.'"

"*Sir*. I'd rather be called dipshit than sir." He grimaced. "All my dad's minions call him that."

My smile faded. I'd been teasing. He knew that, but I could hear the anger from him. It sounded deeper than mine, and I wondered how long it had been there. "You said before that your dad and Samantha's mom are together?"

"Yep." He shook his head. "If you think your dad's bad, you should meet Analise. That's Samantha's mom. She's a piece of work."

I frowned. He wasn't angry with her; it was all directed at his dad. I wanted to ask more. I wanted to *know* more, what was hurting him, but I held my tongue. We weren't—I didn't know, but I didn't think we were there. I hadn't told him my own hauntings, so I had no place asking his.

"Good. The guy's here."

A car pulled up next to us. Logan opened his window and leaned over to talk, then a guy got out of the other car and went over to the gate. After a moment, it rattled open for us. He handed something to Logan through the window before getting back in his car. With a short wave, he drove off, and Logan pulled inside.

The buildings were all there, just like I remembered, but they had aged like the houses outside. Paint had peeled. Doors were rotted. Windows. Panels. The foliage had started to grow over things. The ticket booth was encased in a bunch of bushes. Trash blew over the ground.

I was entranced.

"My mom—" My voice hitched on the memory. "—she took me here a lot. Me and Claire. Jason came with us once in seventh grade, but that was it. It closed the summer after that." I shook my head. "I never heard what happened to it. It's been empty this whole time?"

Logan pocketed his keys as we got out. "I guess. My dad brought in some people. They cleaned up some of the graffiti."

The old paintings were still there, but after he said that, I could see where white had been painted over parts of everything. "This is surreal, Logan. I can't believe your dad owns this place now."

He snorted. "He'll build something, and then he'll probably sell it. He won't have it for too long."

"Are the buildings safe to go into?" I started forward, moving past the bumper cars, the arcade, the kissing booth, the haunted house, the animal barn. I remembered everything. A large tiger had been painted on top of the building, but the middle of its face was whited out now.

Logan stopped beside me. "Some asshole painted a cock up there." He was holding back a grin. I saw his mouth twitch.

"Don't laugh. That tiger was gorgeous."

"Sorry. I don't get sentimental about places anymore."

"This was part of my childhood." I couldn't stop taking everything in. The pink flamingo statue was covered with vines. "How can you not get sentimental about places like this?"

Logan shrugged. "I don't get attached to places. I was always moving and living in different places in high school."

"You were?"

He nodded, and suddenly he was the one looking around, and I couldn't look anywhere but at him. "We were at the house in Fallen Crest when my mom left. I stayed with my aunt and cousins for that summer. Then Sam's mom moved in, and everything changed. We lived in a hotel for a while, then Nate's parent's house. I think we lived somewhere after that too. My mom moved back to town—oh, I was in Paris with her for a month. When she moved back, I went to live with her. Sort of... I felt like I was half living with her and half living at Sam's house our senior year. I guess that was the last place I lived before going to Cain. And we had a different house my freshman year."

"That's a lot of moving around."

"Like I said..." He raked a hand through his hair, grinning at me. "I don't get attached to places. I go the opposite."

"What do you mean?"

"I get attached to people."

He looked right at me as he said that, and my entire body warmed. I swallowed over a knot in my throat. "Who are you attached to?"

"Nope." He laughed softly and grabbed my hand.

I held my breath at the touch.

He pulled me forward. "That's enough reveal talk for now. Come on. I want to show you my favorite place."

He led me through the rides until we came to the roller coaster. When he started through the gate toward the track, I stopped. "Nope. No way." I shook my head.

"It's safe."

"Doesn't matter. No way." I held my hands up and took a step backward. "I escaped death once. I don't want to revisit that feeling." Logan's eyes widened at my words, and I could've hit myself. I cringed. "I'm sorry. I didn't mean to say that, but—"

He waved that away. "I said some stuff. You said some stuff. We'll have sex and cuddle later. Everything's good."

I laughed. "You're pretty damn sure." His gaze sharpened, and I got the distinct feeling he was looking into me. He was seeing past my walls.

"We both knew where we were going to end up tonight when you opened the door," he murmured. "I saw the look on your face, too."

The air shifted. I'd been aware of him since he got to my house, and he was right. As he said those words, everything got hotter. I always felt pulled to Logan—I had since I first met him—and that pull was almost irresistible right now.

I coughed, forcing myself to look away. "Maybe." I moved ahead of him, going through the gate toward the roller coaster track.

"Maybe?"

I grinned over my shoulder. "I just don't want you to get too cocky."

He groaned, tipping his head back for a moment. "Too cocky? Taylor, I'm not being cocky. I'm just stating the fact."

"You're not cocky?"

He came over, holding my gaze, and leaned close. I stood firm, holding my breath, as his lips came close to mine. He stopped an inch away, but I could feel his body heat, and I fought the urge to grab hold of him. This guy. I was almost panting for him, and he knew it. I saw the smug look in his dark eyes, and that made me want him even more.

He grinned. "You think I'm too cocky?"

"I *know* you are."

"That just means I'll have to prove myself all over again tonight."

My blood began to sizzle. It was coursing through me, and I bit my lip. I had forgotten what we were even talking about. I leaned toward him. My body rested against his, and those lips—I grew closer and closer. Just a few centimeters held me away. My lips brushed his, but I caught myself.

He was going to prove himself tonight?

I gulped. God, yes.

"Firecracker," he whispered.

I loved how he said my nickname. I had, all month long. I felt drunk as I asked, "Yeah?"

His eyes went from my lips to my eyes and back, again and again. My brain shut off. The nightmare had taken away so much of my strength, and right now, being with Logan, feeling him so close, I wanted to completely turn off. The need to be in his arms again was burning me up, consuming all of me, and I didn't give a damn.

"Logan," I said. My voice was little more than a whisper.

He groaned and pulled back.

I felt him leave, and it hurt. My body actually ached, but I caught myself and held firm.

He laughed, his voice shaky. "I was two seconds from taking you here."

"I was two seconds from letting you."

He turned and shook his head. "I didn't come over to your house for a sex marathon, I swear. But I've got a feeling that's where we're going." It was where we always went.

His eyes darkened, skimming over my face and falling to my lips once again. A guttural groan left him.

"Why did you?"

"What?" He met my eyes again.

"Why did you come over?"

"Oh." Somehow, the heat cooled. My question put a damper on him. I tried telling myself that was for the best.

I tried…

He cleared his throat, glancing back to the roller coaster. "Honestly? I came to make sure you were okay. You didn't respond to my messages."

"Oh, yeah." The nightmare. I shoved that away.

"But you slept late." His eyes narrowed, seeing through me again. "Right?"

I nodded. I had. That was the truth. I just didn't tell him the reason why. I'd already slipped too much, though I'd begun to feel I could say anything to Logan. The thought of letting it out, talking about it for the first time without being forced, had my throat swelling with emotion. Did I even want to talk about it? It had been locked away for almost a year. My dad had read the report. He knew what had happened, but we hadn't discussed it. Claire. Jason. They didn't know.

Unless they talked to Eric, a voice said in my head.

Eric.

Everything went flat inside of me. The heat simmering and brewing in me from Logan went cold—as if a pot of water had been poured on it. I was left with bitter smoke instead. It filled my mouth with a sour taste.

"We're going in there?" A car sat on the track, its door open and waiting for the next passenger.

"No, no." Logan caught my hand before I could touch the car to get in. He pointed to a narrow walkway alongside the track. "We're going up there."

"Up there?" The roller coaster wound in circles, and the tallest point was the highest place in the entire park. "I thought we were just going to sit in the car or something. What about a plain boring warehouse? Or haunted house? Up there looks dangerous. Does that work? Is that safe?"

"It doesn't, but my dad had a crew come out here. It's safe to walk on. He can't get sued, even if there are no trespassing signs." He pointed to one pinned on the animal barn behind us. I could hear the chuckle in his voice. "You never know what idiots might come out here, scoping to see if they could throw a party."

I turned back to him. "Is that why you come here?"

He hopped down onto the path and held his hands up for me. I went to him, and his hands rested on my hips as he lifted me and placed me on the path behind him.

"Yeah, the first time," he said with a nod. "Then I realized the place is too big, too dangerous for a party."

I didn't want his hands to leave. "And since then?"

They did, but then his hand found mine. It fit perfectly. "And since then, it's just for me. I rigged something up here. I don't come here often, but sometimes I do when I want to be alone. Don't start thinking I'm a pansy. It's a new place for me. Trust me, my usual place to go think is the bar, but I don't know. You can see all of Cain up there. A warehouse is easy to find, but not this. Come on." He started forward. "I want to show you something."

CHAPTER 22

BUCKET LIST
#SEXONAROLLERCOASTER
TAYLOR

We were in another world.

That was what it felt like as we climbed to the highest part of the roller coaster. I refused to look down, and thankfully the path didn't loop-the-loop when the tracks did. My stomach couldn't have handled that. Once we reached the top, I saw what Logan was talking about. A solitary car sat at the crest of the biggest drop. It was clean and shiny. Logan's must've wiped it down. When he opened the door so I could climb inside, I saw a blanket folded neatly in the back of the two-seater.

"Nuh-uh."

"What?"

I pointed at the car. "I'm not getting in that thing. We'll die."

He laughed and shook the car. It rattled against the track, but it didn't move. He shook it a little harder, and it still didn't go anywhere. "I rolled it up here and bolted it down. This baby won't go anywhere, and it can't come off the track. Only way it'll fall is if the track goes with it. It's safe. I promise."

My stomach had been clenched in knots the whole trek up here. They weren't going away, and we still had to get down. "Logan, I don't know."

"Come on." He patted the car. His tone gentled. "Please?"

"Did you bring me up here to kill me?" I plastered myself against the railing.

"I brought you up for a reason, but that's not it."

"You rolled this car all the way up here?"

"Yeah."

I took a step forward, then thought better of it. I pointed at him. "You go first."

He frowned, but hopped in. The way he moved, so lithe and agile, I gasped. My stomach leaped, and I reached for him. It was reflex, but I swear, I thought he was going over. "Logan!" My heart pounded, fast and furious.

"I'm good." He patted the seat next to him. "You afraid of heights?"

I groaned, inching into the car. Then I was torn. To close the car door or not? Should I keep easy access to the walking path and railing, or feel more secure? I took a deep breath. My fingers clenched around the door, but I shut it. Once it clicked in place, I needed a minute. I forced myself to keep breathing. Even breaths. In and out. In and out, and when the car didn't fall or move, I started to feel a bit more secure. Just a bit.

Logan watched me. "Guess that answers my question."

"You're crazy."

"I've been told that."

I shook my head, but his eyes were warm, looking at me, and his dimples showed—I was already forgetting where we were. I was with him. That was at the forefront of my mind. All else was stripped away. That was the power Logan Kade had over me, and it grew stronger with each minute we spent together.

I let out a soft sigh and felt the world right itself again. I was no longer scared.

"Better?"

"Better."

His grin widened. I caught a twinkle of something mischievous in him and only had a second to brace myself before he twisted around to reach behind the seat.

I grabbed for the bar in front of us and clutched it.

Logan laughed as he pulled the blanket from the back. He unfolded it and shook it out over his side of the car. Then he turned back to me and pulled it over our laps. The evening had started to fade, and so had the temperature. I hadn't noticed the cool breeze until now, but once the blanket hit my lap, it warmed my legs.

"Okay. This is nice," I told him.

"Good." Logan pointed out in front of us. "This is why I brought you up here. Look."

Then everything made sense—why he'd taken the time and effort to bring the car here, why we'd climbed all this way: the view. As I lifted my head and looked beyond us, I saw my hometown looking beautiful, serene, the way it used to be to me. I gestured to the town laid out in front of us. "This is beautiful. Thank you, Logan." I looked at him now. "I mean it. Thank you. I'd forgotten that my home could be beautiful."

Logan grew quiet, but it didn't matter. For some reason, the words were coming to me now, and I didn't want to stop them.

"My mom died last year, and since then, I've forgotten about things. I forgot about views like this." I pointed to the hospital. It was the tallest building, set on the outskirts of town. "She died there."

Bang! Bang!

I flinched, my hand closing again around the bar in front of me. I could hear the shots again. "I was coming home for the holidays. I finished my finals a week earlier. I got lucky somehow. Eric, my boyfriend, wasn't done. He wanted to stay and study all weekend, but I talked him into going home with me. I promised I'd help him study, so he agreed. I knew my mom was working a double—she was a nurse—so I talked him into stopping at the hospital on the way into town…" I faltered, remembering the day once again.

Going inside the hospital.

Going past the front desk.

Turning down the hallway to the nurses' station—then the first gunshot.

"My mom was in the ER that night. She loved working there. She loved the adrenaline, the excitement, but that night..." My chest felt like it was shrinking. I was moving backward even though I sat still. "I was told later that a man came in with a gunshot wound. He was still alive."

Feeling panic, I started to run down the hallway—boom.

"In the chaos, another man walked back there and shot him. He wanted to finish what he'd started. After the first gunshot, it was quiet. Eric and I were walking down the hallway to the nurses' station, but everyone stopped. Then the second gunshot sounded, and everyone started running. A big guy turned and slammed into me. Apparently, I still wasn't out of his way enough because he kicked me then, and I fell to the floor. It was funny because I couldn't feel any pain, but I knew it must've hurt because I couldn't walk."

Bang!

"The gunman turned the gun on my mom. He shot her twice, and he killed the doctor in there, too. Then he started shooting everyone in the hallway."

"Taylor, come on!" Eric grabbed my hand and started to pull.

"Eric tried to drag me backward."

"No. My mom."

"Taylor, come on!"

"No." *I looked back to the nurses' station. No one was there.* "She's back there. I have to find her."

"He wanted to run, but I could only think about my mom. She was back there somewhere."

"Taylor," Logan said.

I shook my head. I heard the sympathy in his voice, and I knew he was going to say all the right things: I didn't have to talk. I didn't have to share. I didn't have to fill-in-the-blank. He was wrong. I did have to. I had to get it out now or I never would.

"It didn't matter anyway," I continued. "Even if Eric had tried to drag me out, I couldn't move. The big guy had fucked my knee up bad. And then…" *The fourth gunshot. It had sounded right around the corner.* "The gunman was coming toward us. We could hear him."

I heard the screams again.

"Eric left me there." I flinched. "There were bathrooms across from us; we could've gone in there. It didn't matter, though. Eric left. He ran while I was pleading for him to help me."

"What happened to the gunman?"

"A cop got him. They're always called when there's a GSW. They just didn't get there in time. They came in through the emergency entrance, so they were behind him. He was leaving, you see. He had just come around the corner to the hallway where I was when they shot him."

"This happened at Cain Memorial?"

I nodded. "The whole thing was kept quiet by the cops. The gunman was involved in another shooting so there wasn't any media coverage. The media respected their wishes."

"I had no idea that happened last year."

"A lot of people still don't know all the details, and now the hospital has better security. I think they have metal detectors."

"Taylor."

Logan's voice was so soft. "I'm not telling you for sympathy," I explained. "I'm telling you for thanks." My chest lifted, and I drew in a deep breath. "Thank you for bringing me up here. Thank you for showing me this."

The corner of Logan's mouth lifted in an adorable half-grin. He ran his hand over his hair and laughed softly. "If we're being completely honest, I was hoping to check something off my bucket list."

"What's that?"

"Getting laid on a roller coaster."

There was no pity in his eyes. There was no awkwardness, like he had no idea what to say. It was just—sex on a roller coaster. And the absurdity of it made me laugh.

The half-grin was still there. It was more of a half-smirk now. "So, does that mean there's a chance?"

I shook my head, still laughing. "Not a chance."

"I figured it was the best time to ask." He winked at me. "Because you gotta be feeling close to me, right?"

That spurred another round of laughing, and I wiped tears from my eyes, but the happy kind of tears. Logan kept teasing me. I kept grinning like an idiot, and before I knew it, the evening slipped into nighttime. The lights of the city shone full, bright, and strong. They were breathtaking, and after a moment of comfortable silence descended on us, I snuck a look at him from the corner of my eye. He was staring out over the town, his jaw clenched.

"I came here before," he said.

"Before?"

"When I was little." He glanced to me, his eyes warming. "My mom was supposed to bring me. We didn't do a whole lot together when I was growing up. I don't really know why. I think it was because other stuff was going on already." The lines around his mouth tightened. "My dad cheated on her a ton, and she started drinking because of it. Things got bad in the house, but she promised me one morning that we'd come here. I remember it so clearly because I heard this amusement park had elephants, and I really wanted to see one up close." He grinned to himself. "I wanted to see how big their penises were."

I wasn't even surprised. "How old were you?"

He shrugged, still grinning. "I was young. I was in sixth grade, and Mason was in seventh."

"What happened?"

"My dad brought a woman home. My mom found her underwear that afternoon. I think my dad had already snuck her out, but the damage was done. The whore left her underwear behind. They did that sometimes. They liked leaving things behind. They hoped my mom would find them, and she usually did."

"Is that what ended things?"

"Not that day, no. They divorced later, probably after the fortieth mistress. No." Logan's grin faded away. "That day my mom got drunk at the kitchen table, then decided going to a spa was the best idea in the world. I came home from little league practice, saw the underwear, saw the wine bottles, and knew it was a wash."

"But you still came?"

"Mason took me. He and Nate." His voice sounded stronger. "I had fun that day."

Despite his mother.

I heard the unspoken meaning and I didn't have words, so I covered his hand with mine. He turned his hand, lacing our fingers together. When he looked at me, I could see the whites of his eyes, and I saw his mouth lift in the slightest of smiles. His thumb rubbed over my knuckles.

"My mom never remembered that day. Well, that's not true. She remembers the mistress, and she remembers what color the underwear was, but not that she was supposed to take me to the park." He cursed under his breath, leaning forward so his arms were folded on the bar. My hand was still in his, tucked firmly between his arms. It drew me closer to him. He turned to look at me, and our faces were so near. "She had no clue we went without her."

My heart had lodged in my throat. "I'm sorry."

He grinned, but it didn't reach to his eyes. "You shared. I wanted to share something, too."

The more I stared into his eyes, so close to mine, the more I could see the deeper pain hidden there. I was getting a glimpse few others had been granted. My heart picked up its pace, and the longer I stared into his eyes, the faster it beat. The world had melted away.

I was pulled even closer to him.

This was Logan. He drew people to him, and I was no different. My heart was perpetually pounding in my chest, trying to get to him. With another slight movement, my lips rested against his. Our eyes held, staring into each other. I wanted him to kiss me. I swallowed, and when his eyes closed, his lips pressed more firmly into mine.

Then we heard a gunshot below.

CHAPTER 23

CAR BOMBS.
#HEREWEGOAGAIN
LOGAN

For a moment we were frozen, staring at each other, not sure what we heard. Taylor seemed paralyzed, and after that, I didn't think.

I launched out of the car, told her to stay put, and headed to the ground as fast as I could go. She needed to be safe. That was my first thought, but I needed to know what was happening. If people were coming in here shooting, Taylor was going to be the farthest place possible. I ducked, weaved, and jumped from one section of the walkway down to another. When I got close enough, I leaped over the fence around the roller coaster, and once my feet touched ground, I ran toward where I thought the shot came from.

I kept low, running for my Escalade, and hugged as close to the buildings as I could. When I heard the yelling on the other side of the gate, I relaxed a little. Only a little.

"I told you to get the fucking money!"

"I tried, Rankin. Okay?"

"*Not okay!*"

There were more shouts, but they were muffled, and I slowed down so they couldn't hear my approach. I went to the gate. Thank shit I'd decided to park on the inside, not out on the street like normal. I moved so I could see through a tiny hole in the wall. I couldn't make out their faces, but there was a group of them. They surrounded one guy in the middle.

He stuffed his hands into his pockets and said, "I'll get the money, okay?"

The other voice replied, "Fuck that, Delray. You've been missing payments for three months. It won't fly anymore."

"Delray?"

No—I glanced behind me and Taylor was there, her eyes wide, her mouth open. As I watched, the blood drained from her face. She'd braked suddenly a few feet from me, and I went to her and grabbed her. Pulling her to my chest, I held her close and froze in place. Not one move. Not one word. When she pulled back to speak, I shook my head. My finger went to my mouth, and I pointed at the gate. They were ten feet from us. Ten fucking feet. They couldn't know we were here.

"Logan?" she said, so quietly that I almost didn't hear her.

I looked down and shook my head. It was all I could do; my mind was spinning. She heard her buddy out there. I didn't know Delray well, but I knew enough to know he was screwed. He did illegal shit for Sebastian last year, and word from Blaze was that he'd gotten into even worse shit this year.

But even if I hadn't known that stuff, I still would've known those guys out there were bad news. The gunshot must have come from them. I didn't want to think about whether they'd already shot someone.

I held Taylor's shoulders. She started to say something again, but I shook my head. I mouthed *No* to her and moved back enough so I could pull out my phone. No calls. No talking. I texted Mason instead. My phone buzzed back in seconds. **Got it. Coming.**

I showed Taylor the text, then pointed to my vehicle. I wanted her to get inside.

She shook her head.

I pointed again.

She shook her head again.

I thought about carrying her in there, but could tell from the set line of her mouth she wouldn't go for that. As if sensing what I was thinking, she crossed her arms over her chest. I was still considering what to do when I caught a tear in the corner of her eye. Her hand whisked up and brushed it away as quickly as it had appeared. She raised her chin, and her eyes cut to the gate.

She wasn't hiding. I rolled my eyes. Girl drove me crazy sometimes. I'd known from the beginning that she had trauma in her life. I could sense it, and instinct had me holding back. I wanted to swoop in and take her home with me that first night at Blaze's party, but I refrained, a very unLoganlike quality.

But tonight, after hearing what she went through, I knew it was worth it. I'd been right to move slowly, and I knew another thing about her: she wasn't going to hide. I couldn't begrudge her that. Delray was her friend, her family. If it had been Nate, Mason, or Sam—no fucker would hold me back.

I gave her a reluctant nod. Her relief was evident immediately. Her arms dropped from her chest, and she nodded back to me. I saw the silent thanks on her face.

I looked back to the gate. I didn't know what Mason was planning. He did the planning and I did the talking. Then we both did the busting. I figured I could improvise until he showed up. I could feel Taylor's anxiousness behind me. She wouldn't look away from the gate, but she was waiting for me.

I sighed and looked again through the little hole. No one was leaving. A few of the guys sat on the curb. A couple sat on two abandoned cars, and Delray was still smack in the middle. The leader dude was facing him.

They were waiting for someone.

Well, fuck.

I felt something nudge my hand and looked down. Taylor had typed out an unsent text message to me: **Police?**

I took it, erased the word, and typed: **Mason might've called them, but your buddy's screwed then. If he goes in, they might think he'll narc on them.**

Her forehead wrinkled, and she nodded. She wrote back, **Mason is coming? That's your plan?**

You have one?

She shook her head, typing, **Jason's in trouble no matter what. I just don't want him to get hurt right now.**

I know. Let's wait and see.

She nodded and put the phone away, turning back to the gate. She moved until she found a little eyehole to see through, too.

I took a moment and studied her. Taylor was a little thing, but she was tough. Most girls would run, hide, or cry. She was doing none of that. She was white-knuckling it out with me.

Nate had been digging at me. He knew I had feelings for her. I don't know why he gave a shit, but he did. I hadn't been willing to talk much, at least partly for the sheer enjoyment of pissing him off, but honestly, after dealing with Tate and being the one who hurt Kris, I was over talking about girls. I didn't even want to talk chicks. Never had. If I liked someone, if I wanted to screw someone—bang her, get a quick dick suck—that was always my decision alone. Nate too. He bagged girls all the time and rarely talked to us about it. I knew some guys liked to gab about vagina. They bragged about past pussy or their future pink taco buffets, but we didn't.

That was one thing I'd learned from Mason. That was beneath us. We did our own thing. If there was blowback on the group, we felt bad, but that was how it was. So Nate wanting to know about Taylor was pissing me off. If he wanted a go at her, he'd get a good beating, but I didn't have to talk about whatever was going on with her and me.

Taylor sucked in her breath and stretched up on her tiptoes for a better view.

I looked, too.

A pair of headlights swept over the group, lighting up the area, and my gut sank. There were more guys than I'd thought. I started to reach for the gate, ready to run out if that vehicle was Mason, but when a different voice joined the group, I pulled my hand back.

"This is the guy who owes you?" The leader moved forward, and this time I saw his face: Square jaw. Big, thick eyebrows. Scraggly cheeks and tattoos that covered his neck. He had a scar next to his eye, like a bullet had grazed him there. He was an ugly motherfucker.

"What is this?" The newcomer's voice was high. He was nervous.

"Did you bring the money?" Delray asked.

"What money?"

Okay. This was going nowhere fast. I had to think.

Putting myself in Delray's shoes, his problem ran deep. I could tell. He owed money, or he wasn't getting payments. This dude, whoever he was, obviously didn't have the money. We probably had another few minutes before something popped off. What I typed to Taylor was right. If cops showed up, the pressure would be on Delray. They'd push him to narc, and even if he didn't, these guys would worry that he had. That was the *best-case* scenario in my head. There'd been a gunshot before... I still didn't have it in me to sweep the area for a body. I didn't want to know.

The best way to help Delray was a distraction. I needed to get him out of here. Remove him from the situation and give him a day or two, and he might be able to make things right with these guys. I looked around at what we had on our side of the gate.

I had my Escalade. And...an entire amusement park.

I started off. I had to find something fast. Taylor stayed right next to me. When we got to the first building, she watched me bring out some dirty rags and spray cans. Then we trotted back to where I had some booze in the back of my Escalade. When she saw all the ingredients together, her eyes got even bigger, but she nodded.

I pressed my mouth to her ear. "I'm going to go farther down and toss these into the street. I'm hoping it'll distract them. When they run to check, be ready."

She nodded and moved her lips were to my ear. "What do you want me to do?"

The gate was locked. I needed it unlocked. And I needed my Escalade ready to go. Everything would have to happen within seconds, and I bit back a curse. Mason was the thinker. I wanted to text him, see where he was, but I didn't have time. This shit had to happen now.

I pressed the key to the gate into her hand. "Be ready to unlock the gate as soon as the first bomb goes off."

She nodded.

I kissed her and went to my vehicle. I opened the doors and put my keys in the ignition. Everything was good to go when we had to move. I could hear shouting now from the other side, but I wasn't listening to them anymore. I liked a good brawl. I liked going in alone or with my brother—either was fine with me. But those brawls were against dickheads from high school or fraternity boys—not real thugs like these guys. I didn't think Delray had been involved with this crowd last year when I approached him. I'd just been looking for a little fun. This was not fun. If I stayed to fight for very long, I knew it wouldn't be good. Everything had to move at an almost breakneck speed, and I'd need to go as far as I dared.

And now it was time.

Everything turned off in me then. I couldn't think about Taylor or those guys. This had to be done. I let out a breath and grabbed a lighter. Jesus. God. Christ. I prayed to all three. We needed to get out of this alive.

Opening the liquor bottles, I stuffed rags into the necks. Before lighting them, I pulled out everything else in my pockets. There had been some firecrackers left behind. I closed my eyes.

I was going to die someday. I hoped it wouldn't be tonight.

I lit the first rag and tossed it as far as I could over the gate and toward the assorted abandoned cars on the other side. I didn't wait before lighting the next, then the third and throwing them as far as I could. I heard the crash of the bottles breaking, then the shouts. They'd seen the fire. I braced myself, hoping a *boom* was coming, but I kept moving.

I lit and tossed the firecrackers, which sounded like gunshots. Someone cursed on the other side of the gate, slamming against it. *"Get down!"*

The spray cans came next. These things were going to light up the sky. I didn't light them, as they would've seen it coming from inside the gate, but I tossed 'em and hoped they landed close to the soon-to-be-bombs.

After that, fuck being quiet. I sprinted back toward Taylor. I was halfway there when the first car exploded. The air filled with shouting. Taylor saw me coming, and I gestured to the gate.

She unlocked it and pulled it back as I raced to the Escalade, diving in and starting the engine. She threw herself into the passenger seat just as I hit the accelerator.

The only two still outside were Delray and the leader fucker—Rankin, I think Delray had called him that name. I pushed Taylor down. I didn't want the leader to see her face as I braked between him and Delray.

"Get the fuck in!" I yelled.

Delray's eyes were wide, but he wasn't in shock. The street behind him was filled with smoke, different colored smoke, too. It was covering up his guys, but it was helping us, too. They couldn't see us. That meant it was only Rankin to fight and he knew it at the same time I did. Delray threw himself into the backseat as Rankin came charging and tried to open Taylor's door.

"Fuck no!" Delray's boss growled.

Delray slammed the door shut behind him, but his boss had Taylor's door open.

I reached for her and yelled, "Don't look at him!"

She grabbed my arm as the guy caught her leg and started to

pull her out. He was yelling over his shoulder, "Get back here! It was these guys! No one's down there!"

"*Fuck!*" someone yelled.

Delray lunged forward, and I shouted at him, "Don't you say her name!"

He bit down on whatever he'd been about to say. I punched the guy manhandling Taylor as hard as I could. His head whipped back, but he didn't let go of her. His face twisted in an ugly snarl. His assholes were coming back, and they were coming fast.

I punched him again, but he still didn't let go.

Then Mason appeared behind him and ripped him away. The guy fell to the ground. Mason whacked the guy with the bat in his hand, and he fell unconscious.

"Get in!" I yelled at him.

He jumped in Taylor's seat, covering her with his body, and I hit the gas.

CHAPTER 24

HERE. SAFE. MINE.
LOGAN

I took a crazy path to be sure we weren't followed, but I drove us to the house. We all trooped inside, and Sam, who'd been lying on the couch in the living room, jerked upright.

"Holy shit. What happened to you guys?" Her nose wrinkled. "And why do you smell like fire? Is that what I'm smelling?"

Mason went over and dropped a light kiss on her forehead. He brushed a hand down her face, tucking her hair behind her ear. "We're fine, and kinda." He straightened and gave me a look. "Logan went back to his roots."

My insides were roaring, but I grinned. "Hey, any time I can set a car on fire, I'm all for it."

Sam didn't seem to think this was funny. A worried look came into her eyes. She looked to Taylor and Delray, her gaze lingering the longest on Taylor. Then she sighed and pointed upstairs. "Nate got home a second ago. He rushed upstairs. I asked him what was wrong, and he said something about needing a second bat." She looked up toward Mason. "Did you guys fight someone?"

Mason laughed and sat next to her, pulling her to rest against his chest. His arm dangled over her shoulder, their hands laced together. "Only one guy, and it was to get him off of Taylor."

Taylor let out a shaky laugh, sinking down into one of the other chairs. "Thanks for that, by the way."

This was awkward. The entire scene. Moments like these, after a fight, I was the joker. That was what I did. Nate was usually cursing, and Mason planned how to make things right, but he was holding off this time. This was my girl, and my problem. As if sensing my thoughts, my brother lifted his head and motioned to the back. I nodded. We needed to talk, then maybe I'd take my anger out on Delray.

"Hey." I touched Taylor's shoulder. "Mason and I are going to talk in the back, okay?"

Delray stood up. "I should be there." His face was locked down. There was no readable expression, but his voice was low and foreboding.

My anger flared at him. "You." I growled. "That was your boss back there?"

His eyes grew wary, but he nodded. "Yeah. Rankin. That's his name. He kinda runs a lot of the crime around here."

"So, he's a fucking crime boss?" I wanted to interrogate the shit out of this weasel, but Delray looked ready to piss himself and we had to regroup first. I pointed to the chair in the corner. "You sit your ass down and don't move a fucking muscle."

We'd ridden home mostly in silence, but the tension was brewing. I wanted to explode now, and I was damn near ready to let loose. I took a step toward him, but a hand touched my arm, and I swung around to see Mason.

He took a step back. "We can deal with him in a minute. Let's talk first."

Fuuuuck. I wanted to pound something or someone, but I nodded and let out a ragged sigh. I turned to follow Mason to his bedroom, and my eyes caught and held Taylor's for a moment. The pain I saw there pulled more of the anger from me. I seared Delray with a look, but reminded myself he was her buddy.

"Dudes." Nate's voice broke through my reverie. He was standing at the bottom of the stairs, a bag full of bats thrown over his shoulder. "You guys are back?" His hand slid off the railing with a thud. "Oh, man. I just grabbed these from my room upstairs."

"You were coming back?" Mason asked.

"Yeah." Nate nodded. "We haven't had a decent rumble in forever." He gestured to me. "Most times it's because his mouth gets us in trouble. This time was legit, right?"

My eyes narrowed. "Are you kidding me? You were the entire reason we had problems last year."

Nate moved back. "What?" His hand tightened around the bag strap.

"That's not fair." Sam stood up from the couch.

"Sebastian would've come after us anyway," Mason added.

"But not the fraternity."

That shut them all up. As I said those words, whatever fight Nate had left him. His eyes darted to the ground.

"They wouldn't have gone after all of us, on three different occasions, if *you* hadn't fucked things up," I added.

His jaw clenched as his gaze found mine again. "That's not fair, Logan." His voice was heavy, raspy. "I made a mistake my freshman year of college. *You* make mistakes all the Goddamn time. Every fight we had against people in high school—"

"—was because of Mason," I cut him off.

"Logan!" Sam's voice was a reprimand.

I shook my head, looking at all of them. "It's true. All of our fights have been because of Mason in some way." I turned to him and held up a hand. "I'm not throwing shade at you. I'm really not, but it's because someone wanted to control you or girls wanted you." I flung a hand toward Sam. "Girls going at Sam because of you, or it's just some dickhead like Sebastian who wanted to take you down because you hurt his ego. I deal with my fights. I always have."

"You didn't tonight." Sam crossed her arms over her chest. Her eyes sparked with anger. I'd gone after Mason as far as she was concerned, but I was speaking the truth. It needed to be put out there, or—I glanced at Taylor and my anger damn near raged a bonfire in me—maybe I was pissed and taking it out on other people.

A savage curse slipped out, and I brushed past Mason as I went to his room. "Let's get this talk done."

"That asshole—" Sam said behind me.

But Mason shut her down. "He's upset."

"I don't care."

"His girl was in danger tonight," Mason added softly.

I sucked in my breath and closed my eyes. *Goddamn.* He was right. I'd been lashing out, and…I was a dumbass. As soon as Mason and Sam came into the room, I apologized. "I'm sorry—"

They were holding hands, and Sam shook her head. "Don't worry about it. I get it."

"Sam."

"I mean it." Her voice softened. "I really do, Logan."

The understanding in her voice had me gritting my teeth. It was like she saw something for the first time, and it all made sense to her. I wasn't sure how I felt about that. Something dark in me wanted to lash out again. I didn't want anyone to see inside of me, or understand me. Not unless I gave them that right. I felt stripped bare. No fucking way.

"Can we discuss this and get it over with?" I asked.

Mason nodded. "Sure." After shutting the door, he turned and leaned against it, his hands tucked behind him.

He was waiting for me. So was Sam. Both remained quiet, and somehow that irritated me, too.

I growled at them. "What?"

Mason shook his head. His mouth remained shut.

"That's your girl out there," Sam said.

I cut my eyes to her. "What the fuck does that mean?"

Her top lip quivered, like she was fighting a smile. She made a concerted effort to control her features and schooled them so they were blank. "Nothing."

"What?"

"Look, whatever happened out there, for whatever reason, it happened," Mason finally said. "We could have a serious problem on our hands."

"Because of Delray."

"Because of you."

I looked at my brother. "What?"

"What were you doing there in the first place?"

I lifted a shoulder. "We were going for a drive, ended up there somehow."

"You were going for a drive?" Sam narrowed her eyes. "I don't believe that."

"I don't care."

She looked like I slapped her, but she continued to study me. "Are you this upset because of how you feel about Taylor? I mean—"

"Look, they were there," Mason said. "It doesn't matter why." He cast me a look. I got a feeling he knew exactly why I was there. "You drove out of the amusement park. That guy, whoever he is, could do some digging and make a guess who we are. I don't think a lot of people have keys to an abandoned park unless they know the owner."

"Shit," Sam murmured. "Did he see your face?"

"It was dark," I said. "I think I lit three cars on fire. He probably wasn't seeing so well. He could've yanked Taylor out in a second, but he didn't. He was pulling at her leg, not reaching in and getting a better hold on her. So maybe he couldn't see."

"Maybe." Mason frowned. "What about the guy out there? Her friend. He'll give up our names."

Sam groaned. "These guys are involved with some bad stuff?"

"Yeah, someone was trying to collect a debt—the hard way, if necessary," I explained. "Delray is Taylor's friend, so I was trying to buy him some time. I was also trying to minimize the contact we had with him, but we couldn't leave him there."

"Delray..." Sam frowned. "Why does that sound familiar?"

"He's the gambling guy I talked to Blaze about the other week."

"Oh, yeah. He was connected to Sebastian last year."

I nodded. "Blaze said this guy's new connections are worse. He's into some serious bad shit, and after tonight, we know that's true." Delray needed to stay away from Taylor. No matter what I should or shouldn't do, I knew I was going to have a good, long one-on-one with him. The fucker didn't like me being around Taylor? He was the dipshit who could be bringing guys like this around her. His priorities needed to be corrected, and fast.

Mason straightened. "We can't do much, but that guy needs to stay away from Taylor."

"He will." I'd make sure of that.

Mason nodded. "It'd be smart if he could leave town for a while. You think you could persuade him to do that?"

"Sure going to fucking try."

Sam snorted. "You don't even know it." She gestured to my face. "But you have this whole cocky, dark smirk on your face. You look dangerous, Logan."

Dangerous was good. It was very, very good, and I planned to use it. I turned to Mason. "If we need to get at that Rankin guy somehow, we could—"

"I'll reach out to that company I hired last year or if we have to, you know Dad will take care of this for us." He glanced at Sam for a moment. "I'm sure we could figure something out to handle this guy if he becomes a problem." His gaze came back to mine, and I had a feeling the dark and dangerous expression on my face was the one I saw on my brother's. "We won't let this guy become a danger to us." He cast Sam one more look. "No way in hell."

I couldn't have agreed more. Delray had brought this Rankin guy into our world, a world Taylor was in, and one where she could be used against him. The guy had already tried to get her. If he did it once, he'd do it again. Delray was the bridge that led from Rankin to Taylor, and that was a bridge I needed to splinter.

I turned and left Mason and Sam in the room. As I returned to the living room, I felt Taylor's eyes on me and looked over to see stark need on her face—need for me. I felt the same need rise up in me, and I reached for her. My hand tangled in her hair as she stood from her chair. Her head came to my chest. My arm wrapped around her, holding her in place, and I took a moment to breathe her in.

She was here.

She was safe.

She was mine.

I felt all of that on a primal level as I forced myself to look for Delray. I wanted to talk to him as soon as possible, but his chair was empty.

"Where is he?" I asked.

"He left."

"What?"

I whipped around to where Nate had been, but he was gone, too. "Where'd Nate go?"

"He went to put the bats away."

A guttural growl came from me, and I started for the door. Delray couldn't get away with this shitstorm—not until I had a word with him.

"Logan, stop!" Taylor ran in front of me. Her hands came to my chest. "Stop!"

I kept going until her back was at the front door. Then I reached up and held on to her arms. I was two seconds from lifting her up and out of the way.

"I mean it, Logan. I know you're worried about me."

"Do you?"

"Yes." She softened her voice. "But he won't hurt you."

"He already did." I touched the cut on her face. Blood had seeped from it, and I showed her my finger.

Her hand went to her face and touched the cut. She hissed as soon as she made contact. "I have no idea when that happened."

"I do. When his boss was trying to yank you out of my car." I cupped the back of her neck and lowered my forehead to gaze right into her eyes. "Taylor, do you have any idea what the guy would've done? If he'd gotten you out?"

Her eyes widened. "I can't think of it." Her voice grew hoarse.

I closed my eyes. The deep need in me—the one that would only be quenched when I was moving inside of her—was transforming into a need to protect her.

I laughed harshly. "You can't think of it? I can. Because I have to." She started to look away, but I didn't let her. I turned her face back to mine, gently but firmly. "It will happen again. He's going to go back. He's going to want back in, and maybe they'll let him. Maybe all will be forgiven. That's what they'll say, but it won't be the case. Rankin will want to know who we are, and who you are."

She started to shake her head. "No."

"Yes." She had to hear me. "You need to stay away from him."

"Logan."

"I mean it." My hands fell to her shoulders. "Please, Taylor. I know he's family, but he's sick. He can't be around you anymore."

A tear slid down her cheek. She didn't brush it away. I don't think she even knew it was there. Cupping the side of her face, I brushed it aside with my thumb and rested my forehead to hers.

All the walls I had, all the shields I'd erected over the years—all of those were gone in this instant. Knowing she'd been so close to danger, seeing the fear in her eyes—that shattered what I hadn't been wanting to admit to myself. From the first time I saw her at that party, saw how she was ready to help Sam when she was a stranger, I had fallen for Taylor Bruce. Since then I had fallen farther than I was ready to admit to myself.

I closed my eyes and held her, but I was rattled.

TAYLOR

Logan led me upstairs to his room a few minutes later. It was just Logan and me now. As soon as we were inside and the door closed behind us, he pulled me in for a hug. "Are you okay?"

I burrowed into him, my head resting against his chest, and I breathed in his strength. I held on to him as tightly as he held me.

I nodded, but I couldn't talk. My throat wasn't working.

His chest loosened suddenly, as if a ball of tension had been released. He cradled the back of my head and held me close. We just stood, relishing the feel of each other's arms. I didn't want to pull back, but after a few minutes, Logan slowly peeled himself away. He groaned and dipped down to press his lips to mine.

I gasped. I hadn't realized how much I needed that touch from him. It gave me strength and assurance all at once. I pressed against him, never wanting the kiss to end.

"Fuck it," he groaned against my lips. He grasped my waist and lifted me.

No more words were shared that night. Only touching, caressing, loving.

He carried me to his bed, and we undressed each other. As he lifted my shirt, I pulled his off. My bra unclasped at the same time I undid his jeans. I pulled them off, and he started on my pants. I was soon naked, panting, and ready for him. He paused just above me, the condom on, and looked down into me.

That moment. That look.

I knew it was coming, and my heart had clamored for it. It was the moment when I saw into him, past all his walls, shields, jokes, and the facade he wore for most people. He shed it for me, and as

I closed my eyes, feeling him enter me, I knew this was the real Logan.

He was giving himself to me.

CHAPTER 25

SHITSTORM
TAYLOR

"You and Logan Kade?"

I was letting myself inside my house the next morning when Jason materialized in the hallway, already inside. I looked up, my keys still in the door, and shook my head. "Like you're one to preach." Last night's events came rushing back to me, and I yanked the keys out, slamming the door behind me. "That was a shitstorm, Jason."

His scowl lessened a notch as he shoved his hands into his pockets and slouched down. "I know I'm screwed. You don't have to remind me."

"I told you to come here to regroup, figure out your next move. Not to think about how pissed you are at my choice of bedmate."

"Speaking of bedmate." He tapped his wrist where a watch would've been. "It's nine in the morning. You stayed with him?"

"Yes." I leveled him with a hard look. "And piss off again if you're climbing on that pedestal. That ship has sailed. It's left the dock, and anything you're riding right now that gives you the *audacity* to lecture me, you're flat-out wrong."

And I was done with this conversation. Brushing past him, I went to my room. He didn't follow, not that I expected him to. I was almost to the point where I didn't give a crap what he did. Almost.

But as I tossed my stuff on the bed, I knew that wasn't true. I did care. I cared a lot.

When I came back from the shower, dressed for the day, Jason had made coffee. He extended a cup to me when I came into the kitchen. "Peace offering?"

I took it. "This doesn't get you off the hook."

"I know."

He was less growly than before, and the knot inside of me loosened. I reached for the bread, but he waved me off. "Go sit," he said. "I'll make you breakfast."

"You will?"

He opened the fridge and pulled out a container. Lifting the lid, he showed me a pile of eggs. "I'll make you some of these."

"You made me coffee, and you're going to make me breakfast?"

"Yes, and don't clench your butt cheeks about it. Sit. Let me do this for you, okay?"

"Because of last night?"

He turned on the stove and waved a fork at me. "Listen, I never asked you and your boyfriend to save me."

I opened my mouth, but he lifted the fork higher and spoke over me. "But I'd probably be dead if you hadn't, so thank you. And yes, this is because of last night. Let me appease my guilt in some way."

I grinned, feeling more of the tension inside of me leaving. If Jason weren't too worked up about last night, I wouldn't be either. I needed to follow his lead.

As he made me toast, scrambled the eggs, and poured me a second cup of coffee, we relaxed enough to laugh a little. He sat across from me with his own plate filled with eggs and toast.

I pointed to it. "We need bacon."

He closed his eyes. "That would be heavenly." His eyes flicked open, and he pointed his knife at me. "That's on you. Your dad's been slacking on the domestic duties. If you want food, you gotta do the shopping."

I glared, but it didn't have any heat behind it. Snatching his knife, I put it beside my plate. "That's enough of you waving utensils at me, and I *do* do the shopping. I've been busy lately."

He snorted. "Yeah. Busy getting boned by Logan Kade."

I wanted to groan, but I held it in. Here it was. I knew he'd bring up Logan again. "Okay." I sat back, pushed my plate away, and nodded. "Go for it. Have your say right now."

His eyebrows lifted. "I have the floor?"

"You have the floor." I held up a finger. "This one time." Then it was my turn.

His lips pressed into a disapproving line before he sighed. "You're so frustrating, you know? It's Logan Kade, Taylor. What are you doing with him?"

"Feeling."

Whatever he'd been about to say died in his throat. His mouth closed, and he gave me a wondering look. "What?"

I wasn't going to bullshit this away. He deserved the truth. "I'm *feeling* with him. I'm alive again. I want to do things, like go up to the top of stupid roller coasters and look out over the city. I want to do things like that with him because they make me feel things I haven't felt in a long time."

He didn't say anything, and I didn't care. I kept going.

"Yes, I'm having sex with him. Yes, I'm falling for him. And yes, I know he's going to hurt me."

But I was too far gone to care. Logan had already given me more than he could take away. A wave of thankfulness rose in me. "I lost my mom. My high school sweetheart—the guy I thought I was going to be with for the rest of my life—abandoned me in the worst possible way. My dad's body is here, but not him. He went away, too. Logan Kade's been the first one who made me feel something other than sadness, emptiness, and loneliness no one should ever have to feel."

"Taylor." Jason reached over the table and rested his hand on mine. "I'm so sorry. You never said anything."

"Because I couldn't." I squeezed his hand. "I didn't have the strength to talk about it, much less let myself feel any of that."

"I knew it was bad, but I didn't know…" He fell silent. He looked down to his plate. "I'm so sorry."

I felt the familiar feeling of tears coming and coughed. A person could only cry so many times. "What are you going to do now?" I asked instead. "After last night."

Jason withdrew his hand and straightened in his seat. An expression flashed over his face, but it was gone instantly. I couldn't place it, but it left an uneasy feeling. I pushed that aside and waited for his response.

His voice was low and wary. "I don't know."

"Jason."

"Honestly." He looked up at me, his eyes unusually focused and clear.

I swallowed. That uneasy feeling bounced inside of me again. It wasn't going away.

"Thank you for letting me come here last night," he said, his voice raw. "I know Logan would've pounded on me if I'd stuck around, and he still will." A warning flared in his eyes. "If he finds me, he'll threaten me to stay away from you."

"But you're not going to do that."

He stared at me.

A nervous feeling fluttered in my stomach. "Right?"

"Look…" He cleared his throat. Leaning forward, his hands gripped his silverware—a knife in one hand and a fork in the other. He started talking, but I couldn't look away from his hands. His voice drifted in from a distance. His knuckles turned white. They were the only thing I could focus on. My nerves crawled up my throat. They were going to choke me.

"…okay?"

I looked up to him, tearing my gaze away from his hands. "What?"

"I'm going to make this right. With Rankin. I will. I promise."

"Okay."

"I really will. I mean it."

"Okay." I nodded. "I know you will."

"So when your boyfriend wants to know where I am, you can tell him that: I'm going to make things right, and Rankin will never know your name. I promise." He spoke with vehemence.

"Okay." Jason loved me; he had since seventh grade. "You didn't put us in that situation last night. It just happened that we were there. I know that. You'd never hurt me."

"Never!" His hands squeezed the utensils again.

"I know." I reached forward and eased the knife and fork out of his hands. "But these guys, I'm not so sure." I cracked a grin. "They were my mom's. I can't let you harm the cutlery."

He stared at his hands, as if he hadn't realized he had the utensils in a death grip. A second later, he laughed. It was abrupt, as if he'd surprised himself with it, too. A second laugh, this one smoother, slid out and then a third. The last one finally sounded genuine, and some of my uneasiness uncoiled.

Good. I smiled back at him. Nothing to worry about, right? I wasn't completely sure. I still didn't really understand what he'd gotten mixed up in. And I didn't want to know.

CHAPTER 26

REAL VS. PUBLIC
TAYLOR

"Where's your boyfriend?"

I was sitting in my sociology class when that question came from the aisle next to my seat. I automatically thought it was Jason, but when I saw it was Logan, my retort died in my throat. "What are you doing here?"

He smirked down at me before sinking into the chair beside me. "*Tsk tsk*, Taylor." He waved a finger. "The real question is why did it take me so long to properly stalk you? Duh. I can't stalk the chick I'm sleeping with if I'm in a different sociology class. That's Creeping 101."

I played along. "Oh, yeah. What took you so long?"

His head bobbed. "I'm not on my A game. It took me way too long to catch up." He patted my leg. "I sincerely apologize for that."

I laughed as his hand went quickly from patting to groping, I moved it back to his lap. "If you're a creeper, that went into the stalker zone."

He wagged his eyebrows at me. "I can be a stalker. Any day. Any time. Any..." His gaze fell to my lips. "...position."

I shook my head. Last night he'd been setting cars on fire, driving like a maniac, and punching someone for me. Fast forward through an intense hour back at his house and a night of slow and delicious sex, and now he was hitting on me like nothing happened?

I pointed my pen at him. "You give me whiplash sometimes."

"Why?"

"Last night. I mean, it was…"

His eyes darkened in a sensual way. I felt an ache between my legs as he pointed to his face. "This is Public Face Logan," he said. "I'm all smiles, jokes, and innuendos. You saw Real Face Logan last night."

"I'd rather have Real Face Logan over Public Face Logan any day, any time, any…" I licked my lips. "…position."

He groaned, dipping his head closer to mine. "I see what you did just there."

"You do?"

We both wore stupid grins, getting stupider by the second, but I was beyond caring.

"Mr. Kade." The professor's voice boomed over the classroom.

We jerked apart, and an embarrassed flush heated my cheeks. I slumped in my seat and tried to remember we hadn't been doing anything wrong. *Just flirting,* a voice said in my head. I felt guilty for flirting. That was ridiculous.

"Yo, teach." Logan was the exact opposite of me. He sat as straight in his chair as possible and lifted a hand in a casual wave. "Thanks for letting me switch classes. It's much appreciated."

Our professor looked at me as she mused, "Mmm-hmmm. I'm sure your reasons were valid."

"Completely. My allergies always flare up for nine a.m. classes."

"A couple of hours later seem to be working just fine for you." She motioned to him. "I don't hear any sniffling or wheezing."

"Yep. Told you this would work better."

She harrumphed once more before turning on the projector, and a smattering of laughter rippled through the class. I could feel the other students' eyes and remembered the first day of school. So many girls had watched me, trying to flirt with Logan. Now it was even worse. I felt like they could tell we'd been intimate. I wanted to hide in my chair. As if sensing my embarrassment, Logan threw his arm around my shoulder and squeezed me to his side.

"Oh my God," I muttered under my breath.

The professor stopped talking and turned to us. "Is there a problem, Miss Bruce?"

I cursed under my breath, but before I could respond, Logan lifted his hand in the air again. "She sneezed. Her allergies are acting up this time."

"She's been fine all week," the professor replied coolly. "Perhaps she's allergic to you, Mr. Kade?"

I tensed. That left it wide open for Logan. I knew he was going to say something, and then everyone would know. He laughed before his delivery. "Not possible. I was all over her last night, and there's not a hive in sight." He studied me for a moment and gave her the thumbs-up sign. "She's breathing just fine."

Yep. He went there.

I closed my eyes and hung my head. Hearing how the whispering picked up, I knew this was going to spread like wildfire.

Logan was so pleased with himself, but once class ended, I grabbed him and pulled him to an empty room. I whirled on him as soon as the door closed. "Do you know what you did in there? You announced that we're sleeping together."

"Why's that a problem?"

"Because…" I shook my head. *Did he really not get it?*

Suddenly, the Logan everyone else knew became the Logan only I knew, and the intensity in the room jumped two levels. We were back to thick, palpable sexual tension. He always had this power over me.

"No, I get why you might not want that put out there, but I do. I thought about this. I'm claiming you. It's not the other way around. Girls try to claim me all the time, and I never let it happen. But not this time. Not with you. I *want* to claim you. I want *everyone* to know we're together." His eyebrows pinched together. "Aren't we?"

"Are we?" My mouth went dry.

He stared at me. I stared at him. I didn't think either of us had expected this talk.

"Wait. So, you want people to know we're sleeping together?"

His voice dropped low. "You were never a secret to me."

Oh. This...had me reeling. "I have major baggage, Logan. My mom. My ex-boyfriend. Now I'm worried about Jason—"

"Speaking of Delray. I was serious before. I asked where your boyfriend is, and where is he?" His eyes grew hard. "I want to have a talk with him."

"That's who you meant by boyfriend? I thought you were joking about yourself."

"Normally, yes. This time, no. I really want to know where he is."

I shifted my feet. "I can't, Logan." I'd promised Jason time.

"You can." He moved closer. "Where is he?"

I moved back. "He said he'd take care of it. I have to give him that chance."

"He put you in danger."

"No." I shook my head. "We put ourselves in danger. Jason didn't know we were there. He had no idea. And it didn't look like coming there had been his idea anyway. We helped give him extra time, but he's never put me in danger before." At least, he never realized he had. "I have to believe him."

"He's addicted to that lifestyle."

"If it were Sam? She's like family to you. If she was messed up in something, what would you do then?"

Logan's eyes went flat, and his face became an unreadable mask. I had stepped wrong, but I needed to make him understand. Before he could say anything, my voice dropped to a whisper. "He's my family, Logan. He was there for me when my real family wasn't. You have to understand that."

"I do, but he's sick. You asked me what I'd do if it were Sam, and I'd do the same. If she were in that position, she'd be sick, and

Mason and I would take care of her." He moved closer. His hand took hold of mine, our fingers linking together. "I'd do the same for you."

I knew he was right. "I don't know what to tell you, though. He took off. I don't know where he is, just that he promised to make things right and that Rankin would never be a problem for us."

Logan wasn't happy. I saw the anger on his face. He ran a hand through his hair, making the ends stand up in sexy disarray. He looked ready to say something when a thump sounded against the door.

Claire's hand had smacked the window. She opened her mouth to say something, but her eyes went to Logan and she seemed to change her mind. Her eyes widened, and she stepped back, but she didn't go away.

"You really don't know where he is?"

I shook my head, turning back to Logan. "He was at my house this morning. He made me breakfast and then took off. I told him I'd give him time to fix things."

"Taylor."

I saw the worry. It dripped off of him, from his tense shoulders to the crease in his forehead.

"What are you going to do?" I asked.

"I'm going to find him, and I'm going to find out what he said to Rankin."

"And after that?"

"Then we'll deal with Rankin."

He started to leave, but I caught his arm. I tugged him close. "Be careful, okay?"

The corners of his mouth relaxed into a slight grin. "What are you doing tonight? I'll want to see you. Sorry for being an ass in the room."

"I'm working, and that's okay." I squeezed his hand. "But if you wanted everyone to know we're sleeping together, and I didn't, doesn't that make me the awesome one?" I winked. "Think about that."

He chuckled and bent down to give me a soft kiss. Lingering there, his lips brushed over mine once more before he pulled back. "No one's on my level." His hand slid around my waist. "But I think you've exceeded it."

After another deep kiss, he was gone, and I felt a little breathless.

Until Claire popped into the room.

CHAPTER 27

PUNCHING'S MY THING
TAYLOR

Claire stepped aside so Logan could leave, then made a beeline for me. I braced myself, thinking she was going to ask about Jason, but she didn't. She'd already heard the Logan rumor and wanted details. I wasn't sure if that was better or worse.

I told her the basic truth, that we were sleeping together. She knew it, but I guess she hadn't known how involved the sleeping together part meant. She wanted to know more, but I didn't have anything else I wanted to tell her. Logan and I hadn't nailed things down, and I didn't really want to. Most girls might jump at the chance to lock him down, but I wasn't lying when I'd told him I had baggage. Even though I was starting to deal with things, I had a long way to go. And I had to go to work, so Claire was pushed off… for the moment. I knew she'd want more gossip later, but for now, I was almost eager to punch my timecard.

Telling Logan about my mom and how Eric had left me helped open that door to healing, but it was all so fresh. My worry about the Jason situation helped to distract me, but as I left for my shift at Pete's Pub, I thought about my mom. I thought about Eric—what I'd say to him if I saw him again. After a moment I felt overwhelmed with pain and bitterness. I felt panic coming on, so I shut it down.

I started off again, but heard my name behind me. It was Jeremy Fuller. "Hey, Taylor."

He had stopped a few feet behind me, but came forward when I waved. I could feel the disapproval emanating from him.

"Hey back."

His eyes narrowed. "Logan Kade, huh?"

Yep. There it was. "You heard."

He nodded. "I did, but I'm not surprised. I saw him outside of my party. I saw how he was looking at you."

Of course, he did. "I don't want to be rude because I don't know you very well, but…" I had no clue how to handle this, but he had an opinion. "I'm not sure if I even want to hear what you have to say."

"I could see that. But…"

But…it was coming anyway. I could see the wheels turning in his mind. I waited.

"He's going to hurt you."

I nodded. "I've been told."

"What are you doing then? I don't get it." He took a step closer. A stream of students milled around us. A few glanced over their shoulders or gave us sidelong looks as they went by. A few had knowing looks on their faces, but others seemed curious. A few were irritated because we were in the middle of the sidewalk; I liked those guys the most right now. They had no opinion on my love life.

"Are you supposed to?" I shook my head. "Get it, I mean. I can understand my two best friends having an opinion, but you… You're my TA." Suddenly, I knew why he had an opinion. Thinking back, I should have seen it right away, my first day in his class. I'd blamed it all on paranoid girls who were into him, but he had a part in it, too. "It's because you like me."

"It's because I care." His eyes were full of caution. "Logan Kade hurts people. That's what he and his brother do. I don't want that to happen to you."

"Why do you care?" Because he did. More than maybe he should've. There had to be a reason. "Who did Logan hurt that you cared about?"

He shook his head. "It was no one. No one to him, but it was someone to me, and he's going to do it to you too. I know what you went through last year."

I stepped back. "Stop. Right there. Just stop." My mom, Eric, my dad's absence—he had no right bringing that up. "I'm sorry for whoever you cared about that Logan hurt, but you don't know anything about last year."

"I know what happened. I know that's why you moved back." He was becoming so intense. "I know your dad's been emotionally absent."

The students around us all started to spin together, becoming one long line that wrapped around us, that wouldn't stop. My hands clutched my bag straps. I hung my head. I wanted to bury it in the ground beneath me.

"Kade is going to shatter you," he said. "He's the wrong guy for you to be seeking comfort with. He doesn't know how to give it, or to be loyal, or to be—" He bit back the rest and closed his eyes. I saw the strain on his face. "Logan Kade destroys lives. That's what he does."

I was seething inside, but I asked, grinding out, "Who? Who did Logan hurt that you cared about?"

He didn't answer right away. He stared back at me, the anger flaring in his eyes, and then it faded and he murmured, almost brokenly, "It was no one to him. She was a girl who had a crush. That was it, but she meant the world to me. She liked him, and she told him at a party. He was drinking heavily. That's what she said, and she approached him. They had sex, and afterwards…" His voice grew hollow. "He didn't remember her the next day. It shattered her. That's not what she did normally, but he didn't even remember…I cared for her. I would've been there for her."

"What happened to her?"

"She left school."

So Logan was drunk, a girl came up to him and said she liked him. He slept with her and…that was all Logan's fault. I shook my head. Jeremy was wrong. He was so very wrong, but watching him, I could see that he didn't care. He was still holding on to the past, on to losing that girl. He wasn't being rational when it came to Logan.

And I didn't have any words. There was nothing I could say to make things better, and I didn't know if I wanted to. He came to me with anger in his heart about Logan, about the girl Jeremy thought he should've had, and he used his knowledge about my mother to intervene about another girl, me.

I edged backward again, slowly moving away.

I had nothing else to say to him. The students still moved in a constant line, but my mind detached from my emotions. I knew that line would bend around me. I wasn't scared of it, not when there were so many worse things to be scared of. Like monsters.

Like people who shot my mother.

LOGAN

Pete's Pub was busy when Mason, Nate, and I walked inside. The dance floor usually only had a few regulars, but it was packed this Friday night. And as we entered, the people closest to the doors turned and stared at us. Nate and I got attention when we came here, but this was more than normal. It was because Mason was with us. College star and all that jazz. He came out with us because the team didn't play this weekend. It was rare, and I was planning on taking full advantage. Sam stayed home, so it really was just the guys, but I wanted to check on Taylor. She said she was working tonight.

I usually didn't care if a girl was mad at me. I enjoyed that—made things more entertaining—but I was finding I didn't like when Taylor was mad at me. It didn't sit well. Made my insides all mushy, which pissed me off. But I refused to let anyone know. Whatever stick was up Nate's ass would be wedged even higher if he knew.

Mason leaned close to me. "I didn't think this was a college bar."

"It wasn't." But I recognized the students, too.

"The girls from last week tagged us on Instagram," Nate said. "I'm sure word spread from there."

"Well." Mason looked at me. "We're here." He pointed to an empty booth in the corner. "You go check on your girl. Nate and I will be over there."

There was a line to get to the bar, and I could see Taylor's head bobbing back and forth as she filled orders. She'd only started a month ago, but I wouldn't have known it watching her now. She wore a cool, calm look, with her hair pulled back in some kind of braid. She had on her black uniform shirt over jeans, and the V dipped low enough that when she darted to the back storage section, I got a glimpse of her rack, and a delicious view at that.

I wanted to go back there and lock us into the storage room. I'd just convinced myself it would be better if I didn't when I saw another guy break free from the crowd. He was heading right for the storage room. He would've walked right past me, but I shifted, leaning my shoulder against the wall and folding my arms.

Nothing.

The guy should've stopped, if only to check me out.

When he reached for the door handle, I moved fast to stop him. My arm completely blocked him now, and as he leaned back to take me in, I leaned forward to give him a better view.

"Don't see a Pete's Pub shirt on," I said.

He frowned and glanced down. "No. I don't work here."

"One point to me." I grinned. I felt the asshole coming out. This guy was going to get the full effect. He had no idea what was coming his way.

"Point? What?" He pointed to the storage room door. "I just need to see Taylor. She went in there."

I cocked my head. "You work for Rankin?"

"Rankin?"

Enough chitchat. I was about to straight up ask if he had a hard-on for Taylor when the door swung open under my hand. I stood back, but kept myself between the doorway and the guy as Taylor appeared. She stopped, braking at the sight of us. I looked over my shoulder at her, but her eyes moved past me. I knew the second she saw the guy. Her eyes went round, and the blood drained from her face. Her lips parted, and she leaned backward, though her feet stayed rooted in place. I started to reach for her when I heard her quiet gasp.

"Eric."

The fuck? The ex? I looked at him, and his face flushed. He looked guilty. And with good reason.

"You're the ex?"

"Yeah."

I grunted. Enough reason for me. I swung my fist and made contact with his neck. He went down, but not enough. He wasn't on the floor, so I punched again. This time, I hit the sweet spot—going through the cheekbones toward the nose—and his body dropped.

Taylor looked down at him. "Why did you do that?"

"Because he's a fucker." It was as simple as that.

She groaned. "I'm going to get into trouble for this."

"No, you won't."

A security guard shoved through the small crowd that had gathered. Mason and Nate were right behind him.

"Logan." One of the security guards frowned down at the douche. "Why'd you hit the guy?"

"Because he's a fucker." I was going to add that I would hit the guy whenever I saw him or I wanted to hit him every time I saw him, but Taylor's hand clamped down on my arm. She squeezed, stopping me.

"He's an ex, and my history isn't great with him," she explained. "Logan was just worried about me."

"Punch first, talk later?" The guard looked confused.

I laughed. "More like punch first, never talk later." I pointed to him. "I did you a favor. The guy is a dipshit."

The security guard looked from me to Taylor and back again. "Was there a violent history we need to know about?"

"He won't be a problem, if you're worried about a lawsuit." Mason stepped forward.

"Let him try," I said.

"Logan." Nate shook his head, giving me the motion to cut it out.

Fuck them. I motioned to Nate and Mason, bending down to grab the dipshit. "We'll take care of him."

"Wait. I mean—" The guard gave us a nervous look. "What are you going to do? Give me something here to work with."

Mason grabbed Eric's legs, and Nate pushed his way through the crowd, making an opening for us. When we lifted Eric in the air, I said, "We'll take him to the hospital, make sure I didn't do any permanent damage. How about that? Can you work with that?"

"I don't know, man." The guard still seemed torn.

Taylor moved next to me. "I'll go with, if that's okay?"

"We'll be down a bartender then."

"Let her go. I'll step in." A guy arrived and took in the scene. The name tag clipped to his shirt read *Manager*.

"Are you sure?" Taylor asked.

The guy waved her on. "Go. Get him out of here before he wakes up. I don't want to deal with paperwork. As far as I'm concerned, this is a domestic problem. Not a bar problem."

He stared at Taylor as he said the last part, and I got his message. This was on her. I was about to let him know this was on me, not her, when she nodded.

"Yes, sir." She touched my arm. "Let's go. Please."

I nodded, and Mason and I carried the ex-boyfriend out of the bar. When we got outside, Taylor pointed to her car. "You can put him in the backseat."

"No way in hell," I said. "He's going in my Escalade."

"You sure?" Mason asked.

I nodded. No way was I letting this guy further hurt Taylor, not if I could prevent it.

"Taylor?" A voice came from the parking lot.

Taylor cursed, and I recognized the same friend who'd interrupted us after sociology this morning. Claire...? I think. Taylor talked about her a few times. She was the female counterpart to that dipshit Delray. Both were Taylor's friends. Earlier she'd been on cloud nine. This time she seemed transfixed by the unconscious dude. She stopped a few feet away and pointed. "Is that...?"

Taylor nodded.

Her friend's arm dropped. "Oh."

Nate laughed. "He walked into Logan's fist."

Mason grinned and added, "Twice."

Taylor's friend turned to me. I flashed her a grin.

"Oh." I could see the wheels turning, and she got stars in her eyes.

I would've stepped back and held up my hands, but they were occupied. I could only shake my head. "Don't get ahead of yourself. I'm not some knight in shining armor. The guy had it coming."

She turned to Taylor. "I'm not disagreeing with you, but whatever. It's all over social media that the Kades are here tonight. You weren't answering my texts, so I figured I'd see if you were with them."

Mason frowned. "It's on social media?"

Nate groaned, cursing under his breath. "Uh..." He gave us an apologetic look. "I might've posted that we were going to Pete's tonight."

"Why would you do that? All these people know our hangout now."

Nate rolled his eyes. "Because unlike the new you, I want chicks to show up."

My eyes narrowed. "I still feel like punching someone. *You* could be that someone."

"Stop." Mason threw both of us a warning glare. "Let's deal with this guy, then hash out whatever is going on."

"Taylor, stay." I nodded toward Claire. "Talk to your friend. We'll load him up."

And once Eric was in my backseat, Mason shut the door and rounded on us in the parking lot. "Nate, what's your problem?"

"Nothing." He pointed through the window to my unconscious passenger. "Let's head out. This guy is going to wake up soon."

Mason held back, still watching me.

I gestured for him to go. "I'll be fine. I mean it."

"You sure?"

I nodded. "Get the fuck out of here. I've got an ex to interrogate. We can figure a plan later."

Mason grinned and lifted his hand in a wave. As the two of them left in Mason's car, I glanced back to the bar and saw Taylor heading my way. I walked over to meet her. I didn't want her to have to see her ex any more than necessary.

"Jason's gone," she said before I could speak.

Good. "Really?"

"Claire's been trying to call him, but he wasn't answering. So she called his roommate instead. He's completely gone, like he packed up and everything." She stopped and tried to clear her throat. Her voice came out hoarse. "He said there were two letters left behind. One for me and one for Claire." She looked over to my vehicle. "What the hell are you going to do with him?"

I shrugged. "I wasn't thinking that far ahead, to be honest."

"Logan."

"What?" I grinned at her. "I'm being the supportive guy. I punched your ex for you. Punching's my thing. It's what I do."

"I thought you were the talker?"

"That, too. Tonight it was punching."

"I never asked you to."

I tapped my head. "You were thinking it. I caught the vibe." I winked. "I can read minds, too, didn't you know?"

She laughed, shaking her head. "I can't deal with this. Can you just drop Eric off somewhere where there are medical professionals?"

"He'll be fine. Don't worry. And you shouldn't go to Delray's place. Call his roommate. Have him meet you somewhere else, somewhere safe. Crime Boss Dickhead could be waiting there for Delray. You don't want me to go with you?"

She shook her head, her smile fading. "No. I'll go with Claire. And we'll call. We'll have him meet us somewhere safe. Can you just—"

She looked over my shoulder at my vehicle. "Why did he come back?"

"Look at me. I'll find out why he's here."

"You won't hurt him?"

I flashed her a grin.

She added, "Any more?"

"You really don't want me to hurt him?"

She let out a sigh. "No. He's an asshole and a coward, and I think he deserved getting hit, but he doesn't need to get beat up anymore."

"Okay." I let her hand go and held both of mine up in the air. "I'll be nice. We'll just…chat."

She shook her head. "Why don't I believe you?"

I winked. "Because you know the real me." Pressing a kiss to her forehead, I motioned for Claire to come over. When she did, I said, "Take care of her, at least until I can come and take over."

She gave me a firm nod and took Taylor's hand in hers. "I'll take care of her."

Taylor gave me a tentative wave and smile as she followed her friend to her car. But there was a look in her eyes—the same look she'd worn when she told me what happened to her mom. And that didn't sit well with me.

Not at all.

CHAPTER 28

THE LETTER
TAYLOR

"What do you think is in those letters?"

Claire hadn't shut up since we'd gotten in her car. Normally, I didn't mind her chatter. I liked it even. It had helped while I'd been on the too-quiet side this past year, but tonight—with a headache forming and a feeling I already knew what lay ahead—she was too much for me. I rubbed at my temples.

"Okay." Claire pulled her car over and leaned forward, craning her neck to see the park we told his roommate to meet us at. "We're here. Do you see him?"

It was empty, but it was a small park in a good part of town. It was only a few blocks in length, and it was surrounded by homes. We were safe. I was sure of it. I shook my head. "I don't, but he'll come. He'll bring the letters."

"Good." She glanced over and confessed, "Because I didn't know how to get to Jason's apartment building. I was hoping you knew."

"You didn't?" That surprised me.

"No." She looked down to her lap, fiddling with her keys. "Jason and I, we…uh…we kinda faded once we graduated. I never came over here, and I think he moved this summer, too. So this could be his second place. I'm not sure."

Jason had mentioned their "fade," but Claire never had until now. For some reason, it hurt me to hear about it. "You guys put on a brave face for me then?"

She looked up, her eyes searching mine. "Yeah. Kinda. I mean, we *are* friends, but we just weren't close. You were the closest to both of us. I just don't think you realized it."

"When did that happen? I mean, I thought you two were good."

She shrugged, turning to look out the window again. "It always was a little difficult. It got worse later in high school when…" Her voice trailed off.

I finished for her. "When you started dating student council members, and Jason started dating…guys?" I closed my eyes. My heart sank. "Why didn't I notice?"

"Because you loved us both," Claire said. "And because we hid it from you."

"But—" I shook my head. It made sense. The guys Claire dated weren't the nicest to Jason, and I knew others had been even worse— like the guys who were friends with Eric. Only Eric had been decent to him. "I should've paid attention."

"You were loved by everyone. Even the bullies usually left him alone. No one wanted to piss you off."

"Why?" I opened my eyes.

"Because…" She shrugged. "People like you, Taylor. I don't think you notice how much. You've been off since last year, but it's still there. Logan Mr. Sex Machine Kade is interested in you." She rolled her eyes as she said his name. "He's let everyone know you two are together."

I had to laugh at that. "There's no one else breaking down my door."

"Stop it. He likes you—like, really likes you. That's not something to dismiss."

"I know. I just don't understand it. I don't understand why me."

"Because you're Taylor," Claire said. "What more reason do you need?"

I tried to smile, but her words had punched through a wall, and a whole host of emotions streamed through. I reached over and grabbed her hand. "Thank you, Claire." I had to whisper. My throat wasn't fully functioning.

Her hand squeezed back and held on. "You have no idea, but you've been there more times for me than you think." A tear slid down her cheek, and her voice turned hoarse, too.

"Look at us." I lifted our hands. "Holding hands. Both crying."

She laughed, flicking her tears away.

"And we're going in there to read some letters from Jason," I added.

She grew quiet before she asked, "You think he left, don't you?"

I didn't answer. I couldn't. I was still hoping it wasn't true.

Just then a pair of headlights was visible as a car neared the park, pausing at an intersection. It turned right and went the entire way around the park. "Look." I pointed to it.

"I see."

We both watched as the car was moving slow, until it passed us. It paused and we saw a guy press his forehead to his window, trying to see us. I relaxed. The guy didn't look scary or thug-like. I was sure that was Jason's roommate. I waved and once I did, his face visibly relaxed. He blew out a breath and lifted a shaky hand back. He pulled forward, then turned around so he could park behind us.

I looked at Claire. "You ready?"

She shook her head, but her hand went to her seatbelt. "We have no choice. Let's go and get these letters."

We both nodded. We both reached for our doors…

…neither of us moved an inch.

Taylor,

If I know you—and I think I do by now ;)—you probably already know what I'm going to say in this letter. But I have to say it anyway because I have to put in words how much I love you and how much I've cared about our friendship.

I'm leaving. Surprise! (bad joke) (sorry)

That's what this letter is about. I never meant to have my "other" life affect you, but it has. It was bound to happen eventually. Gambling—that whole world—is my addiction. I can't get enough of it. I think about it the moment I wake up. I miss it when I'm being good, and I am literally counting down the hours, minutes, seconds until I can get back to it.

I thought it would be better if I was the one taking the bets, but it wasn't. I still gambled, and it got all sorts of fucked up. I can't tell you anything because if something ever happened to me, I don't want you to be involved any more than you already are. Just trust me when I say that this life is a toxin, but one I can't live without. It's sweet fucking poison <-ha! That's as poetic as I'm going to get here.

(After reading this over, it sounds like I was laughing as I wrote it. I wasn't. I was bawling, but damn—I do have to laugh at how sucktastic this whole situation is.)

Anyway, if you're reading this, you went to my apartment and saw everything. All my stuff is gone. And no, I wasn't the one to get my shit out of there. I had some friends do it for me. They were told to box everything up and see if they could sell whatever they could to pay Rankin back. I owe him a lot of money, but it doesn't matter. He'll want to know who you are and who the others are. I know him. He won't let it rest. A part of me thinks that even if I do disappear, it won't matter. He'll still try to figure out who punched him and who knocked him unconscious. And if he does, I'm so very sorry.

The good thing, though, is that I know those guys can take care of themselves. (I'm not putting their names in here, in case something happens to this letter. I don't want any more damning evidence, but just in case, burn this when you're done reading. I know it's addressed to you.)

So, going back to my dramatic goodbye here (So dramatic! Can you feel the thick sarcasm?), for real, I love you. You were my family when my real family kicked me out.

I know I told you things with Claire fizzled last year, but it really happened long before that. I don't really know what happened, but I never fought for it. As long as I had you, I was okay. I really was. You were my rock for so many years. It meant the world to me that I was able to be your rock this last year. You'll never know how much I loved being able to support you, even though it was because of a seriously shitty situation.

Please don't worry about me. I took enough to get by for a while. I'm not telling where I'm going, but some of my friends have friends who can help me out. I'll be fine. I really will. I may even seek treatment for my problem. I'm told it doesn't stick well, but I'll try. Maybe we can figure out some secret spy way to send coded messages. Probably not, though, because I'm sure I'd forget the code and all would be lost.

Okay. My ride is here. I have to sign off. Oh, hey, you should know that Claire is going to be a mess when she's done reading my letter to her. It's filled with a lot of "I'm sorry. I wish we had fought to keep our closeness." And "I'm so glad we were a united front for Taylor this past year."

I love you, Taylor. I'll always be your best friend. No matter where I am or where you are, we're still family. Physical distance can't hamper our bond, and since I'm not there, do not let a certain someone hurt you. If he does, let him know that I'm coming back to kick his ass. I'll get bigger guys to do the deed for me. I got your back, Taylor.

(But having written that, I did see how much he was worried about you that night. I may have to eat all my words. I think the guy does care for you, and if that's the case, you have tamed the beast. Good luck. I've heard some of the crazy stuff he's done. It'll be a wild ride for you, so have fun with him.)

Okay. Shit. They're honking. I really have to go.

I LOVE YOU, Taylor Laurelin Bruce. (I'll be seeing you again, so this isn't a goodbye letter.)

SEE YOU LATER— Jason

PS I made a call on your behalf. Please don't be mad, and if you are, you can chew my ass out the next time we see each other. Because there WILL be a next time.

Using the back of my hands, I wiped the tears from my face. Claire was still reading her letter. Jason's roommate (ex-roommate) handed us the two letters earlier, both sealed in envelopes, and mumbled something before taking off.

Once we got back into the car, Claire ripped into hers. I only held mine. I listened to her sniffling for a full minute before I had the strength to open it. And now, feeling gutted, I waited for Claire to be done as well.

Jason wanted me to burn the letter, but that wasn't happening. I folded it up neatly and put it back into the envelope. When I saw him again, I'd burn it. Until then, this letter would never be destroyed.

It was my last contact with him.

CHAPTER 29

A PSEUDO KIDNAPPING.
NOT REALLY.
REALLY.
LOGAN

Taylor's ex-douchefriend's head had started to bob up and down, back and forth, before the first moan came from him. I put him on a couch in the garage and kept the lights turned off—except for one spotlight trained solely on him. The only door was locked, and I stood right in front of it. The dipshit wasn't leaving without giving me some answers.

"Wha…" His head raised from his chest. "Huh?"

"You good?" I called over to him.

"What?" His eyes opened, but shut again right away. He groaned and coughed before asking, "Where am I?"

"You and me." I walked over to lean against my Escalade. "We're going to have a chat."

"Wait." He still seemed so confused. Looking around, he lifted his hands and touched his face. "I was at the bar. I wanted to talk to Taylor, but this guy—" He stopped and squinted at me. "Was that you? Did you knock me out?"

I didn't see the point of lying, so I shrugged and walked out from behind the light. As soon as he could see me, his head fell back against the couch. "You."

"Me." I smiled.

"Who are you?"

My smile switched to a frown. "I thought you'd recognize me."

"No." He blinked a few times before focusing on me again. "Who are you?"

"I'm the guy screwing your ex-girlfriend." I leaned down in his face.

His eyes jumped to mine, and a flare of anger appeared, but he didn't say anything.

"Now." I went back to smiling, though I knew my eyes weren't showing it. My eyes were saying a whole host of other shit. He should be scared of me. He should be scared of Taylor. He should leave and never come back.

A wary expression flickered over his face, and I knew he'd registered each and every one of those messages.

"You're going to tell me why you came to see Taylor," I said.

"Why I—no." He shook his head, his voice growing stronger. "No, I won't. That's between her and me. I don't care who you are."

"Dude." I felt a speech coming—a good rip-into-'em speech— and the more I felt it, the more I knew I was going to enjoy it. I hadn't delivered one of these in a long time.

I'd started to lean down again when I heard a door shut outside. Cursing softly, I whipped around as I heard Mason's voice.

"I'll catch up with you later," he said. "I'm going to find Logan."

This needed to be handled ASAP, so I pointed a finger at the douchefriend. "Stay. We're not done."

"What?"

Heading back around my vehicle, I opened the side door of the garage just as Mason walked by, raising his phone to his ear. He jumped at my sudden appearance.

"Holy shit." He clapped a hand to his chest. "Where the fuck did you come from?"

"Shhh." I looked around him. Nate was heading across the front lawn to his car. He was too far away to hear our conversation, and

I was grateful. Nate had gone back to his weaseling ways. I didn't want him anywhere near this guy. "Where's Nate going?" I smirked. "Who's he going to hang out with? Sam?"

"Fucking A." Mason let out an aggravated sigh. "What the hell is going on with you two? I thought the petty bickering was done."

"Never." My grin turned frosty. "I was all fine and dandy till he started taking pot shots at me."

He gave me a hard look. "I don't like having a family rift. We've got enough to deal with." He nodded behind me. "He's here?"

I hadn't known where else to take him. "Figured I shouldn't go back to the amusement park, in case Street Thug has guys out looking for us."

"Logan." Mason twisted around, looking at the house. "This is our garage!"

"I don't know of any empty warehouses," I said. "I'm sorry. I've only been here a year."

He groaned, tipping his head back. "But five feet from Sam? She lives here, too."

I clapped him on the shoulder. "Relax. This guy's just an ex-boyfriend. And it's not like I'm holding him here against his wishes or something, like I kidnapped him."

"You pseudo kidnapped him."

"Not really."

"Really. You did."

I shrugged. "He can leave whenever he wants."

"Does *he* know that?" Mason asked before following me into the garage.

Fortunately, Eric was still on the couch, squinting toward where he could hear our approach. We stopped, standing right behind the light. He couldn't see us, but he knew we were there. Mason shook his head.

Whatever. We'd done stupider things. It wasn't like we'd get arrested for this…I didn't think. Not wanting to dwell on that, I started forward. "I'm back, and that means you need to start talking."

"But—"

"Now," I said.

He let out a breath. Some of the fear had faded from his face, but he was still wary. "Or what? I don't understand why I need your permission to talk to my girlfriend."

"Ex-girlfriend, bro."

I grabbed one of the folding chairs leaning against the wall and set it up in front of him. I dropped in to straddle it, now glaring from eye level at the guy. This was better. I could intimidate up close and personally.

I smiled, waving my fingers. "Let's cut the bullshit. I know what happened that day."

He grew still. "What do you mean?"

"I *know*."

"Bullshi—"

"You ran like a coward."

He paled and fell silent.

"Dipshit," I leaned closer, tipping the chair on its back legs, "I'm sleeping with her."

"No." He shook his head. "I don't believe you."

I laughed. The guy didn't *want* to believe me. "What are you doing? Are you holding on to her? Is that it?"

"I know Taylor. She would never get over me that fast."

"Well." I gave him a pitying look. "She did. Sorry."

"No." He kept shaking his head. "Jason told me she would need me tonight. He said I could make everything better. I—" He stopped, studying me, before his head moved from right to left again. "No way."

"She has a firecracker tattoo on her thigh."

That shut him up. His eyes turned ragged. "No. No way."

"When you're inside of her and kiss her throat, she arches her back, and it's the hottest thing I've seen in a long time. She makes a little sound that makes you want to go harder, just to make her do it again because you don't want to disappoint her. She makes you want to satisfy her, makes you need to satisfy her—"

"Shut up," he snapped, his chest heaving. "Shut up."

"I could tell you a lot more. I won't, though, because this isn't about further hurting Taylor. This is about helping her. You being here is not helping her. It's going to hurt her."

He put a hand to his forehead and started rubbing. "Jason told me…" He cleared his throat. "Jason said, uh—"

I moved the chair closer, folding my arms over the back of it. "What did he say?"

"He said I could come back and make things right. This was the time to do it, if I was going to. That…" He hesitated. "That…he was leaving. I don't know why," he added hastily. "He wouldn't tell me, and our conversation was really rushed. He was already heading out of town, but he said she'd need her family."

"The fucker left town?" Wait. "Why'd he send you?"

"Because he—uh—." He wouldn't look at me. "He doesn't like you, and he thinks I still have a chance. He doesn't know about…"

I grunted. Delray would have a different opinion if he knew what Eric had done. I'd be the knight in fucking shining armor then.

Mason moved up behind me. I knew what he was thinking already. If Delray was gone, so was part of our problem.

"Yeah. That's the only reason I went to find her."

"How'd you know where she was?" Mason asked.

Eric looked up, his gaze shifting to my brother. "He told me a few days ago she'd started working there. I figured it was Friday night. It's the best night to work. I'm not in contact with Taylor, and she doesn't update any of her social media, so I guessed. That's it."

I grunted. The fucker had guessed right.

"Why'd you punch me? I wasn't going to hurt her."

"Because I wanted to." I stood and put the chair back against the wall. The guy either had no clue, or he was just choosing to be stupid. "Delray has no idea what you did to her. You must know that, right?"

He continued to glare at me, but after a beat, he jerked his head in a nod. "Yeah. I figured."

In that moment, I saw into him. He wasn't there to hurt her; he didn't think he would. He had no clue. "You're delusional, you know that?" I scoffed, running a hand over my face. Before he could reply, I said, "You had her. You were with her for years. Even she admits that she would've married you. You *had* her." I shook my head. "You have no idea how lucky you had it, but you did the one thing that would cut her deep, and it will continue to cut her deep for years. You left her. You could've saved her, and you ran like a dog with its tail between its legs. You were a coward."

"You don't know—"

"Yeah, I do." I leaned over him. I wanted to make sure he didn't walk out of my garage with the same delusions. I wanted every single one of them dead and shriveled up like dust. "Family never leaves each other. You save each other. If it ends, it ends together. That's all you can do, because even if you get out, you're alone. Don't you get that? When you left her, you chose yourself. You chose being alone. You did it. You decided. Not her. If you hadn't? Shit, you'd still be with her. You'd probably be cozied up to her right now instead of me being there in a few hours. You ended the relationship. Not her. Don't put that on her, *ever*. You got that?"

Mason's phone rang, and I heard him answer as he left. "Yeah?"

The guy never looked away from me. I straightened back up and gave him the biggest fuck-off look I could. I pitied him. "You lost her. Don't think you can come back and just pick things up."

"You're—" He tried to muster something to throw back at me. I saw the anger, the resentment, the bitterness. But just as the strength to protest gathered in him, it faded. His head hung, and he sat there like a lost puppy. But I didn't feel bad for this asshole.

I pointed to the door. "You can go whenever you want."

"What?"

I jerked my head toward the door. "I was never holding you here. And now I'm done talking."

"But—" He closed his eyes and rolled his head from side to side. "I came for a second chance with her."

"You came to weasel your way back in. You said yourself you only thought of it because Jason called. Stop lying. It's making me want to take an actual shit on you. You knew she wouldn't want to see you. That's why you haven't been back since. But the first moment she might be vulnerable? She might be feeling exposed? You decided to be here. You wanted to come in like the hero you're sadly not. That's all you wanted, not to actually make things right."

"What's the difference? I mean, it's my way of helping her."

"It's straight up manipulation, dipshit. You know it, too. Or at least you should. Your chance to help her is long gone."

Just then, the door opened, and Mason's voice called, "Logan? Phone."

"Okay." I had one more thing to do. "Stay away from her," I told Eric. "Delray doesn't know what you did, and if he did, I think he'd have a different opinion of you. Your presence will hurt her. If she wants to see you, she'll come see you. That's on her. That's her right to decide when to deal with you—or not. Let her have that right." I glared down at him once more. "That's the only good thing you can do. Just stay the fuck away."

I left him sitting there. He was nothing to me now.

As soon as I stepped through the door, Mason held his phone out. He glanced behind me. "You're going to make him walk?"

I shrugged. "Message was received. He'll stay away from Taylor now. That's all I wanted."

"Mind if I give him a ride to his car? Make sure he actually leaves?"

"I don't care. He's slime to me. If you want to dirty your car with it, that's fine."

Mason moved around me. "The longer he stays here, the more resentful he might get. I'll feel better if he's as far away from Sam as possible, and from you."

I nodded. This was my big brother doing his big-brother thing. Some of the anger inside me chilled, and I gave him a half-grin. "Thank you."

He nodded. "It's what family does." He pointed to his phone in my hand. "Before I go, give me my phone back."

"Hey." I stopped him. "I have to go find Taylor after this, but call Dad. I don't want to worry about Rankin, and even if Delray's gone, I'll still worry about him." He could get to Taylor. A darkness was in me, twisting, churning, threatening to spill over. "He can't get to her."

Mason held my gaze, studying me. "You know he'll want something in return, right?"

I clenched my jaw. "He can try."

"Okay. I'll give Dad a call." Mason nodded as he went into the garage. I stepped away as I lifted the phone to my ear. "Yeah?"

"Hey. Took you long enough," Nate griped from the other end. "Did you and Mason have a nice chat?"

"Shut up. There are things going on here." I frowned, hearing loud music through the phone. "Where are you?"

"I came back to Pete's," he shouted over the noise. "I wanted to see if the girls came back here or not."

"Girls?"

"Yeah, asshole," he retorted. "Your girlfriend. I came here for you, and that's why I'm calling. Your phone's not on, so you might want to check it, see if there are any messages from Taylor."

"Why?" I reached into my pocket and pulled it out.

"Is she there?"

"No, but the other one is."

"Other one?"

"That friend of hers, the one she left with in the first place. She said she left Taylor at some abandoned amusement park place."

"*What?!*"

Nate sighed heavily into the phone. His voice dipped low. "Look, I know we're bickering like we always do, and I know it's a little worse than normal. That's on me. Everything's changing, and yes, a part of me didn't want you with Taylor because—well—because you've been more my friend than Mason has lately, and I didn't want to lose another friend. But having said all that, I don't know her that well, but she's at the amusement park all alone. Something's not right. So...what I'm saying is, go get your girl, Logan."

And like he said, I went to get my girl.

CHAPTER 30

I FUCKING CARE
TAYLOR

I sensed Logan's approach long before he finally appeared. Sitting on top of that roller coaster, so high above the rest of the world, it's remarkable what you can hear, feel, and see. I saw his Escalade's headlights blocks away before he slowed outside the gate. I had Claire drop me off. She didn't even question why I asked to be dropped off there. I think she was happy to go and deal with her own feelings, away from me, away from the one that had been close to Jason.

"Hey."

I'd been sitting here, feeling Logan's ascent as he climbed. The full moon lit us, but his face was in shadows. I heard caution in his tone and grinned. "You sound scared of me. I didn't think Logan Motherfucking Sex Machine Kade was scared of anything."

He laughed, and the sound was so smooth, so low, so genuine that it washed over me like a warm breeze. Instant tears pricked at my eyes, but I steeled myself. I wouldn't let them fall. I was done with crying over people.

"Can I sit?"

Instead of answering, I scooted. This put me on the outside this time, so the only way off was through him or by plunging to the ground. That thought would have terrified me last time. This time I almost welcomed it. Once Logan sat, I expected questions, concerns, even words that would never comfort. My pain couldn't be eased. I lost another family member.

He didn't say anything, though I glanced over to find him watching me steadily.

"What?" I asked.

One of his eyebrows lifted. "Okay, I know this is the part where I'm supposed to ask you what's wrong. You're supposed to tell me, probably break down in tears, and then we express our undying lust for each other. You're also supposed to somehow straddle me, and we have amazing hot sex."

"I'm sensing a but?"

"But..." I could hear bitterness even as he laughed. It mirrored what I was feeling. "I don't do that shit. I don't follow rules or guidelines. I do my own fuck-ups, thank you. So..." He lifted an arm around me, resting it on the back of the car as his hand traced circles on my shoulder. He leaned back, kicking his leg up to rest on the front end of the car. He looked completely relaxed and let out a deep breath. "I already told you my dad used to be a major whore. Surprising fact: He's no longer married, and he's been the most committed partner ever. It's sad that she's a psychotic, evil bitch. I'm sure you'll meet her one of these days. Apologies ahead of time. But that's not the point of me filling the silence right now. I want to tell you something about me."

"Logan." I shifted toward him. My hand went to his leg.

He shook his head. "Nope. I'm telling you. You're going to have deal with it."

I smiled again, and this time it didn't fade so quickly. The more Logan talked, the more his words and voice soothed me, helping the world go away. I scooted down to rest my head in the crook of his shoulder. I felt safe there.

"This happened a long, long time ago, and it's not a great story. It actually pretty much sucks, but for some reason I feel compelled to tell you." He stuck out his bottom lip. "My parents got divorced when I was still pretty young. To be honest, I don't remember a time when they were happy. I'm sure they were once. I'm sure there are memories, but I can't remember any."

"This is the story?"

He patted my shoulder. "Patience, Firecracker. I'm getting to it."

Another warm sensation flooded me. "Okay."

"So my parents divorced, but that wasn't the part that sucked. It was the before part, when they were still together."

My chest tightened. "Logan," I murmured.

He ignored me and kept going. "My mom was a closet alcoholic. I think she started drinking because of my dad's cheating, or maybe he started cheating because of her drinking. I don't know what came first. I'm sure Mason does, but we don't talk about those years much. Neither of us wants to remember. It sucked. It majorly sucked. It was like living in a house where you know there's something dead."

He looked out over the city for a moment. "We were there. It was supposed to be our home, but it was just walls. The house was huge, so we had a lot of stuff, but it was empty. I could never shake the feeling that something was wrong. Mason loved me. I knew that. But from my dad, even my mom—I never felt anything. I know now that they do love me. They've showed it in different ways. Like, my mom moved back to Fallen Crest, and I lived with her for a year before graduating. If we ever need her, she'll always fly in, no questions asked. That's nice. And my dad, he's been trying more lately. He's committed to Sam's mom, so I know he loves her, and he's helped me a few times. He bailed me out last year so I didn't get expelled, and he's helping with… Well, he tries to show his love, so maybe that'll come in a few years. I don't know. I don't have much hope for a real relationship with my dad, you know?"

I listened to him, and the more he said, the farther my heart sank, even though Logan sounded almost cheerful.

"I remember one time when I was little," he added, his voice wistful. "It was Christmas Day, and this was at the end so Christmas was a joke. My mom usually passed out by the afternoon. My dad was always at the office, or with some woman. And Mason was usually pissed off. I always knew he was mad at Mom and Dad, but he was mad at what they were doing to me, too. That's the part that always gets me: He was mad because of me. He worried about me. I might not have grown up with a happy or loving mom and dad, but I grew up with him. He loved me. He was like my mom and dad all together, and he never treated me the way a regular brother might. Some older siblings don't want shit to do with the little brother. Mason was never like that."

He shook his head. "In some ways, I think I had it better than him. If Mom and Dad did love each other once, he experienced that. But he lost it. I never had it. I'm only a year younger, but I guess that year makes a different. I don't know if I'm making sense. I just—I had him to raise me, and he had no one to raise him. Mason raised himself. It's why he hates adults so much. He's gotten less angry since Sam came into his life. She's helped ground him, and she loves him back. They're good for each other like that."

He trailed off again, lost in thought. I slid my hand into his and prompted, "You started to say something about a Christmas morning?"

"Oh, yeah." He squeezed my hand, resting his head on top of mine. "It was weird, now that I'm thinking about it, because it wasn't normal. I was up early. My mom was sober. Mason was sleeping in. Our dad must have been already gone. But there was this peaceful feeling in the house. It was like we got a break, just for that morning. No one was mad. No one was hurting. No one was lying. There was no anger. I mean, it came in a few hours, but not that morning. I remember going to look at the presents. I sat down in front of the tree, just looking. I thought it was so pretty. I liked looking at them because it made me feel normal—like I had a normal family, a normal holiday. I knew it wasn't real, but I liked to escape there. My mom came into the living room with me that morning. She brought hot chocolate and cookies, and she sat down with me and looked at the tree."

I moved so I could look up at him. A smile played over his face as he spoke.

"She asked what I was doing, and I lied. I said I was planning which present to steal. Usually she'd get mad, send me to my room or something. I never cared. It was better to be alone than hear the anger take your mom away, you know? But that morning, she didn't believe me, or she chose to ignore me, and she nudged me and pointed at one of the ornaments. 'What do you see there?' she asked me."

He shook his head, as if he were back in that room talking to his mother. "'It's a baseball ornament,' I said. And she replied, 'No, it's one piece.' I didn't know what she was talking about, but she pointed to another ornament and said the same thing. That one was a picture of Mason in a frame, but she said it was the second piece. She kept going until she'd pointed out all of them. When she was done, she turned to me and asked, 'When you put all those pieces together, what do you see?'"

He laughed, shaking his head. "I thought I was so smart. I answered, 'A bunch of stupid-looking ornaments?' But she said, 'A life. Each of these ornaments signifies a memory. Look at them individually and you only see a small section. It's like a puzzle. But when you put them all together...'" He raised his hands. "And she lifted her hands up like this, showing me the entire tree, and said, 'This tree is our life story. All together it's a masterpiece. And some day, you'll go off and start your own tree. You'll start making a whole new masterpiece.'"

"Logan," I said softly.

He shook his head, his eyes hooded. "She told me she liked to stare at our Christmas tree, too, because it reminded her of our family's story, and that always helped her. I didn't know *what* it helped her with, and I don't know if it *continued* to help her—I'm guessing not—but that morning, I had my mom. And it felt damn good. I got a little glimmer of what it's like to feel a mother's love."

He looked at me then. "I don't really know what you're going through right now. You lost your mom, your ex-boyfriend is a jackass, your dad's MIA, and I know your two best friends have left you high and dry. One left you in the literal sense."

I closed my eyes. I didn't want to see the pain on his face. It was hidden in the deepest places where only someone who felt a similar pain could sense it. I did, and it brought up all my turmoil once again.

"Taylor," he said.

He'd never felt his mother's love except for that one morning. I'd felt my mother's love so many times. So many mornings she'd woken me with pancakes for breakfast, made me a sack lunch even when I didn't want it, proudly displayed my school pictures on the wall, went to any competition I was in. The tears were starting. I didn't fight them anymore.

"I've heard people talk about you, and your 'family'," I told him. "Your brother, Sam, even Nate. I overheard some girls in the library talking about you, and they were jealous. You guys are so close, so tight-knit, and your walls are so high. No one can break 'em down, and no one can climb over."

His hand squeezed mine.

"I heard those girls saying that stuff, and I thought, even though I'd just lost my mom—and dad in a way—I was lucky. I had Jason and Claire, even though I know Claire isn't that great of a friend, but I was actually kinda happy. You and I became friends—maybe more than friends—and I felt good. But now…" I clung so tightly to his hand. "I feel like I only have you, and I don't even know what this is. Jason left, and I lost one more person in my life."

He didn't say anything, and I wasn't looking at him anymore, but I felt him turn to me.

"I can't cling to you," I said.

"Taylor—" he started.

I shook my head, forcing myself to let go of his hand. "I'm in a place right now that's not good, and I'm not going to be one of those girls who pretends this is more than it is."

"Wait a minute—"

I had to be strong. I had to shut it down, shut him down. "It's like I'm in a tornado right now, and instead of having something solid to cling to, I'm holding on to a tree branch. It'll break, and it'll be destroyed, and I will, too. Whatever this is, you and me, I can't destroy it. I can't."

"You want space? Is that what you're saying?"

"I want..." I would not break down. That was all I could focus on, but I forced myself to say, "I don't want space, but I need it."

I finally looked up and saw a stricken look in his eyes. I'd surprised him. *Good*, I thought. There was no hurt. I hadn't made him feel pain. "I need—I can't hold on to you right now," I continued. "I can't destroy whatever we have. I can't do that, Logan."

He turned away and gazed out over the city. After a beat, his jaw hardened. "That's bullshit."

And there it was. The backlash. "Logan, I—"

"I fucking care about you. I told you about my mom. I told you about Mason. I don't let people in, and I let you in."

"Logan..."

"No—" He launched himself out of the car, rocking it a little with the sudden movement. He glared at me. "I'm not being conceited. That's not what I'm doing here, but I let you in, Taylor. So many people want in, but *you* got in. You got in when my last girlfriend tried for an entire year to get in, and she didn't. But you did. You!"

"Logan—" Letting him go now meant he couldn't walk from me later. *This was for the best. We would've ended anyway. Everything ended. Everyone walked away.*

His nostrils flared. His hands curled into fists. He shook his head. "So because you surrounded yourself with shithead friends means I'm getting the boot? That's fucked up, Taylor. Fucked. Up."

"I can't." My voice was a whisper. "I'm not doing this to hurt you. I'm doing this to prevent even more hurt later on. Don't you see that?"

"What?" He leaned down, bracing his hands on the car's door. His eyes stared directly into me. "You're wrong. You're so completely and fucked-up wrong. I live, Taylor." He pointed to his chest. "I don't turn shit off and hide. I live, and if that means going at the storm, I'll go. I don't hold back. I don't flinch. I never second-guess. I do life. Otherwise, why the hell are we alive? Why are we here if we let our demons win? They don't give a shit. They're off doing their thing. You should, too. You've been through the fire already. Why are you still afraid? There's no way in hell I'm going to let some 'less than' experience I had rule how I live the rest of my life. Whatever. Fuck you, Taylor. Fuck off. Oh, by the way, I took care of your jackass for you. He should leave you alone."

And then he was gone.

I closed my eyes and knew it was done. I'd tried to walk away clean, but whatever I'd had with Logan Kade had been destroyed anyway, at my hand. I drew in a ragged breath. Fully alone now, I let the tears come.

Everyone left.

He would've gone, too. Eventually.

It was better to be broken now than beyond repair later.

CHAPTER 31

ASSCHEEKS & CUPCAKES
LOGAN

Nate was in bed when I pushed open his door, flipped his lights on, and threw some clothes at him. "Get up."

"What?" He jerked upright. His hand lifted, the fist formed already, but he relaxed when he saw it was me. He rubbed at his eyes. "Logan? What are you doing?"

"Whatever our problem is, I don't care. I need a drinking buddy, and Mason's all curled up with Sam. You're it."

He picked up the shirt I'd tossed on his bed and glared. "Gee. How could I resist that invitation?"

I chucked a pair of his jeans over from his chair and paced as he dressed. I needed more than a drinking buddy. I need a friend, and I needed someone who wouldn't make me feel like shit because I wanted to screw three different girls tonight. Mason would have the damn I-know-you're-hurting-but-is-this-really-smart? look on his face, and Sam would press her lips together and look away if she saw me heading off with a chick in hand. Neither of them understood that a good climax was the best escape at times.

Nate did, so Nate it was.

"All right." Nate followed me out the door, running a hand through his hair.

He'd put on the shirt I gave him, but I could see now that it was ripped at the bottom. He looked ready to tear down the city. That was what I needed.

"I'm here, and where are we going?" he asked.

Downstairs, I pushed open the door, tossing and catching my keys in the air. "Blaze has a party."

He grunted, following me to my Escalade. "Blaze always has a party. Does that kid sleep?" But when we got there, the house was dark.

"What the fuck?" Nate wondered.

I was about to text Blaze when the front door opened, and he darted toward the car, his hands in his pockets and his shoulders hunched forward. He climbed into the backseat and waved.

"Hey, guys."

"Dude." Nate twisted around. "Where's the party?"

"What?"

I pointed to the house. "Where's the party?"

"Oh." He laughed. "No way. Not at my house. I know *of* a party. That's what I said." He propped his hands on the back of our seats. "But I have to warn you. This party is a little sketch."

"Sketch?" Nate asked.

"Yeah. There might be hard-core people there. So…" He looked at us. "I mean, we don't have to go. We can go somewhere else."

Nate looked at me. "Some girls from Pete's Pub told me about a party. We could go there instead."

"Wait." Blaze's eyebrows pinched together. "What's wrong with my party?"

"Define 'sketch people,'" I said. I was pretty sure he wasn't talking our crowd.

"Oh. Uh… I don't know. Harder drugs, if you know what I mean."

"Yeah," I said dryly, turning the vehicle onto the street. "That's what I figured, and sorry, pal. We do not need to be hanging with the local crime circuit."

"Huh?"

I ignored him. "Nate, where's the other party?"

"Asking now," he muttered, already typing on his phone. A few blocks later, it buzzed. "Ah-ha. It's not far, and the girls are down to get dirty, if you know what I mean."

"Show me the address." Once he did, I took a sharp left turn. In between telling me where to turn, Nate and Blaze started to talk. Normally, I was a connoisseur of bullshitting, but this time, I tuned them out. I had other things in my head, or other people.

Taylor wouldn't leave me alone. Her face kept flashing in my mind—the way she'd looked when I first saw her up on that roller coaster. She'd looked so small and defeated, but there was still a look of defiance on her face. Like the world sat on her shoulders, but she was ignoring it because she didn't want to let it push her into the ground.

She was strong like that. She wasn't an in-your-face kind of strong. She was quiet, but sturdy. The kind of strong that you didn't know was there until you pushed up against it, and it threw you back on your ass.

Pain sliced through me as I remembered how I'd gone to her. I'd thought I could share a few stories, let her know everything would get better, and she'd be happy. Nope. I was the one bounced back on my ass. She was cold and locked up. I hadn't read the signals correctly. Nate had told me I was hardened about letting new people in, but I had nothing on Taylor. She was made of ice. It was shiny and pretty, but it was thick. I could see her through it, so I didn't even realize it was there until too late. Taylor was the hardened one, and I don't even think she knew how much.

"Hey, right there." Nate tapped my arm and pointed to a house at the end of the block.

Finally. I had a huge fucking knot tied up inside of me. At the sight of the party, I felt a little relief—like a knife had swiped at the knot, cutting away some of the tension. I was about to embrace my inner manwhore, and I wasn't going to have any regrets about it. The first chick who hit on me, I was pulling her to a room.

"Logan, you look ready to tear into someone," Blaze commented as we walked to the house.

I grunted, and Nate narrowed his eyes. I needed to get it together a little. I found them a smile and clapped them on the shoulders, pulling them in for a quick side-hug. "Fellas, you have no idea what night this is."

Blaze frowned.

Nate muttered, "Oh, no."

"No." I shook my head. "No naysayers. No haters. There won't be any of that negativity shit. This is our night, guys. This is the night we remind ourselves we're men."

"Yeah." Blaze pumped a fist in the air.

"I know I'm a man. I don't have to remind myself." Nate stepped away and folded his arms over his chest. "Please don't say we're doing an orgy or a brawl. I don't know if I'm up for that tonight."

Good God, a brawl sounded like fun. I tilted my head to the side, knowing the grin on my face was weirding him out.

Nate shook his head. "Oh man, Logan. What are you planning?"

"Well…" I pulled him back to me and threw my arms around their shoulders again. "I'm planning to screw at least three girls tonight, but the brawl sounds like a good idea, too."

Blaze stopped. "Wait. Seriously? I don't want to fight."

I dragged him with us, propelling us forward until I could kick open the door. A girl stood on the other side, drink in her hand and hunger in her eyes. I didn't know her name, but she said, "Logan! Hey!"

I took in the sight of her: platinum blonde hair, tight shirt showing off her trim waist, and long-ass legs. Her miniskirt hid very little—I loved those. She motioned us inside the house, and as she turned, I could see her asscheeks. They were smooth, firm, and supple. And they were just asking me to touch them.

"Asscheeks and cupcakes," I mused to myself. Oh, how I loved both things. A flicker of the old Logan ignited in me, the one who did what I pleased, who I pleased, and gave no shits about it. That Logan. Single. Carefree. If I wanted to streak later, I sure as shit was going to, and as I took a deep breath, I remembered how much I enjoyed that Logan. He was selfish, and he could indulge as much as he wanted, and this chick with her asscheeks right here to warm his hands was the first one in line. Tonight would be carnal fun.

I dropped my arms from around the guys, and Nate and Blaze moved farther into the house. I stayed behind, and so did the girl. Moving close to her, I looked down, and she grinned up at me. We weren't touching, but one inch closer, and I'd be all over her. I just stared down at her, letting her see how much I wanted to fuck her, and when she saw it, she leaned closer.

"Hi there," she breathed.

Enough with foreplay. "Got a room for us?" I had a quota to fill.

Her eyes widened, and she nodded, clutching her drink. "Yep."

I took the drink from her, finished it in one gulp, and took her hand. "Lead the way."

"Okay." She giggled nervously, and she stumbled as we moved down the hallway. My hand went to her waist to steady her. As she weaved through the crowd with her head down, I watched her. If she were drunk, I'd have to find someone else. I didn't like the wasted girls. I grabbed 'em before they got there, while they could still make decisions. A minute later, another girl fell backward, and Asscheeks ducked away from going down with her like a pro. She was fine. She'd stumbled from nerves.

She was about to sleep with Logan Motherfucking Kade. Why wouldn't she be nervous?

My chest swelled. Girls wanted me to screw them. They'd line up if they could. Guys either wanted to hang out with me, or they wanted to get their faces ripped up by my fists. *This* was my life, not taking some broken chick to my spot, not pseudo kidnapping her ex-boyfriend and interrogating the shit out of him, not working so damn hard at making her smile, and certainly not loving it when she did, thinking it made everything worthwhile. Fuck no. That guy was a sap.

I'd learned a lesson with my first girlfriend, and if Nate thought I was hardened before, he had no idea how thick the wall was now. As I followed the blonde up the stairs and into a room at the end of the hallway, I told myself this was what I'd be doing with girls now. Dick only. No emotions. No heart. No nothing. Just sex.

The girl turned and started to undress.

I couldn't close my eyes. If I did, I knew I'd see Taylor.

"Feel better?" Nate asked two hours later when I joined him at a table out in the backyard.

I glared at him, a drink in my hand. I didn't want to think about it. It had been Taylor in front of me. Taylor I was kissing. Taylor I slid inside of. Taylor making those sounds. Thinking of it now, I downed half of my drink. It burned my throat, but that was good. I needed some searing pain to erase some of that shit.

"Oh, joy." Nate's sarcasm was not subtle. "Look! Another girl's coming over with sex eyes. You going to bang her, too?"

"Fuck you."

"No, Logan." Nate shot forward, glaring at me across the table. "Fuck you."

There were others at the table with us, but whatever they said fell on deaf ears. I wasn't listening. I wasn't there to be social and joke, or play the happy Logan Kade. I was there for one purpose: to get Taylor Bruce out of my head. And it wasn't working. She was still with me. I could feel her beside me. I could see her eyes, and I knew how hurt she would look when she realized what I'd done. I could already feel the disappointment.

Fuck. I finished my drink and shoved back from the table. I needed another one. Knowing the rest of the night would be a drunken stupor, I took out my keys and tossed them to Nate. "You're going to have to drive."

He pocketed them, giving me that knowing look Mason always wore. "Sure," he said. "If you actually go home with me."

"Hey, Logan!" The sex-eyes girl got to the table and leaned her chest toward me. She wasn't there for anyone else—that was obvious. As I looked at her, she tugged her shirt down and licked her lips, the invitation more than clear.

I grinned at her, not even looking at her face. My gaze was trained solely on her rack. They were full. A good C cup, bordering on a D. And even though I wasn't touching them, I knew they'd have good bounce. They were probably fake, but I didn't give a shit. They'd be nice to look at if she rode me.

"Look, I don't know if I can go another round right now," I told her, thinking about that image. "But find me in a couple of hours. Then I can make some magic happen."

She giggled. "Sounds good." She leaned close and whispered, her hand running down my chest. "You can just come home with me. You can have me all night and any way you want. How about that?"

That sounded...empty. Why would she want that? But I flashed her a grin. "Sounds like a plan."

Her hand dropped to my dick, and she pressed against it through my jeans. It was quick, but enough to give me a good preview of the night to come. As she turned to leave, her breasts grazed my arm, and I was right. Firm. They were possibly my new favorite thing after asscheeks. Once she headed back inside, I could feel Nate's gaze on me, and I ignored him.

He knew I was pissed, but he didn't know about what, and he didn't know how deep this burning pain went. It went all the way to the core. That was how far Taylor had gotten in.

"Like I said…" Nate stood up. "That's *if* you're going home with me tonight." He brushed past me, tossing his beer bottle into the trash and heading back inside the house.

I glanced around. Still feeling Taylor—smelling her vanilla scent and hearing the last thing she'd laughed about—I gripped the glass in my hand. I needed shots, and a lot of them.

TAYLOR

After Logan left, I sat up there on that roller coaster for another hour. I stayed until I could finally feel the cold. Before that, I felt nothing. I welcomed something finally slipping inside of me, something other than emptiness.

I climbed down, and I was able to squeeze back through a hole I found in the fence. I sat on the curb, wrapped my arms around my knees, and bent my forehead to rest on my legs. If I could have closed in on myself, I would have. But that position warded off some of the night's chill, so I sat back up. I wanted to feel that. I sat and shivered and waited for the cab I'd called.

I wouldn't be the type of girl who clung to a guy when I was hurting. I wouldn't be that person. Nothing good could come of it. I was broken inside, and even though Logan's *Fuck you* still echoed in my head, I knew this had been the right thing to do.

He'd see that, too. Eventually.

I was still telling myself that when the cab arrived, its lights sweeping over me. And I was still reminding myself when it pulled up at my house. Stepping inside, I dropped my purse by the door and my keys on the counter. I'd been at Logan's, and I'd gotten used to how alive his home was. It was full of people, of life, of love. I perused the darkened entrance hall, then moved to stare at the living room.

Empty.

Dull.

Nothing.

That was what I felt as I stood inside my home.

"Taylor?"

My dad came from the kitchen wearing his plaid robe over pajama pants and a white T-shirt—what he always used to wear at night. He also wore the slippers he always used to wear around the house.

I pointed at them and said hoarsely, "Those stupid things. You're wearing them again."

He looked down and lifted a leg in the air. He laughed. "Oh, yeah. I didn't even think. They were by the nightstand, so I just slipped 'em on. Habit."

I'd given them to him as a Christmas present three years ago. The slipper was a mallard duck, but the green coloring had faded. One had a rip that my mom had tried to stitch up a few months before she died.

"I made that rip," I said through tears. "Mom was carrying them, and one snagged on a nail from the stupid DIY project I was trying to do." I'd been rushing past, in a hurry to meet Eric. The words would hardly come now. "I told her to toss 'em, that I'd buy you a new pair, but she wouldn't listen. She said you loved them. That they were your 'habit' slippers. I didn't know what she meant, but I didn't care. Eric was waiting for me."

My dad laughed, still gazing down at the slipper rather than acknowledging my tears. "Your mom was right. I'd gotten used to them, but I would've loved the new pair, too." He passed by me, patting me on the arm.

I used the back of my hand to wipe my eyes.

Pausing at the steps, he turned back and frowned. "It's almost four in the morning. What are you doing still up?"

Oh, Dad. My heart felt like it had been torn in half. "I had an all-nighter at the library," I said.

"Oh." He nodded. "Good to know. Study hard, Taylor. You always do so well. 'Night, honey."

I hadn't slept at the house in five nights. The library closed at midnight, and he was wearing his mallard duck slippers. I didn't know if I should laugh or cry. Tomorrow was Saturday. My dad would leave because that was what he did, and I wouldn't see him for another few days.

I sat at the bottom of the steps and laughed.

CHAPTER 32

HOLY SHIT!
TAYLOR

"We're going bowling tonight," Jeremy Fuller explained. "It should be fun."

I had the phone tucked between my ear and shoulder. "Mmm-hmmm."

"You're going to come? Professor Gayle will be there. The professors are joining us tonight."

I had been tying my shoelaces during that last part. I planned a quick jog before going to work, but Jeremy's call had caught me by surprise. I answered without looking at who it was and then panicked. For a moment, I'd thought it was Logan calling, but then I recognized the voice.

Jeremy had been calling more and more over the last three weeks. He apologized with the first call, saying he had no right to say what he had against Logan...and I kept quiet on that subject. I knew he knew. Everyone knew, but I couldn't lie that it felt nice to have someone else calling me. Logan, on the other hand, hadn't called or texted. Silence. He didn't sit by me in sociology. He sat with a group of girls in the back of the room instead, but he didn't act like I was a total stranger either. He offered a polite hello and nod once in a while. Each time it was like a knife being shoved into me, then twisted around for maximum pain.

I had no one to blame, and that was my attitude. I'd chosen this, and every time it happened, I reminded myself that in the long run, it would be worth it. I could still walk, talk, and think. I hadn't been reduced to a pile of nothing. I would find a way to get stronger, get through this, though I hadn't known it was possible to feel this alone.

Every time I saw that guarded mask looking my way, I returned the polite greeting, and we moved past each other, like mere acquaintances.

"...you up? If you want."

I shook my head, clearing my thoughts. "I'm sorry. What did you say?"

"Oh, no. That's fine. No worries about it."

"What?" I sat on the edge of my bed with my foot in front of me. I lowered my leg to the floor and sighed. "No, I'm sorry. I was distracted for a moment. What were you saying?"

"Oh." He was quiet for a beat, then he coughed. "Uh. I was offering to pick you up, and don'tworryI'mpickingupsomeotherstoo. It's not just you."

"This is tonight, right?"

"Tonight? Oh, yes. Tonight. Yes."

"I have a shift at Pete's Pub today, but I get off early. I can come later?"

"Did you want me to give you a ride?"

"No. That's okay. I'll drive over myself."

"Great. I'll make sure we stay later, then, till whenever you get there."

"Okay. Perfect. Thanks for the invite, Jeremy."

And I did mean it, I realized after signing off and tucking my phone into my pocket.

It was ten in the morning. I did a few warm-up stretches and started off. I could do three miles, shower, and be at work right on time. As I ran, I thought about the phone call. This bowling was the first social event I'd been invited to in the last month. Jason was still gone, and Claire had stopped talking to me. I didn't know the reason, but I also didn't have the energy to go and find out. If she stayed away, then she stayed away. She hadn't reached out after hearing that whatever I'd had with Logan was done either. And I knew she'd heard. Just walking around campus, I overheard stories about him at parties—who he'd hooked up with, who only gave him a blowjob. I'd heard about a few fights, and how he 'finished' them. His notoriety hadn't weakened since our demise. But then again, no one else seemed surprised by the stories. To them, this was the normal Logan. Manwhore. Partier. Fighter. No wonder he was legendary, as he would've called himself.

I smiled in spite of myself, thinking about that as I turned down another block of houses. I didn't notice the guy at first because I was busy realizing it hadn't hurt as much to think about Logan this time. But then I realized he was near.

His Escalade caught my attention first. Then I saw a guy leaving a house and heading for the street. He moved toward the car, drawing closer as I did the same.

My stomach sank. It was Logan, and as my head turned, he saw me at the same time. His eyes widened before his mask slipped in place in the next instant, but I couldn't react as quickly as him. My mind was whirling. Logan didn't live here. Why would he... It clicked then, and I didn't want to look, but my head moved of its own accord. I stared at the house he'd come from, and I saw a girl there, watching from the window in a skimpy tank top and barely there boy shorts. Seeing me, recognition flooded her eyes, and she disappeared from the window. Her door opened the next second, and she moved out to her front porch, her hands resting on her slim hips.

I came to a stop, not realizing it, until Logan said, "You run?"

"Huh?"

I couldn't tear my gaze from the girl. She had no bra on. Her shirt fell low between her breasts, and they looked abnormally large on her very tiny body. Pain took my breath. God. I had heard the stories, knew he was sleeping around, but seeing it firsthand, the dam I'd had built to contain it all burst open. It flooded me, and I felt dizzy. I almost didn't hear his next statement.

"—figures."

"What?" I pulled out my earbuds, and the music blasted between us. It was jarring, but that went for the whole situation. This wasn't supposed to be happening.

Logan didn't even have his shirt on. It was in his hand, and his jeans rode low over his hips. When he realized I was checking him out, a hard look flashed in his eyes before a smirk appeared. He tossed the shirt over his shoulder and transformed into the cocky Logan Kade so many knew.

I saw this façade, but I also saw through it. I saw the sweet Logan. The Logan who took me to sit on top of a roller coaster so I could see one of the most beautiful views in town. I saw the Logan who'd punched my ex-boyfriend, no questions asked. I saw the Logan that liked to make food for his family, and who took me away from one party to show me what a *real* party was like.

I drew in a shuddering breath.

God.

I looked past the hardened smirk he wore to hurt me. This was the guy who'd brought me back to life. He'd made me feel again, and realizing all of this, tears came to my eyes.

What had I done?

Blood rushed to my face, but somehow it drained from there, too. I was a mess inside because I now knew I'd made the worst mistake of my life.

I'd let him go. Worse, I'd forced him away.

I turned to the girl. She had a smug smirk on her face, similar to Logan's at first glance, but so different. Hers was real. She honestly thought he was hers. But he wasn't. He was mine.

He was supposed to be mine, and I'd lost him. I shook my head.

She wasn't his. If she thought that, she was a fool. I knew, without a doubt, that he'd never date her. Screw her, yes. Date her, not in a million. But as if sensing my thoughts, her smirk grew, and she lifted her chin, daring me.

I started for her, not even thinking about it, but Logan stepped between us. He blocked my view, and once I saw his chest instead of hers—his perfectly shaped and sculpted chest—I jerked backward. I burned, and I wanted to touch him. I wanted to take everything back. I wanted him back. All this screamed inside of me, but I couldn't do anything. Not here. Not like this. It was done.

I forced myself to step away from him, though one step forward and I'd be against him.

"I'm sorry." I heard my voice before I realized I'd spoken.

Logan's hands lifted toward mine. He'd been going to touch me, but at my words, he stopped. His head cocked to the side. "Huh?"

"I'm sorry." I gestured to the girl. "This isn't you. This isn't the real you, and I did this."

His hand ran through his hair. "Taylor—" he started.

I shook my head. He wasn't going to be himself, and I didn't want to hear it. "Don't."

"You seem to be mistake—" he said anyway.

"I'm not," I cut him off. I knew the real him. "You're sweet. You're kind. You want to be loved. You still miss your mom's love. You yearn for a dad who'll choose you over his lover. You want a girl who'll hold your hand on top of a broken roller coaster." I could only whisper the words as they tumbled out now. "You want a partner in crime, but also someone you can protect, and who'll do the same for you."

He didn't say a word, just stared at me with a dumbfounded expression.

I pressed a hand to his stomach. "No one knows the real you, but I do."

A stricken look passed between us, but he still didn't speak.

"I see you." I looked over at the girl. "That's not you. That's not the real you."

He still said nothing, and I didn't want to look up at him. I didn't want to know whether he couldn't talk or didn't want to. I'd said what I needed to say. I just wanted him to know.

Keeping my head low, I stepped back again and put my earbuds in. Then I turned and kept running.

After a few paces, I found an extra bounce in my step. I'd said what I needed to say, and I realized I was okay.

My mom.

Eric.

My dad.

Jason.

Even Claire.

All of them.

I was okay, and that was because Logan had healed me. For that reason alone, I loved him.

I stopped—right there, right then—in the middle of the sidewalk. It was as if I'd hit a cement wall. I gasped for breath, feeling my insides smashed and jumbled up.

I loved Logan.

I couldn't move.

I loved Logan…

I gasped for breath.

Holy shit.

LOGAN

I couldn't move. Fucking hell. Somehow Taylor had just ripped me all the way to my core, and I couldn't even fucking breathe.

"Hey—"

"Stop," I cut the girl off. I didn't want to hear it. She was going to cut Taylor down, and I wouldn't have it.

"What?"

I turned and looked down the sidewalk. Taylor had kept running, but suddenly she stopped. She stood frozen in the middle of the sidewalk. I held my breath. I was exposed and raw, but holy fucking shit—that was what I'd been waiting for. All these damn years, that right there. Just that.

Taylor saw me. She saw through me. She saw into me. She saw me, and she claimed me.

"Logan?"

The girl touched my arm, but I moved away. I didn't want her touch. I'd been revolted by it as soon as I woke up next to her, and I'd slipped out. I hadn't known she was at the window until Taylor looked and saw her.

I wanted to apologize to Taylor. She caught me leaving another girl's bed, but then *she* apologized. She went deep, deeper than anyone else in my life. I was so wrong. I saw her running and instantly wanted to claim her as mine again, but I fought against myself. These days I always fought against myself when it came to her. Every damn time in class I forced myself not to sink into the chair next to her. I forced myself to keep moving. I forced myself to sit with other girls, to hear their annoying come-ons.

That was all I'd been doing the past month, forcing myself to stay away from Taylor, and then she pulls this shit?

She gutted me.

I couldn't move, but I couldn't tear my gaze away from her. I wanted to go after her, ask her why if she could see me she couldn't be with me.

But I didn't. Like every damned day this month, I didn't. I didn't text. I didn't call. I did nothing, and I was starting to hate myself for it. Because I needed to go to her. It was normal to be with her, because she was mine. My insides knew it.

Because she was still mine, just like I was hers.

Fucking hell. I was in love with her.

I was in love with Taylor Bruce.

Fucking…hell…

"Logan." The girl lifted her hand again to touch me. I saw it coming and stepped aside, evading her. She let out a frustrated sound, but said, "Your phone is ringing."

"What?" I looked at her. "What'd you say?"

She pointed to my pocket. "Your phone is ringing, and I'm pretty sure that's your brother. It's the same ringtone from when he called you last night."

I closed my eyes, wanting to scream at the girl because she was the one in front of me, but I didn't. That'd be an asshole thing to do, and my asshole limits were set at sleeping with girls, not taking anything else out on them. I heard the ring this time, and I pulled out my phone and answered. "Yeah?"

"You need to get back."

"Why? What's going on?"

"Because Dad just called," Mason said. "He said he reached out. Rankin won't be a problem. I don't know how he did it or what he did, and we're not supposed to ask questions, but he did it. Rankin is supposed to stay away."

I waited. I knew Mason had something else to deliver.

And then, he did. "And he's coming to town. He's calling in his favor."

CHAPTER 33

LOVE YOU BACK, FIRECRACKER
TAYLOR

I couldn't run anymore after that realization, but eventually I could move again. I ended up walking back to the house, but when I went inside, I just stood there. Nothing made sense. I had no idea what to do. The door shut behind me, but I barely heard it. My keys fell from my hands, clattering to the floor.

I loved Logan.

I couldn't—I loved him. I hadn't thought I could love again.

A dazed cloud settled on top of me, but my mind was spinning at the same time. I wanted to shout and throw my hands in the air, then I wanted to shed more tears. All at once. I was all over the place, so I sat down.

Right where I was. In the middle of the front entryway, I crossed my feet over my lap, and I leaned forward. I...I loved Eric. Or I had. It felt like all my life he'd been at my side. He was my best friend in elementary school, my crush in junior high, and my boyfriend for the next four and a half years. He was going to be my partner for life, and he'd taken my heart with him when he left me.

Or so I thought.

I couldn't...I couldn't believe it. And then a wave of yearning crushed me. I wanted someone to talk to. Jason...he was gone. The person I really wanted to talk to was my mom. And she was gone, too. I wrapped my arms around my knees and rocked back and forth. She would've been ecstatic for me. She would've hugged me, told me to go after whoever made me happy, and she would've waved in the window as I left to do just that.

She should've been here. "Mom," I whispered.

"What did you say?"

I looked up to see my dad standing there with a cup of coffee in one hand and a book in the other. "You're home." I had to blink a few times before it processed in my head.

He frowned. "Yeah. Why wouldn't I be?"

"You're never home."

"Oh." The frown deepened, and his chest lifted as he took in a breath. "Um. Okay."

He put his book on the stand, took a sip of his coffee, and placed the mug next to it. He took a step toward me and folded his hands behind his back.

"Yes. I know I've been…" His hand tugged at his collar before it went back behind his back. "…absent for the last few months."

"You think?" I retorted. I grabbed the ends of my shirt and fisted my hands around it, stretching it tight. It was becoming harder to breathe, and a hot and burning feeling started in my chest. "Why are you home?" I asked.

"Honey…" He stepped back, his eyes closed. "I'm sorry, Taylor."

"You're sorry?" I couldn't have heard that right. "For what? For not being around? For not helping with Mom's funeral plans? For not being here, ever? What *exactly* are you sorry for?"

"Honey—"

"Stop." I stood up, shoving off from the floor. "I don't want your apology."

"Taylor—"

I shook my head. God. I could see it all over him. He felt bad. His face was filled with regret. He wanted to take everything back. I saw all of it, and none of that helped. "Don't." My voice dropped. "You can't take anything back."

He looked at me, drawing in a deep breath. His lips pressed together before he said, "I've not been here for you..."

I kept shaking my head. He had no idea. None at all. "I lost my mom, and you. I lost *both* of you."

"Taylor, I...you're right. I can't take it back."

I held up a hand, stopping him again. "Why are you here today?"

"We don't have a game, and..." He scanned my face, seeming hesitant to say his next words. They came out in a rush. "I got tired. I got tired of hiding and avoiding. I did leave this morning. I was going to stay at the arena all day, but no one was there." His head hung low. "I couldn't think of a reason to stay away, so I came home."

A guttural laugh ripped through me. I didn't know how to take this. He was my father, and he'd left me high and dry.

But he lost me, too, honey. A lump formed in my throat. I could hear my mom in my head. Even now, even gone for so long, I knew she would've been forgiving. She would want me to forgive, too.

"You weren't there for me," I said, my voice hoarse.

"I know." His eyes shut tight and his forehead wrinkled. "I am so, so sorry, Taylor. I really am. I...it sounds stupid when I say it out loud, but I woke up today. I've been...escaping takes a lot of work, I've realized. I need to use that energy for something else, so I'm here. I'm not leaving tonight, tomorrow. I'll be home in the evenings. I really will. You and me, it'll be like we're father and daughter again. Not—"

"—roommates?" I supplied.

He stopped, and his shoulders slumped. It was like I'd taken whatever oomph he'd had in him. My father was gone.

I was staring at a husband who'd lost his wife, and seeing him that way, I understood the grief still there. They'd been best friends and soulmates. He lost his other half. I could see the battle and how it weighed on him. A knot formed in me, and seeing my father as a man, not just as my dad, made it even tighter. It was bittersweet, and it was necessary.

"I'm sorry, too, Dad," I whispered.

His eyes lifted, haunted. "I'm so sorry, Taylor. I really am."

I had to say some things, and I knew they were going to hurt him, but if I held my feelings in, they would never leave me. "I'm angry at you."

"Oh, honey. I know. And you have every right to be."

I shook my head. I wasn't done. "I'm angry at you for so many reasons, but mostly I'm angry at you because you haven't been around." I flinched, remembering what I'd said. "Your daughter shouldn't be your roommate. Ever." He was supposed to be here. "You were supposed to hold my hand at the funeral." He made sure someone else sat between us. "You were supposed to hug me when we buried her." He stood on the other side of the casket. "You were supposed to tell me everything would be okay." Never. I hadn't known if it would be or not. "I get it. You're mourning her, too, but so am I. I wanted to mourn *with* you, *beside* you, *together*. Instead I lost you too. I'm not supposed to lose *both* of you—not when one of you is still walking, talking, breathing. Not when you're right here in front of me."

"Taylor," he whispered, tears falling down his face.

"We don't talk. I don't talk. I learned that from you and Mom dying, we need to talk about that. We have to talk about her. We have to just talk, Dad."

"I know. You're like me. Your mother was the talker. She made everything better for us, but you're right. We need to talk more." He tried to smile, but couldn't. He nodded instead.

"Are you going to be okay?"

At that question, a ragged breath left him, and he shook his head. I was staring at a battered man. I saw the bags under his eyes, the wrinkles I never noticed before. There were extra lines around his mouth, and his entire face seemed to hang loose. The skin sagged where it had been tight before. He aged ten years.

"I'm going to try," he finally said. He looked at me. "For you."

I nodded. That was the best answer I could have received. "Okay."

We stood there together, and nothing more needed to be said—at least, not for a while. I could feel her. She stood with us, smiling. I knew my mother wanted us to be a family again. It'd happen.

Love you, Mom.

Love you back, Firecracker.

LOGAN

Mason's head appeared over the roller coaster as he made his way to where I sat in the car at the top of the track. So much for this being a secret. He finished his ascent, I could see him looking around, a slight frown on his face.

I had to laugh.

Mase called and said our dad wanted to meet up for a later dinner. The favor he wanted had to be done in-person and that meant it was a big one, one we wouldn't be happy about. That was like issuing a challenge. Usually I'd pounce on that shit like a starving lion. Challenge accepted. A month ago, I would've shoved through those doors, walked into the room like I owned it, and ripped into our dad. Fuck. A day ago I'd have had the same response. But not today. Today I came here.

This day...was so much not like the rest.

"What..." Mason paused next to the car door. "...the fuck are you doing up here?"

I grinned, leaning back. "I usually come at night." I gestured to the view. "The entire city's out there."

"It's dangerous, Logan." He eyed the empty seat next to me. "That's safe, right? I mean, you wouldn't be up here if it wasn't... right?"

I scooted over and patted the seat. "All warm and cozy for you."

He groaned, but climbed inside. "Tell me I'm the best big brother you got." He grimaced. "I fucking hate heights."

"You'll never jump out of a plane." I cocked my head to the side, teasing. "You'll never experience a high-ropes course."

He frowned. "Fucking A. I can't even think about some of that shit."

I was just getting started. "You'll never go parasailing. You'll never zip-line anywhere...ever." That one did suck. "Holy shit, Mase. What the hell are you going to experience in life? You may as well shrivel up and die now." I laughed and slapped him on the back. "Does Sam know?"

He gripped the bar in front of us, but threw me a half-smile. "That I'm your big brother?"

"That you'll never be an extreme sports junkie. Her dream of making love on the side of a cliff will never come true." I patted my chest. "You know, a year ago I would've offered to fill in for you, but—" The joke died. I didn't have it in me. I liked to get a rise out of him, but my spark was gone. Taylor had snuffed that out. Pretending to hit on Sam no longer gave me joy.

"Shut the fuck up." His eyes flashed a warning. "I'm here. I'm sitting on a Goddamn roller coaster ride— one that I'm sure Dad would have a heart attack if he knew we were on."

I laughed. "I don't actually ride. I just come up here and sit. It's peaceful." It used to be peaceful. I remembered finding Taylor here, weeks ago. Alone. I could see her tears, hear the sadness in her voice. Dammit. I could smell her all over again. That damn vanilla scent.

"Are you done making me feel like a pussy?"

I looked at my brother and nodded. "Yeah."

"Okay." He rubbed his forehead. "Can we have this talk on the ground? Why'd you make me come up here?"

I shrugged. "This is my thinking spot."

"You can think just fine down there." He leaned forward to peek below us, then jerked back, cursing under his breath. "I love you, but right now some of that is fading—fast." He made a circling motion. "Let's get this conversation going. What's going on with you?"

Well, there was no reason to beat around the bush. "I'm in love."

Mason said nothing.

And nothing.

Still nothing.

I looked over and lifted an eyebrow. "You going to say something?"

He was watching me steadily, but there was no reaction on his face. I couldn't read him. He moved his arm to rest on the back of our seat, lifted his hand, and smacked the back of my head. "You're just now figuring this out?"

"Hey." I shoved his arm off the back. "What was that for?" I scowled. "You knew?"

"Everyone knows."

"Everyone?"

He nodded. "Me. Sam. Nate."

"Nate did not know."

"Why do you think he's been an asshole to you? He knew before I did. He's pissed because he's losing his bar buddy." Mason shifted to sit sideways, facing me. His arm rested on the back of the seat again, and he leaned forward. "You've not been yourself. You're more serious. You don't want to screw everything— except for the last month, but that's because she sent you down the highway."

"What highway?"

"The road." He motioned ahead of us. "You know what I mean. She sent you packing."

I shook my head. "You need better metaphors."

"Whatever," he said. "I'm not the funny one, remember? That's your job."

"Trust me, I'm well aware. I'm hilarious."

Mason bit out a laugh. "You fell in love, Logan."

I slumped down and cringed. Fucking hell. Love. "Love's for pussies."

He coughed.

I shot him a sideways look. "Yeah, you're a pussy."

His hand moved faster than I could react, and he slapped me on the back of the head again.

I groaned. I didn't even argue.

"Look, I've not approved of your choices. Tate was a royal bitch."

"She was a whore," I added.

His head moved up and down. "Yeah, she was that, too, and Kris..." He shook his head. "She was too young. She had too many issues, and you—"

I looked out over the city as I said, "—didn't love her."

"Yeah. There's that."

He sighed.

I sighed.

This was a fucking sigh-worthy event.

"I don't want to be in love," I announced.

"Well. You are so deal with it, or lose her. Those are your two options." He turned to look out of the car with me. Only I wasn't seeing the city laid out beneath us. I wasn't seeing anything except Taylor, how she looked on that sidewalk. She'd been running, and I wanted to hurt her, like the dipshit I was. I wanted to hurt her, and she saw right through me.

"You're sweet. You're kind. You want to be loved." I could hear her voice. She was so strong, so sure—like she had a secret no one else knew, one the entire universe wanted to know. *"You want a girl who'll hold your hand on top of a broken roller coaster. You want a partner in crime..."*

And that girl I fucked—I didn't remember her name. She was forgotten as soon as I woke up, and if I passed her on the street, I wouldn't recognize her. But she came forward to stake her claim, and Taylor stopped her.

There hadn't even been a chance for a battle. *"That's not you,"* Taylor had said. *"That's not the real you."*

"Fuck," I muttered.

She'd touched me, and my hand moved there now, resting on my stomach. *"I see you,"* she'd said.

I groaned, closing my eyes. "What do I do?"

I felt my brother look at me, and he said, so simply, "You go get her."

CHAPTER 34

I HAD HIM
TAYLOR

King Cain Bowl had been partially renovated in the last few years, but as I entered the front lobby, I smelled the same musk that I remembered from childhood: thick, red shaggy carpet; the smell of old, worn shoes; the aroma of burnt popcorn; and teenage sweat. All of that hit me as I walked inside, and I was instantly comforted. Some things never changed.

The front desk sat a half-level below the lanes. The wall was open so I could see shoes going back and forth when I went to pay. Sounds of bowling balls hitting the floor and slamming into the pins mixed with loud music, talking, and laughter. It was busier than I remembered. Then again, I got off early from my shift, so it was close to seven thirty. It was prime time for some bowling magic.

"Size seven." The clerk put my shoes on the counter.

I wasn't sure how many games we'd be playing, so I looked around for Jeremy, but before I could spot him, I turned to see Claire coming in the front doors behind me. And my stomach dropped. Eric was behind her.

I locked up. Everything. All my insides. "What are you doing here?" I asked just as I heard "Hey!" from my left.

Jeremy was coming down the stairs from the lanes. His hand was lifted in a wave, but not for me. He grinned at Claire. As he paused and followed her eyes to me, his smile changed, but it didn't disappear.

Claire paused, coming no closer, but she glanced sideways at Eric. She frowned, her hands folded in front of her.

I looked at Eric. "What are you doing here?" It'd been almost eleven months since that day, and as I stared at him now, I no longer knew him.

"Okay. Here goes." His shoulders lifted with a deep breath. "I came to apologize, because…" He glanced around to Jeremy and Claire before focusing on me again. "I'm sorry, Taylor. I'm sorry that I didn't protect you. I don't know what happened to me that day, but I'm sorry I let you down. I'm sorry I didn't protect you. I'm sorry I didn't stay."

"What?"

He nodded. Disappointment. Shame. Guilt. Regret—all of those emotions filled his face. "I couldn't live with what I did. I know Jason told you I went back to school, but I didn't."

"What?" This wasn't making sense.

Eric lifted a shoulder. "I've been hiding this last year. Jason called me. He told me that you might need me."

"Jason knew you were here?"

He nodded. "I thought he'd hate me, too, but I never told him what I did. I should've, though. I should've just for you, but it was obvious you hadn't told him too and," he glanced away, his Adam's Apple bobbing up and down before he looked back. "I was a coward. I've been a coward this whole time, but I can't anymore, though. That's why I came tonight. I'm going back to school. I'm going up there to see if I can get back in, and I'm going to stay put, find an apartment. I'm going to stop hiding."

This guy had been my first love—my first everything—my best friend, my lover. And I…was speechless. I stared at him now, and all the hate that I thought I would've felt was gone. I felt nothing.

"Oh."

Claire and Jeremy were there. I could feel their gazes at what should've been a touching goodbye scene, or a meeting where I could finally let him have it. He left me to die, but there was nothing there. The only thing I could think about was Logan.

Eric left me, and Logan hadn't.

Logan never hesitated. He didn't run away. He never left me. He ran toward the action. He fought for me. He *fought* for me. He—Goddamn, I couldn't breathe. I had someone who ran toward me, not away from me.

He never left me…

I was an idiot. A Goddamn stupid idiot.

"What am I doing here?"

"What?"

I shook my head. Claire moved closer to me, so did Jeremy. I knew they were all confused, but I didn't care. What was I doing?

"I have to go."

"Wha—where?" Eric glanced around. "I'm apologizing here."

"I know." I frowned, pushing past him. "I don't care." Then I was out the door and hurrying toward my car. I had to find Logan. Why did I wait? I knew I loved him. I knew I had to find him.

I was at my car—

—then I heard the shout, "GUN!"

LOGAN

I saw her.

I saw her car first and pulled mine over, then I saw Taylor hurrying out of the bowling alley. I sat back, letting the image of her wash over me. Goddamn. She was beautiful. I was going to go over there. I was going to make a speech. I'd grovel. I'd beg. I'd do whatever, but I was going to get her back, but then--no.

I saw him then and time slowed.

She was almost to her car. She was digging for her keys. She was stopping so she could unlock the door—and the guy was coming toward her.

Black hoodie. He was hunched over, his hands in his front pocket. I couldn't see his face. It was hidden by his hood, and then one of his hands came out.

I saw the gun—and time completely stopped.

No. That didn't make sense. This was a bowling alley—in a nice part of town, a safe area. My family's dinner was just a block over, in a five star restaurant.

This wasn't happening—the blood was pumping through me and my vision began to blur. Not Taylor. Not her—he moved forward, bringing the gun across his body. Taylor turned her back to him, opening her door so she could climb inside.

No! It wasn't happening. I was out my vehicle and sprinting across the street. I was on his right, but he hadn't seen me. He kept his head down, but as he raised the gun, he glanced up and to the side.

"GUN!" I yelled. "No!"

I sprinted for him, and time snapped back and sped up. I couldn't lose her, not when I was just about to get her back. Nothing could stop that.

I raced the rest of the way as the guy looked around. My eyes met the gunman's, and forget that my heart was in my throat, it was now stuffed all way into my mouth. The gunman was Rankin. Seeing me, there was a split second of surprise, followed by resolve. He knew I was going to stop him, but he was going to do it anyway. The asshole was going to kill her anyway.

He started to turn for her again. I couldn't see Taylor. I couldn't take my eyes off Rankin. If I did, I'd lose her.

"*Get down!*" I yelled as the gun went off—*Boom!*

It was louder than I expected. Not like fireworks at all. Then the air was veiled, like a blanket had been thrown over me. I couldn't move fast enough. The gun went off again, and it was like thunder exploding in my ear.

I never stopped.

I crashed into Rankin, and he turned, ready for a fight, but I body-checked him. I ducked, wrapped my arms around his waist, and threw him to the ground. The gun fell from his hand, and I yelled as I lifted my fist, "Get the gun!" I didn't know who I was yelling at. I was just yelling, but then I was fighting.

Rankin twisted, hoping to dislodge my hold, but I was on top of him. As he struck my face, I evaded, knocked his arms to the side, and rained punches down on him. Hit after hit, I kept making contact. I wanted this bastard so far gone, he couldn't fight back, and as I kept going, he finally stopped resisting.

But I couldn't stop. I heard the gunshot. He wanted to hurt Taylor. That was all I knew. The blood thirst was too much, and I never would've stopped. I would've killed the guy if someone hadn't yanked me off of him.

I struggled against the hold until I heard Mason's voice in my ear. "He's done, Logan. He's done. The ex-boyfriend got to her too. He grabbed her and turned his back. He took the bullet, Logan. Not her. She's safe."

My brother. The ex-boyfriend. His words started to sink in, but my heart was still pounding. My job wasn't done. Taylor. I shoved out of his arms and whipped around.

"She's safe." He turned me so I could see her, huddled inside the bowling alley. "We were coming back for you when we saw it go down. She's inside. She's safe."

I felt myself nodding, but then I was running. "Taylor!" I yelled, my feet swallowing the space between us.

She saw me coming and tore away from whoever was patting her arm. Someone stopped her at the door, but I tore through it, knocking people down. I was there. She was there, and she was in my arms.

I lifted her, my arms around her, and carried her away. I didn't know where I was going, but I kept going until there was no one else.

Once we were alone, a door closed behind us, and I looked at her, holding her face. "Holy shit." I breathed as I kissed her. I needed to know she was okay. Or I needed to reassure myself that I was okay. I didn't know which one—both, and so much more. I loved this woman. Holy shit, I loved her with everything in me.

She responded to my kiss, climbing against me, and I lifted her again. Her legs wound around my waist, and I pressed her into a wall. I pulled back just enough to double-check she was all there. She smiled up at me, her face flushed and her eyes beaming. So bright. So alive. I touched the side of her face. "I love you."

I saw her love swim to the surface then, too. She nodded. "I love you, too."

I rested my forehead to hers. "You're okay?"

"I'm okay."

She looked down and lifted one of my hands to inspect my knuckles, which were bloody and raw. "Are you okay?"

My hands would be sore in an hour. It was worth it. I tucked her hair behind her ear and cupped her face again. "If you'd—" I struggled to say the words. I didn't even want to think them. I gulped for breath. "Fuck, Taylor. If you'd—if he had—"

"He didn't. He got Eric—" She choked up. "Eric—"

She pulled back, starting for the door.

I couldn't let her go. The guy saved her, and I'd thank him later, but for now, I just needed her. "Taylor."

She looked up and saw my torment. Her face softened. She held both sides of my face and pressed her forehead to mine again. She said softly, "I'm okay. I'm okay."

She kept repeating those two words over and over again. I nodded, my head moving against hers. I knew she was telling me she was safe, but I needed to hear it again. I needed to hear it all the way through the night, the next day, the next week, and even the next month or two. I almost lost the woman I loved. Never again.

Never fucking again.

I breathed out once more. "I love you. I don't care if you don't want to be with me. I fucking love you, Taylor."

"No." She laughed, her hands holding my face. "No, Logan. I love you, too. I was coming to find you. I was going to plead, if I had to."

"You don't have to. I was going to do the same thing." I wouldn't get enough. I already knew this. If I had her for a year, I'd thirst for a second, then a third. I stopped, wrapped my arms tight around her, and just held her to me. I breathed her in.

CHAPTER 35

LARGE AND IN CHARGE
LOGAN

The elevators pinged my arrival, and the doors opened for me. My dad's office was large and in charge, just how he was. Two water fountains lined the side of the long hallway. My dad's receptionist's desk was at the end and she was behind it, staring at me. I knew the layout was set up that way to impress colleagues, business associates, and whoever else of my dad's power. He was fucking James Kade. He owned and operated a shit ton of businesses, but this was me. I'd been there when he brought woman after woman into the house, and that must've been years after sleeping with them in his office or at hotels. I'd been there when Mason asked him to come to a little league game and he no-showed. I was there when my mom screamed at him, threatening divorce, and he merely walked out of the room like he hadn't heard a word. I was there...in that damned empty mansion. Long after my mom left. Long after Mason would go and drink with Nate. Long after my dad was hardly even a roommate. So no, walking down this extensive hallway and seeing some stick-thin woman at the end, sitting there in her tight shirt, the buttons threatening to burst at the seams, a black lacy strap peeking out from one side of her shirt, none of this impressed me.

It only pissed me off, and the fact that I didn't want to be here when all I wanted to be with was Taylor.

"Logan," the receptionist greeted warmly and stood up.

She was going to open the door for me. I waved her back down. "I know the way."

She paused, frowning. "I'll need to make sure he's ready for you."

I grunted. Like I cared about that. Ignoring her, I swept past and was at the door before she could get there first. I didn't know what to expect inside my dad's office, but seeing Mason there had me putting on the brakes.

He was standing, glaring at James, but twisted to see me. His face went blank. "What are you doing here?"

I gestured to him. "Probably same as you. What are you doing here?" And why hadn't he told me?

As if reading my thought, Mason cringed. He shifted back on his feet and slid his hands inside his pockets. "I would've told you I was coming here, but a certain someone is always with his girlfriend now."

I smirked. "You jealous of Taylor? Missing your little brother maybe?"

"I'm starting to feel that you spend more time with my coach than I do." I grimaced.

I laughed. "You're jealous of your coach." I winked. "That's cute."

Mason rolled his eyes. "Taylor was attacked a month ago, and you're basically living over there now."

"Well," I corrected. "Not really. I had to meet Broozer first. You know, the official boyfriend/dad of the girl I'm screwing and who I love to screw, that meeting." I flashed a grin.

"Screwing?"

I shrugged. "Make love, but the mushy stuff is on the down-low. I have a rep to uphold. I'm still a badass."

"You're wifed up."

I hushed him. "Let's not talk like that." I zeroed in on our dad, who'd been quiet the entire exchange. Mason and I were standing while he remained in his big leather chair, watching us. I said, "We've got a different 'wifed up' situation to deal with first."

Mason turned with me so we were both facing our father. And I knew without looking that we wore matching expressions. Scowls.

James took a breath in, his shoulders lifting up and moving back down in a slow motion. His hand came to the desk, resting there, before he nodded like he came to a decision. He stood then and slid his hands inside his pockets, mirroring Mason. I started to smirk because I knew what would happen next, and it did.

Mason pulled his hands out and crossed them over his chest instead.

James glanced at me, and I raised an eyebrow. "You going to do that, too, now?"

The slight blank mask on his face fell away and exasperation showed. "You two will never completely forgive me, will you?"

Mason asked, "For what, Dad?"

I added, "For being a douchebag father?"

Mason was next. "For all the women you brought into the house?"

Me again. "For not being there, ever, for us?"

Mason. "For leaving Mom and falling in love with someone *just like* you?"

Me. "Or for deciding to be our father when we really don't need you anymore?" I leaned forward, placing my hands on the desk. "Too little, too late…Dad."

He sat back down and leaned forward, folding his hands together on the desk. His eyes went from Mason to me, and back again. In that moment, he gave in. I felt it from him. He sat down while we both towered over him, and we were united. This was how it was supposed to be, and how it would always be. Me and Mase, together, as we were against him.

"Okay." He gestured to the chairs behind us. "I get it. I do. Please, sit down."

We remained standing.

He let out a small breath of air, shaking his head. "I told you guys two years ago that I was going to make everything up to you—"

"Yeah." I nodded. "You left. Thank you."

He threw me a dark look. "Oh, come on, Logan. Analise is sick, *was* sick. I went to be by her side. I was doing what a devoted fiancé does for the woman he loves, and I know you both hate her—"

Mason cut in, "With good reason."

"—but she's better now, and we're back. We've been back, and I've done what you both wanted." He held a hand toward me. "I stayed away because that's what you wanted. I can't do that anymore."

"Why not?"

I kept quiet. Analise hurt Sam and while Sam was my family, she was Mason's soulmate. This was his fight, more than mine, but only by a little.

James didn't answer, not at first. He focused on Mason, his jaw clenched and his Adam's apple moved up and down.

Shit. This was it. This was the favor he was calling in, and then he said, "Because we set a date."

Mason closed his eyes, leaning back on his feet, away from the desk. His arms fell down, going to his side, and he let out a defeated sigh, half turning away.

I frowned. "A date for the wedding?"

Mason said, "That's the favor." He looked back and glared at James, speaking to me, "He's going to make us be his groomsmen. Aren't you?"

"What favor?" I snorted. "Rankin still went after Taylor."

"That was a miscommunication, and you know it. He was told to stay away from my sons. The girl should've been included, yes. That was a misfortunate mistake, but I still reached out and took some highly unethical and illegal risks for my sons. So, yes, I'm going to be a bastard father to you, too, because I'm still holding you both to the favor I did do for you." He paused, then continued, "I know I've not been a great father to the two of you, and I know you might not realize it, but I've been trying to make things right. I love Analise, and I've been at her side. I'll be a devoted husband, and now it's time for me to be a devoted father to you guys." He stood up. "It's time for you guys to let me be that father to you again."

He was right about one thing. We'd been shutting him out since high school, since he brought that woman into our home, but he was wrong about one thing, too.

I shook my head. "I'll be your groomsman. That's the favor I owe you for helping us with Rankin. You did that for Taylor, so I owe you." I paused before adding, "But that's all I owe you. You've been less of a father to me than Helen's been a mother to me. Mason got the happy family experience for a little bit. It was already falling apart by the time I knew what was going on, so no. I don't owe you the chance to be a dad. No child will ever owe a parent their own obligation. You cannot demand to be let in. It doesn't work that way."

My phone buzzed in my pocket, and I knew what that text said. Taylor was done with her own father/daughter/new girlfriend dinner. She was ready to be picked up. I sent her a text back. I was heading over soon before I put my phone away and locked gazes with my father one more time. I shook my head. "I can't speak for Mason, but that's my deal. I'll be your groomsman, but nothing else."

I said to Mason, "I gotta go. I need to pick up Taylor."

He nodded. "See you at the house later?"

I nodded back and left. I was at the door when James called after me, "Logan."

I paused, glancing back.

He said, "I won't demand to be your father, but I think you do owe me a chance to be your father again."

He already knew my answer. I opened the door to go.

"Logan."

I was half out the door. I didn't look back, but I did stop.

He said to my back, "I'd really like to meet Taylor one day. I'd like to meet the girl that you fell in love with."

I looked now and said simply, "No" before I left, and I didn't spare him another thought. As far as I was concerned, we were even now, if a son could ever be 'even' with his own father...

TAYLOR

Professor Gayle was dating my dad.

"Call me Carol. You must."

She had insisted with a warm smile and a glow on her face. She was my professor. She was the reason behind Jeremy's insistence I join the Honors Study Group, and she was now my dad's girlfriend. I looked between the two as they stood side by side, both waiting for my reaction. And what that was...I had no idea.

I said to my dad, "I didn't know you were dating anyone."

He was wearing a Cain University staff shirt, tucked into jeans, and loafers. His hair was combed in place, and he seemed worried, gauging my reaction. When he called and said he was bringing someone home for me to meet, I joked to Logan that I was going to meet the girlfriend. The joke was on me.

I blinked a few times.

My dad rubbed the side of his face, his eyes darting from Carol to myself. "Yeah. Uh, well, you know how these things happen sometimes." He coughed. "Logan Kade, honey. Logan Kade."

My neck grew warm registering his hidden meaning. We had a similar meeting like this a month ago. My dad was not happy to find out that Logan Kade was not only my boyfriend, but the one who tackled the guy who tried to shoot me.

Rankin went to prison. Word trickled down from his boss that he was supposed to stay away from the Kades. There'd been no mention of me, and hoping to get back into his boss' good graces, he wanted to take me out. It was supposed to be a way to get back at Delray. He thought his boss would reward him and not turn his back on him, which is what happened. The attack on me was his third strike. He had enough on his record to be sent away for half his life, and we were told by a detective that he had no allies on the inside.

And even though Logan tackled Rankin, my dad didn't take that into account. Eric stepped in front of a bullet for me. He had the scar to prove it, along with a week stay in the hospital, but he'd be fine, too. And while I was grateful to Eric, and we were on better terms, I wasn't going back to my first boyfriend. Ever. My dad didn't want to accept that, even when he had no place to hope for that outcome.

I was with Logan.

He had to get used to it, but for the first week, he blamed Logan for why the attack happened in the first place. Even after Jason came back and explained the real reason—his gambling. My dad didn't want to believe one of my best friends, so Claire was brought in for reinforcement. She was more than happy to recall Jason's history and the poor choices he'd made since graduating high school. Jason finished it up with a grudging acknowledgement that Logan Kade wasn't to blame, saying, "Yeah…maybe he's not that bad of a guy. I guess. Maybe." As he added the last 'maybe', he was staring right at me, and a warm feeling spread through me. He was speaking to my father, but I knew it was really to me.

He was giving me his approval, and I grew misty-eyed, giving him a silent 'thank you.' He gave me the slightest of nods back, and that was when I knew everything would be fine. I had my friend back and as I stood there now, I couldn't deny myself what I was seeing.

There was a sparkle in my dad's eyes and laugh lines around

his mouth. Even the bags under his eyes had lessened. My dad was happy.

"So." Carol drew closer. She looked like she was going to take my hands so I tucked them back. I wasn't ready for that stuff yet. She bit down on her lip and wavered back on her feet. "Oh. Okay. Uh." She still smiled at me. "I know you're one of my students so I wanted to wait till after the semester to let you know."

Finals had been last week.

She added quickly, "And this is part of the reason I've been so absent, too, why I had Jeremy do more than normal for his TA position." She continued to eye me. "Are you...okay with this?" She had moved a step forward so my father moved behind her, and she reached back, resting her hand on his chest. The whole gesture came so naturally to them, and that was the problem. It was natural. They were natural...my dad really had moved on.

My throat burned, but I looked into my father's eyes, and I smiled. I really did smile. It wasn't forced or fake. It was real, and he relaxed seeing it. I nodded. "If you're happy—"

He said, "I am."

"—then she'll be happy."

"She?" Carol's eyebrows pinched together, then she got it. Her eyes widened. "Oh."

Water pooled on the bottom of his eyes, but my dad coughed and blinked a few times. The water went away, but his voice was hoarse when he murmured, "Thank you, Taylor." His hand rested over Carol's shoulder, and I noticed how her eyes closed, how she leaned into his touch, how it was the same way when Logan would touch me. His touch gave her strength, and with my dad beaming at me, I was okay.

No. After texting Logan to come and get me, I was more than okay.

Ten minutes later, as he pulled into the driveway, and I got inside, I was so much better than okay. Our lips touched, and I was fucking fantastic.

He pulled back, looked harried, but touched my lip. "How'd it go?"

I told him, but once I was done, I asked, "What happened?"

He grunted, reversing the vehicle back to the road. "My dad's getting married."

"What?"

"When you meet her, you'll understand." He held my hand and laced our fingers together. "You ready for this?"

No. "Yes."

"You want me to read it?"

Yes. "No." I had to.

"Okay." He squeezed my hand. "But I can, if you can't."

"I know." I squeezed back. "I'll get through it."

CHAPTER 36

THE LAST
LOGAN

I stood back.

This was Taylor's time to speak and she did, raising her head and clearing her throat. She began, "It's not for the weak or faint of heart.

It will take a toll on you. Your body will hurt. Your soul will ache. Your family life will suffer. No one will understand what you do or why you do it, but you do it. You will work nights. You will work weekends. Holidays. You will bathe the elderly, the weak. You will clean their body, their bodily fluids. You will have to know every medication, what it does, when to stop it, when to give it, and how to get it into people. You will have to know how to interpret blood tests, when the doctor must know. You will have thirty seconds to start an IV, how to hook up an EKG machine. You will need to know how to interpret tracing or when you should give or take away oxygen. You will experience joy, grief, and sorrow in a day, sometimes within the same hour.

You are the glue between the patient, the family, the doctor. It's you who will keep everyone happy, as comfortable as possible. Code blue. Trauma evaluation. Labor. Delivery. Surgery. Babies. Postpartum. Psychology. These and more will all need to be learned. And when you think you know everything, you don't.

You're just starting.

I was asked to write this essay on why I want to be a nurse. I know that I wrote all that will be demanded of me, and the reason for this was because I know what it takes to be a nurse. I know the joy and the sorrow. I know the suffering, but the real reason I want to be a nurse didn't need an essay. There's really one reason, I will pick up the torch that my mother left when she died caring for the man who would shoot her.

She did a service to others in her life, and now…

…it's my turn."

Taylor was crying, and she folded up her essay, sliding it into my pocket when she was done. I didn't say a word. I didn't dare. Love swelled up in me, and I wanted to take her in my arms, but I refrained.

She stood over her mother, then used both hands to wipe the tears from her cheeks. She stayed there, gazing down at the headstone. I waited. I'd wait an eternity for this woman. I saw the strength in her. I was drawn to her from the beginning, knowing she wanted to fight for Sam, or maybe she just wanted to fight. Something deep in me was drawn to her, so I used an excuse to talk to her. I didn't want to admit that it wasn't really Delray. I didn't care about him. I didn't even really care about messing with him. It was her the whole time, only I didn't know it myself. Now here we were. This visit was different. It wasn't because of the essay, though. I felt it in the air. We came another time, but there was a sense of finality in her voice. Her tears seemed deeper.

She was letting her go.

I straightened, frowning. "Taylor?"

She gazed at me, her eyes uncharacteristically bright. Then she smiled, and the sight did two things. I felt the twitch deep in me, when only she could smile at me, and it transformed her face. The pain was gone. All of it.

"You're okay?" I had to know. My fingers still ached to reach for her.

She nodded. "I am." She took a breath. "Do you have it with you?"

I pulled out the vase, then the sand, and handed over the sparkler. She took everything, bending back down so the vase sat in front of the headstone. The sand went inside, and she stuffed the sparkler in there, standing it upright. I handed her the lighter, and after she lit the sparkler, she stood back, moving to stand beside me. Her hand found mine, and we stayed there, watching the firecracker spark to life.

I used to be a partier. I used to be a manwhore. I used to fight—well, okay. I would still party. I would still fight, and I'd be a manwhore, but it was over.

Tate's words came back to me. *"I hope you fall in love. You can feel what the rest of us feel."*

I scoffed at that. I saw more heartache than good coming from loving someone, but here I was.

I was holding hands with my last girl.

EPILOGUE

TAYLOR

We were setting up for the big party, and when I say 'setting up', the guys went to get two kegs while Sam and I stayed behind to get the food done. I came to Fallen Crest with Logan for the holiday break, and we were at his mother's house, getting ready to throw a 'Kade Party'. From the way Logan said it, these types of parties were a big 'fucking' deal. I wasn't sure what the night was going to be like, but I was ready for anything. I learned to adopt that mantra being Logan's other half. I never knew what he was going to do, say, or when he'd suddenly sweep me up and carry me off to bed, but it was an adventure, like Logan himself.

I'd have it no other way. Where he was, so was I...except now. He was off getting booze, and I was waiting as his sister ordered food.

As if on cue, Sam hung up the phone and announced, "Our part is done. Twenty pizzas are on the way."

"That's all we have to do?"

"Nope. My friend is bringing the rest." And right then, the doorbell rang. Sam pointed to the air. "That'd be her, right on time."

We heard the door open, then shut, and rustling bags approached from the hallway. A moment later, a girl appeared with three grocery bags filled. She lifted them up, a bag strapped on her back. She grunted. "I've got the chips here, and the rest of the booze is in the bag." She gestured behind her. "Back there."

Sam took the bags while the girl took her backpack off, placing it on the table. She turned, saw me, and her eyebrows lifted up. "Well. So this is her."

The girl was stunning, whoever she was. Dark blonde hair. A sexy and toned body, and as she raked me up and down, I could tell she was familiar with Logan. The way she said 'her' had me narrowing my eyes. I wasn't sure if I liked it or not.

"This is Taylor, yes." Sam moved to stand next to me. Her eyes narrowed. "Chill, Heather. She's family now."

At the word 'family', the girl's entire demeanor changed. The frosty reception melted, and she beamed brightly at me, throwing her arms in the air. "Well, hell then. How are you? I'm Heather." She jerked a thumb toward Sam's direction. "We're besties."

I started to nod, saying that I got that when she advanced and I was pulled in for a hug instead. I could feel her smiling as she whispered in my ear, "Sam says you love the kid so if you hurt him, I will hurt you tenfold." She pulled back, still beaming, and clapped me on the shoulders. "Got it?"

Sam started laughing, overhearing. She shook her head, but picked up the bag of booze and moved further into the kitchen. "It's not going to work. Taylor's the one who put me in my place."

Heather's eyebrows shot back up. "Really?"

"Really."

Heather looked at me. "Really?"

I shrugged. "I don't remember."

Sam laughed, starting to unpack the bag. "Right. She doesn't remember." She winked at me. "We're going with that story, huh?" She said something to Heather then, who moved closer to her and the two started talking about a bar, but I held back.

Heather knew Logan. She cared about him. He told me about her, and about their time together. I heard the fondness in his voice when he did, so this girl wasn't just important to Sam, she was important to Logan, too.

I cleared my throat, feeling like I needed to say something.

Heather was in the middle of saying something, but quieted. Both turned to me once more.

I gave them a small smile. "Logan cares about you." I held her gaze. I didn't want her to question if I knew or not. I just wanted her to know. "You're different than the others."

"The others?"

I nodded. I saw the knowing look in her eye. She was strong. She came in here and let me know how much she cared for him. She wanted to protect him. I respected that, and I wanted her to know that too. "Logan's slept with a lot of girls. I'm not stupid. I'm aware. Trust me, I heard all the stories from on campus and I know that was only the time he was at college, but he told me about you."

She'd been leaning against a counter and her arms had folded up over her chest, but they fell down slowly back to her side. She straightened, her head righting itself. "Yeah?" Her eyebrows pinched together. "What'd he say?"

What he said didn't matter. It was how he said it. "I heard how much he cares about you. It was in his voice, and meeting you today, I can tell you care about him too." That was it. There was really nothing more to say, except, "Thank you for caring about him and wanting to protect him. I love Logan, and that means a lot to me."

I felt a little bit like a blubbering idiot, but I felt it was necessary to say something, and I meant what I said. I respected her. This was the rare incidence where it wasn't earned. I gave it freely. I wanted her to see that too so I let it show. I let her see it, and it was that moment when the door opened and male voices were heard. The guys were back. They were coming toward us, and then they quieted.

Logan stepped next to me. "Taylor?"

I ignored him. This wasn't for him to be a participant. I raised my chin up, my eyes still locked with Heather's, and I gave her a small nod.

She continued to study me, looking me up and down. Then a

slight grin lifted the side of her mouth up. "I think I just got a new girl crush. Kade, if I turn lesbian, you need to worry."

Logan laughed, throwing his arm around my shoulders. He pulled me against him, nodding toward Sam. "I thought you'd hit on Strattan first."

"No way."

"Hey!"

Heather added, "Sam's too skinny. Plus, who wants to deal with Analise now that she's back? I'll take my chances with Taylor."

Another "Hey!" came from Sam, but she didn't mean it. She was grinning from ear to ear. "Well, whatever. Nate and Logan have their bromance. I think I might compete with you for a womance with Taylor, too. Her dad will get us good tickets for the Cain U football games long after Mason graduates."

"Hey." Mason's eyebrows bunched together, standing behind Logan. He came forward, holding a bag of liquor. "Should I be pissed about that?"

"No way, big bro." Logan's hand fell to my waist as he moved around me, hopping onto the table, and pulled me back so I stood between his legs. His other hand fell to my left hip, and I leaned back, feeling his arms slide over, anchoring me more firmly in front of him. His chin rested on my shoulder. "Sam's right. We need to start thinking long-term about tickets once you're gone. You only have one more year. And we can't always depend on Nate. His parents might be famous in the movie biz, but he's not always on good terms with them."

"The fuck?" Nate moved from behind Mason and folded his arms over his chest. He glowered at Logan. "Is that why you asked last week if my parents knew any football coaches? To see if they could get tickets?" Logan shrugged, his arm brushing up and down from the motion. "They know celebrities. They're kind of celebrities themselves. It doesn't hurt to see our options once Mason graduates, but you guys are right. The Broozer will hook me up." He tightened his hold over me, and I felt his attention, his voice grew huskier.

I looked up, looking right into those warm, smiling, and mischievous eyes of his. As my heart skipped a beat, I remarked, "Is that why we're dating? You were using me to get to my dad?"

"Uh-huh. Me and the Broozer. We've got the ultimate bromance going. Nate's been replaced." He continued to watch me, and I couldn't look away either. Nate said something. The others laughed. Sam or Heather made a comment, and the conversation soon continued without us, because in that moment, the world melted away. I was standing there, held in his arms, and I saw the love shining down on me.

My body sparked alive, tingling, and warmth swirled all around inside of me. This was the effect he had on me. Always had, and I knew he always would. I let him see what he was doing to me, I let him see the love I had back for him, and as his eyes darkened, he lowered his lips to mine.

I kissed him back, turning and winding my arms around his neck. He pulled me even tighter, taking control of the kiss. The others would leave. They'd grown accustomed to our spontaneous make-out sessions, or Logan would tug me away, leading me to his bedroom. Either way, I'd go with him. No matter the future, I was never leaving.

I loved Logan Motherfucking Kade.

For more stories and information about upcoming books, visit:
www.tijansbooks.com

ACKNOWLEDGEMENTS

Here I am, writing this section and I'm bawling. Usually by this time, I'm numb. Sleepless nights. The ease of one pressure, knowing a different pressure will soon replace it, and when the acknowledgements arrive, my mind is mush. Usually. I worry about who I'm forgetting to thank, or who I need to mention, or who might not even read this part, but I should still add. All of it just swirls into one big mess inside, but this book is different.

I have never felt so much pressure or received such fierce opinions about a book until Logan's book, and the reason for this is Logan himself. He's been loved and protected by so many readers. Logan is loved by others as much as I love him, and I sincerely thank everyone for that. I tried to write a book to give him justice, and I hope I achieved it. I have cried over this book, forgotten phone calls/events/trips/normal daily stuff because I've been thinking about this book. I have laughed. I have agonized and like I said above, I've never felt so much pressure, so I truly want to thank all of the Logan protectors because I wrote this book for you.

I also want to thank my agent! Kimberly, you're amazing and always there. You're one damned amazing agent and I'm lucky to have you on my side. I want to thank all my betas, admins, and promoters: Cami, Kim, Kerri, Amanda, Amanda, Heather, Eileen, Autumn, Stacey, Pam, Crystal, Tera, Lisa, and oh my goodness—so many!! You guys are some of my go-to people and you're always there for me. THANK YOU!! Thank you to the Tijanettes!!! You all have created a family in that group and I'm seriously blessed and lucky to be a part of it. A huge major thank you to my editor, Jessica, and my proofreaders, Chris and Paige. My goodness. All of you have helped me so much, and you keep helping. I can't express how much gratitude I have for you guys. And my formatter, Elaine!! You're more than a formatter, though. You've become a friend and another invaluable source of support and help. I don't think I hugged you enough in Florida. ;) Oh my gosh, I have to give a big shout out to some authors who read Logan and gave me early feedback, then proceeded to always be there if I had questions or worries: Debra (I'm always safe in your bosom *winking here*), Rochelle Paige, and Jay McLean! And to the ladies at Rock Stars of Romance: I LOVE YOU GUYS!

A special thank you to my mom. Even though you won't read this, thank you for writing an essay on why you love being a nurse. You had no clue why you were doing it, but you helped me put a thank you in this book to all the nurses out there.

I'm stopping now, because the emotions have now turned to the normal mush. Lol! That means my brain is telling me to move on, so ending it here with:

THANK YOU, THANK YOU, THANK YOU!!!

CPSIA information can be obtained
at www.ICGtesting.com
Printed in the USA
BVOW06s1010070317
477966BV00015B/246/P